Books by April Wilson

McIntyre Security, Inc. Bodyguard Series:

Vulnerable

Fearless

Shane (a novella)

Broken

Shattered

Imperfect

Ruined

Hostage

Redeemed

Marry Me (a novella)

Snowbound (a novella)

Regret

With This Ring (a novella)

A Tyler Jamison Novel:

Somebody to Love

A British Billionaire Romance:

Charmed (co-written with Laura Riley)

Charmed

A British Billionaire Romance

by

April Wilson
&
Laura Riley

Cover Artist: Steamy Designs
Photographer: Wander Aguiar
Model: Forest
Editor: Christina Hart (Savage Hart Book Services)

Published by
April E. Barnswell
Wilson Publishing LLC
P.O. Box 292913
Dayton, OH 45429
www.aprilwilsonauthor.com

ISBN: 9798637313235

ॐ 1

Fitzwilliam Carmichael, II (Will)

I simply cannot believe the e-mail staring me in the face.

It's over, Will. I'm tired of wasting my time on a man who's afraid of commitment. David Markham isn't afraid. We're eloping tonight to Gretna Green. It was fun, and you're great in the sack, but I want more. I want a diamond ring on my finger. Cheers – Rachel

Eloping to Gretna Green? Really? How very Regency of her. Dumbfounded, I shake my head. *That little bitch.* I gave her the best four months of my life. I would have gotten around to giving her a ring... eventually. Maybe. I was starting to think she might be *the one*. If only she'd been a little more patient. Maybe in a couple of years, I might have felt the desire to settle down. But no, she has to run off with David Markham in accounting. *Seriously? That tosser?*

Connor walks into my office, his nose buried in his phone. He's chuckling about something, probably the latest viral video of a cat doing something stupid.

"What do you want?" I say in a much harsher tone than I had intended. I'm in a shitty mood, and I know I shouldn't take it out on the work experience lad. He's all right. I rein myself in and give it another go. "Hello, Connor. What can I do for you?"

Snorting with laughter, Connor stuffs his phone into his trouser pocket. Only then does he really get a look at me. He makes a face, but refrains from saying anything.

"Go on, spit it out," I say.

He scowls. "What the hell's wrong with you, man?"

Typical Connor, he has no filter and what pops into his head comes straight out, please or offend. "Don't hold it in, kid. Say what you're thinking."

"You look like someone just pissed all over you. It's got to be either girl trouble or money trouble. I know it can't be about money—you're fucking loaded—so it's got to be a girl. Rachel, right? Who else?"

Well, you can't kid a kidder, so I won't even try. I nod. "She's run off with David Markham in accounting. They're eloping tonight."

Connor snorts. "Markham? What's he got that you don't?"

"He's put a diamond ring on her damned finger, that's what. Apparently, that's all that matters."

He wags his finger in my face. "Spoken like a true misogynist."

"I am not a misogynist! I love women."

"You love *fucking* women, Will, but I'm not sure how you feel about them outside of the bedroom."

I press my hand to my chest. "That hurts, Connor. You've wounded me deeply."

Despite his apparent verbal diarrhea, I damn well love this kid. He's so switched on about life it scares me. I don't see an eighteen-year-old boy in a man's suit. I see *potential*. This kid is going places.

He's six-two, the same height as me, blond-haired and blue-eyed, and the ladies love him. He's kind of got a boyband vibe going on. I can't knock his effort. Today, he's dressed in an Armani suit that is clearly two sizes too big for his lanky frame. I'm guessing it's his father's. No doubt his mum ironed it for him this morning.

Right now, he's staring at me like a smug bastard, not showing the least bit of sympathy. "Rachel and I had tickets to the symphony tonight," I say. "Now who in the world will I take at such short notice? I wouldn't be caught dead going alone."

"How about me? I'm available."

I roll my eyes at him. "Be serious."

"Take your housekeeper then. What's her name—Maggie?"

I wad up a piece of paper and lob it at him.

Connor shakes his head. "Poor Will. You'll spend the entire weekend getting shit-faced in your fancy London penthouse, feeling sorry that you lost your newest piece of ass."

"Hey, watch your mouth." I can't really contradict him though, as he's spot on. "I'm paying you to work, kid, not talk."

"You're not paying me a single penny, Will. I'm the work experience kid, remember?"

"Well, you've got to start somewhere. Stop talking and do something productive. Empty the bin."

Connor drops down into one of the two black leather chairs positioned in front of my desk. "Are you kidding? It's five o'clock, and I'm done for the day. Want to go out for drinks?"

I lean back in my chair. "I'm not going out drinking with an eighteen-year-old. At least not while I have an ounce of dignity remaining."

Connor makes a face. "It's your loss. The way I see it, I'm your best bet, mate. What else do you have to do this evening? Your girlfriend dumped you."

"We were only together four months. I'd hardly call her a *girlfriend*."

"Then what would you call her? Your fuck-buddy?"

"Watch your language."

Connor rises to his feet and pulls up what are likely his dad's trousers. "Anyway, I almost forgot what I came here to tell you. I've been promoted."

That's news to me. "Promoted? To what?"

"I'm going to be a PA starting Monday."

I bark out a laugh. "You, a personal assistant? You're not qualified. You can't even make a decent latte."

"I'm not qualified? You are such a sexist, Will. Men can be PAs too, you know. Besides, it's a step up from carrying and fetching for you, which is all I do now."

I shake my head. "You're too wet behind the ears."

Connor frowns as if he's not understanding.

"You're a boy, not a man. An ambitious one at that. Wait until you grow up some, get some facial hair. You'll get there eventually. But I like your style, kid. I really do."

After Connor leaves, I get up from my desk and pace over to the windows overlooking The Thames. There's something about water I find oddly fascinating and comforting. Whether it's this river or the lake at my estate in Bibury, water is constant and steadfast. It's dependable, unlike most people. This river is as old as time itself, and it'll continue to flow through this city long past my time here on Earth.

I glance down at the ground, at all the people scurrying along the pavement. I've spent my life looking down at people, literally and figuratively. It comes with the territory when you're born into an obscenely wealthy family. Women throw themselves at me because I have an abundance of what every woman wants—money. Lots and lots of money.

Rachel wasn't any different. Her defection has hit me hard. Or, rather my ego has taken a hit. She wanted it all—a ring, a marriage certificate, kids, a big townhouse in the city. I'll be thirty-one soon, and I suppose I should start thinking about those things too. I do want them, eventually.

Of course I want a family of my own. I want a wife—someone to go home to who is exclusively mine, and I'm hers. I want kids. Loud, messy kids. I want the whole package. Problem is, I don't know how to get it. The idea of settling down with just one woman terrifies me.

What if I can't do it?

After I've dated a woman for a few months, I'm usually ready to move on. In this case, Rachel beat me to it. I'm not a player by any stretch of the imagination, but the women I've dated have only wanted me for my money. What would stop them from divorcing me and taking me to the cleaners after they've got bored?

The question I ask myself daily is: *Am I enough?*

If you take away my money and my name, my family connections, what's left? In the end, am I enough to make someone happy? Truly happy?

There's work I should be doing, but I'm struggling to concentrate. These four walls are closing in on me, and the collar around my neck is a little tighter. It feels as though invisible fingers are wrapping around my throat and squeezing, making it harder to breathe. Maybe I should go out tonight and get completely shit-faced. Might as well, since I won't be going to the symphony.

The intercom on my desk buzzes, and my secretary says, "Will, your father would like to see you."

Fuck.

This can't be good. Dad doesn't talk to me here at the office unless he has something to complain about. Maybe he's heard about Rachel already. Bad news travels fast.

Rachel's the first woman to dump me, and now I know how it feels to be on the receiving end. Shaking my head, I pull myself out of my pity party for one. I'm trying not to take it personally, but it's hard.

"All right," I tell my secretary. "I'm going."

* * *

I knock on my father's door, and when I hear a faint, "Come in," I push it open and walk inside.

"Hello, Dad. You wanted to see me?"

My father looks up from the mountain of paperwork on his desk and scowls. For a man in his mid-seventies, he's still rather fit, and his mind is as sharp as a knife. His hair's gone completely white, but there's plenty of it left. I hope that's a good omen for me.

He waves a sheet of paper in the air. "Do you know what this is?" He points at the chair in front of his desk. "Sit."

I take a seat, hoping this won't take long. "I'm clearly not a mind reader, so no."

My father narrows his eyes at me. "Don't take that tone of voice with me, Will. I've just been informed that your PA eloped with David Markham in accounting!" He glares at me as if it's my fault.

"So I've heard."

My father sighs. "I thought you had something good going with Rachel Whittingham. Your mother and I actually approved of that one. She's practically family."

I shrug. "Apparently, she disagreed. What does any of this have to do with me? She left me—not the other way around."

"It's got everything to do with you! She's the third PA we've lost in the past year, thanks to your philandering."

I cross my arms over my chest. "Regardless of how many have quit, Rachel running off with Markham is *not my fault*."

"You listen to me, son. I'm sick and tired of you chasing off PAs. I'll arrange for your next one. I'll pick someone you won't want to sleep with for a change. From now on, keep it in your trousers. And for God's sake, keep your sex life out of the office! We've lost enough employees as it is."

I can just imagine the woman my father will choose to be my new PA. The old man can be vindictive when he wants to.

I'm definitely getting shit-faced tonight. And if all goes well, I'll stay that way all weekend.

2

Skye Williams

I wake from a fitful catnap to the sound of the airline captain's announcement over the speaker system.

"Welcome to the United Kingdom, ladies and gentlemen. Please stow all your belongings and prepare for a smooth and delightful landing at Heathrow Airport."

We're here.

Amidst the eager chatter of passengers, the flight attendants jump into action, checking each row of seats to make sure everyone is complying with instructions. I lift up my tray and tuck my e-reader into my purse before taking a moment to gaze out my window at my home for the next year—London, England.

It's the first time I've ever been to England. My mother conceived me here while she was attending University of Oxford. But she left soon after she realized she was pregnant, running back home to the States, where she gave birth to me in Cincinnati, Ohio.

I've lived my whole life in Cincinnati, in a lush green suburb outside the city. My British father, Frank Williams, has come to visit me for a week during my Christmas breaks from school. Even though I only got to see him once a year, he always gave me his undivided attention when he was there. I never doubted that he loved me. I just, sadly, wasn't a big part of his life for the rest of the year, aside from periodic video chats and texts.

But that's about to change.

I'm going to spend the next year living in London while I fulfill a post-graduate internship at the financial investment firm where my father is a managing director.

I'm excited—and a bit nervous—to be seeing him again. He's a good dad, even though we've only ever had a long-distance relationship. He sent my mother a generous monthly check deposit throughout my childhood to help cover my support. He paid for half the cost of my braces and half my tuition bill at UC. He even bought me a reliable used car when I graduated from high school—one that had been awarded an excellent safety rating by *Consumer Reports* magazine.

It will be nice to have the chance to get to know my dad better—along with his new family. He finally married six years ago, and he and his wife, Julia, have two young children. I have a little brother and sister I've never even met in person.

I suppose I should have come to visit them before now, but I was so caught up in my studies and working part-time jobs to help with living expenses. In June, I graduated from UC with a dual master's degree in finance and economics. And now, just two months later, I'm on my way to London.

I guess you could say I went into the family business, because working with money runs in our blood, apparently. Both my parents work in the financial industry. My mother is an economics professor at UC, and my father works in finance. Numbers run through my veins.

My gaze is glued out the window as we approach the airport. I glance down at fluffy, white clouds that float in the air like cotton balls. I'd heard that London was damp and dreary, but right now, I'm looking at a clear blue sky. I hope that's a good sign.

As my plane approaches Heathrow, I scan the landscape for recognizable landmarks. The voices of the other passengers fade to a soothing background noise as I pick out iconic London features. I spot Victoria Park. It's easy to make out the River Thames as it snakes its way through the densely-packed city. There's the Tower Bridge, and off in the distance I can pinpoint the London Eye. Vehicles on the street come into view, looking like tiny toy cars. I smile when I see the quintessential symbol of London—red, double-decker buses.

I did my research before leaving the States, studying the landmarks of the city, the public transportation system, the cuisine, all the little details I could glean from the Internet. I like to plan ahead, to be prepared. And I'm ready for this adventure. Maybe *challenge* is a more fitting description. Since my father is a bit of a bigshot at Carmichael & Son Capital Investments, I have a lot to live up to.

As our plane descends, I eagerly take in the patchwork of London, which is a lovely mix of wide, open green spaces and bustling human activity. I want to explore the streets of London, ride a double-decker bus, and visit Buckingham Palace. But I want to do more than just see all the tourist spots. I want to truly get to know the home of my father—after all, I'm half British, even if I don't have the accent. For one full year, I'll do whatever I can to be a true Londoner.

I find myself fiddling with my bracelet. It's my prize possession. A dozen sterling silver charms dangle from the chain, all representing my most favorite things in the world. And there's room for a few more. I hope to pick some up in England to commemorate my year abroad.

The landing is smooth, and I collect my belongings as the captain rattles off instructions on when and where we'll deplane. A small child seated a couple of rows behind me is giddy with excitement, squealing as he bounces in his seat. I suppose I'm just as excited.

The plane eventually rolls to a stop, and we disembark. After collecting my luggage, I wait in line for customs. As soon as I get a chance, I send a quick text to my dad to let him know I'm here. I also text my mom to let her know I arrived safely. She texts me back immediately, and I can tell she's relieved to get my message.

My mom and I are very close, and this is the first time we've ever been apart. I know it wasn't easy for her to see me off.

As we stood at the airport security gate, we hugged for what had to have been the tenth time that day, both of us choking up as we held each other tight.

"A whole year, sweetie," she said to me as we were about to part. "I'm going to miss you so much."

"I'm going to miss you, too."

She brushed back my hair and cupped my cheek. "You're going to have a wonderful time, honey. Go and enjoy yourself. I'll be counting down the days until you return."

It's always been just the two of us, like two peas in a pod, and I miss her already. Taking a deep breath, I steel myself to move forward. This is my big adventure, and I'm ready for it.

By the time I'm through customs, I'm exhausted. It was an eighteen-hour flight in all, with two layovers along the way. I'm so tired, I'm half-asleep on my feet. I just want to get to my dad's house and crash for the night.

I'll spend the weekend with him and his family. And then Monday, I'll ride in to the office with him and get the key to the flat I'll be sharing with another company intern—also an American—and my temporary life as a Londoner will begin.

* * *

When I reach the arrivals' lounge, I spot my father immediately. Our gazes lock, and he gives me a welcoming smile. With a wave, he heads in my direction, and I meet him halfway.

"Skye." He clasps my shoulders and looks me over. It's August now, and we haven't seen each other in person since last Christmas. "You look well, sweetheart. I'm so glad you're finally here."

My dad looks like the typical absent-minded professor, with his dark gray slacks, white button-up shirt, and brown-plaid jacket. His brown hair, which is graying at the temples, is cut short, and his trim beard is threaded liberally with gray. His cobalt-blue bow tie, which matches his bright blue eyes, is the only splash of color on him.

I imagine his wife, Julia, is the one who bought him the tie.

"Hi, Dad."

He wraps me in his arms, giving me a light squeeze as he sighs. "It'll be so good having you here with us. For once, I'll have all my children under one roof, even if just for a couple of days."

I hug him back, letting the moment sink in.

I'm with my dad.

"I'm looking forward to meeting your family."

"They're your family, too, you know. Julia is dying to meet you, and the kids are beside themselves with anticipation. They can't wait to meet their big sister."

My dad is a no-nonsense kind of guy. He's easy going, organized, and practical. I guess I come by these traits naturally.

"Here, let me take that," he says, reaching my wheeled suitcase.

As he heads for the exit, I follow behind it all in. Everything's different here, from the signage, to the accented voices over the speakers. It's quite a trek out to the parking lot. He pops the trunk on a black BMW sedan and stows my suitcase inside. As I'm waiting, I peer into the backseat and spot two children's booster seats.

"Sit up front with me," he says, motioning me to the front.

It's a bit awkward that I'm climbing into the front seat on the left-hand side of the car, while he slides behind the driver's wheel on the right. Of all the many differences between the US and the UK, I think the fact that they drive on the left side of the road is going to be the hardest to get used to.

I find myself white-knuckling the door handle when we pull out into traffic.

My father notices and grins. "A bit nervous?"

"Yes!" I laugh. "You're driving on the wrong side of the road."

He pats my knee. "You'll get used to it. It took me a while to get used to driving on the other side of the road when I came to visit you in America."

As we merge into traffic, I force myself to sit back and my seat and try to relax. It's time for me to let go and embrace change.

By the time we get to his residential area a little way out of the city, I'm much more relaxed. It's dark already, so I can't see much of the neighborhood. When we pull up into my dad's driveway, I glance out my window at a large, two-story brick ome with a fancy wrought-iron gate and a separate three-car garage.

"Ready to go in?" he asks me once we're parked.

I nod. "As ready as I'll ever be."

He reaches over to pat my leg. "No need to be nervous. They can't wait to meet you."

My dad wheels my big suitcase up the curved walk to the front door, and I follow with my backpack and purse slung over my shoulder. Several lamp posts light the way, revealing a beautifully-landscaped front yard.

We walk up three steps leading to the front door, and my father opens it, pushing it wide and motioning for me to walk inside. A very attractive woman who looks to be in her mid-thirties is waiting for us with a warm smile on her face. She's dressed in a peach skirt and a white, tailored blouse. A string of creamy pearls adorns her slender neck, and her light brown hair is sleek and shiny.

"Hello, Skye!" she says. "Welcome! We're so happy to have you." She steps forward, her arms open wide, and embraces me delicately.

I don't know what to call her. "Thank you, um, Mrs. Williams."

She suppresses a grin. "You must call me Julia, please."

We're standing in a foyer, and a long, narrow corridor leads to the back of the house. There's a sitting room to the right, and another room to the left. A staircase leads upstairs, where presumably the bedrooms are located.

The house is quiet and most of the lights are off. I figure it's close to midnight, so the children must be asleep.

Julia motions for me to follow her into the room to my right. "Come sit with me. We can have a little chat while your father carries your luggage up to your room."

Julia switches on a lamp, and I glance quickly around the space. It's a cozy sitting room with a fireplace, a sofa, and two upholstered armchairs. The room is impressively furnished with an antique upright piano and several bookcases with glass doors. The walls are covered with a pretty floral wallpaper, and the floors are hardwood. There's a large burgundy rug in the center of the room that perfectly coordinates with the wallpaper.

"Can I get you something?" Julia says as she sits on one of the chairs. "Are you hungry? Or would you care for a drink?" She nods toward a liquor cabinet beside the fireplace.

I sit in the other chair and hold my purse in my lap. "Thanks, but I'm fine."

"Nothing at all? Not even a cup of tea or water? How about some custard creams?"

I'm not really sure what those are. "Nothing, thanks. I'll wait until morning."

"Let me know if you change your mind. How was your flight?"

"It was fine. Pretty uneventful, really."

She smiles. "Those are the best kind."

We chat for a few minutes until my dad returns.

"All set," he says, propping his hands on his hips. He stands behind Julia's chair and lays his hands on her shoulders, squeezing lightly.

The two of them are staring at me, and I feel a bit self-conscious. A little bit of awkwardness is to be expected, I'm sure. I'm an interloper in their family dynamic. It's going to take some getting used to, for all of us.

I yawn. "I think I'll go up to bed, if you don't mind. I'm exhausted." I've been up for over twenty-four hours now, and I'm sure jetlag will be setting in soon.

"Of course," Julia says, jumping to her feet. "I'll walk you up and show you where everything is."

I follow her up the stairs and down a hallway. She leads me to one of the rooms at the front of the house and switches on the light as we enter.

It's a charming bedroom, with a full-size bed covered by what looks like an antique quilt. There's an antique dresser and chest of drawers in the room, as well as an armchair beside a little table holding a brass lamp. A large picture window overlooks the front yard.

My suitcase is resting on a luggage rack in the corner of the room.

"Here's the *en suite*," Julia says, pointing to a door that I presume leads to a private bathroom. "And the closet is there. Please, make yourself at home. If you need anything, just let me know."

"Thank you."

Once she's gone, I collapse on the bed, happy to find it soft and inviting. There's no point in bothering to unpack, as I'll be moving to my flat on Monday. So I dig out my pajamas, freshen up in the bathroom, and climb into bed with my phone, my charger, and a power adapter I brought from home.

I try reading for a few minutes, but my eyelids are so heavy I find myself drifting off. So, I shut off my phone and set it on the nightstand, and then exhaustion overtakes me.

3

Skye

On Sunday, I sleep in until ten, which is late for me. Then I shower and head downstairs, where I find Julia in the kitchen making breakfast.

She's already dressed and made up for the day, looking like she just stepped off the cover of a fashion magazine. She's clearly a lot younger than my dad, who's in his late fifties.

I pause in the kitchen doorway, taking a moment to study my two young siblings, who are still in their pajamas. They're seated at the kitchen table, chattering nonstop as they play with little toy figures. When Charlie spots me standing there, he immediately clams up and stares.

Julia turns at the sudden silence and when she sees me, she smiles and waves me into the kitchen. "Darlings, this is your sister, Skye. She arrived last night from America. Skye, this is Charlie, and this is Rebecca."

They're both adorable as they give me wide-eyed stares. I smile and say, "Hi. I'm very pleased to meet you."

Rebecca, the youngest, who's just turned three, has long, silky fine hair the same rich shade of brown as her mother's. Her brother, who's five, has short, spiky brown hair, a bit darker than his sister's. I'm not sure if it's an intentional hairstyle, or if he just hasn't combed it since getting out of bed this morning. Either way, he's as cute as he can be. They both are.

Charlie stares at me nonplussed. "Is our dad really your dad, too?" he asks, sounding more than a little skeptical, as if he's sure somebody's pulling his leg.

I bite back a grin. "Yes, he is."

His gaze narrows. "You're kind of old to be a kid. And why do you talk funny?"

"Charlie!" Julia says. She positions herself behind her son and lays a gentle hand on his head. "That's not a polite thing to say, dear."

I laugh. "It's all right." And then to Charlie, I say, "I am a lot older than you are, sure, but I'm not too old to be your big sister. And I'm from the United States."

Rebecca, who had jumped down from her chair to hide behind her mother, peeks out warily from behind Julia's skirt.

"All right, children," Julia says, shooing her daughter back into her seat. "Time for breakfast. You too, Skye. Have a seat."

It's funny. Julia probably isn't more than ten years older than I am, and yet she's lumped me in with her kids. But I am starving, and I'm grateful she's made breakfast.

The table is already set, but I offer to help Julia carry the dishes.

"Oh, no. You're our guest. Please, sit down and make yourself at home."

Breakfast is warm crumpets with butter and jam, soft boiled eggs and little strips of toast—which Charlie calls *soldiers*—bacon, orange juice, and tea. It's not very different from what I eat back at home. I don't know what I was expecting, but I thought it would be something vastly different, like black pudding or haggis.

No, wait. Haggis is Scottish, not English.

After breakfast, the kids take me outside in the backyard to look at their swing set. The entire day is relaxed, just spent getting to know one another. It's not long before Charlie and Rebecca warm up to me, and pretty soon Charlie follows me around like a puppy dog, while Rebecca wants to hold hands with me.

* * *

Monday morning is a flurry of activity. I can hear the kids talking excitedly downstairs as I dress for my first day of work and pack up my luggage. My dad had already popped his head into my room this morning to tell me he'd carry my suitcase out to the car.

He comes downstairs to join us for breakfast, already dressed for work in his gray slacks, white shirt, and a brown tweed jacket. He scarfs down his food, then rises from the table and kisses Julia on the cheek. "Thanks for breakfast, darling." He kisses both Charlie and Rebecca on the tops of their heads, and then ruffles their hair, making them both giggle.

To me, he says, "Ready to head to the office? I've already carried your luggage out."

After taking my last bite of toast, I stand. "Thank you for breakfast, Julia."

She beams at me. "You're very welcome, my dear."

* * *

My father and I head off to Canary Wharf, which is the center of London's financial district. It's where the Carmichael & Son office building is located. I don't know a whole lot about the company yet, other than it being a privately-held equity firm. I've studied the company's website, their mission statement, and client list. They have some pretty impressive clients from around the world. The company was founded forty years ago by Fitzwilliam Carmichael, and his son, Fitzwilliam Carmichael Jr., works for the company and is slated to take over when his father retires.

As a capital investment firm, the company loans out money to start-ups and established businesses wanting to grow. My internship will be in the area of risk analysis, which is my academic specialty. I wrote my graduate thesis on the topic. Now, I'll get to put what I've learned into practice. My job will be to help identify which prospective clients are good risks and which ones aren't.

We arrive in the financial district, which borders The Thames. I'm excited I'll be able to walk along the river at lunchtime. Right now, it's early morning rush hour, so the streets are jammed with cars and buses, and the sidewalks are equally packed with pedestrians heading to work.

I glance down at my outfit, hoping I'm dressed appropriately. I'm wearing a brown skirt, cream-colored blouse, leggings and brown flats. My hair is down, and I'm wearing small silver studs in my ears and my charm bracelet around my wrist.

I hope it's not too much.

I hope it's enough.

"Here we are," he says, pointing up at a huge stone edifice that takes up half a city block. "Carmichael & Son."

It looks more like an old courthouse building than an equity firm. It's enormous, with a massive multi-story marble façade. It must be four or five stories tall, with huge windows and ornate details on the exterior. Five stone pillars surround an impressive archway. The three turrets make me think of castles and fortresses rather than a modern financial services company.

I stare up at the building. "It's... huge."

"We're one of the largest equity firms in Europe, you know," he says, with a tinge of pride in his voice. He watches me admiring the building and smiles. "We receive over a thousand applications every year for coveted internship positions, and fewer than one percent of applicants are selected." He pauses to smile. "I'm very proud of you, Skye."

"Great, Dad. Make me feel even more nervous."

He chuckles. "Don't worry, darling. You'll do well. I have all the faith in the world in you."

Parking is surprisingly easy, as my father has his own designated spot in the rear lot. My stomach is in knots as we walk up the pristine stone walk to the employee entrance at the back of the building. The grounds are meticulously tended, with lush green grass and colorful flowerbeds.

My dad motions for me to precede him through the glass doors.

Inside, the lobby is spacious, with soaring ceilings. The floors are polished marble, and beyond the receptionist desks are two banks of elevators.

"Good morning, Mr. Williams," says one of the receptionists, a young woman with pale blonde hair twisted up in a bun. She eyes me curiously.

We stop at the expansive mahogany desk, and my father says, "Good morning, Megan. This is my daughter, Skye. She'll be working here for the next year, doing a post-graduate internship."

"It's a pleasure to meet you, Miss Williams," she says.

I love her accent. "Thank you."

Her eyes widen. "You're American." She sounds surprised.

I grin. "Guilty as charged."

As we continue to the elevators, I notice I'm getting quite a number of curious glances. My dad is on the receiving end of quite a few "good mornings" and other respectful greetings. As a managing director, he's probably pretty well known around here.

We step into a crowded elevator and ride up to the second floor. When the door opens, my father motions that this is our stop. He follows me out and walks me down the hall to the personnel office.

"Here you go," he says, stopping at the door to the HR department. "Make me proud. I'll collect you from your office at five o'clock, and we'll go see about your flat."

My heart is hammering in my chest as I open the heavy glass door that leads into the personnel office. There's a sizable waiting room with plenty of chairs, all currently empty. Across the room is a long, high countertop, behind which sits a middle-aged woman who's talking on the phone. When she sees me, she abruptly ends the call.

I walk up to the counter and smile, doing my best to look professional and confident. "Good morning. I'm Skye Williams. I'm here to start my internship."

The woman—Mrs. Stewart according to her name-tag—glances up with a frown. "You're American."

"Yes." I nod, unsure whether I should apologize or not. She

seems to think I should.

"I've been expecting you." Mrs. Stewart waves at the plethora of empty chairs. "Have a seat. Someone from Risk Assessment will be along to collect you momentarily."

I give her my best smile, trying not to show any trepidation. "Thank you."

While I sit, she picks up the phone. "Hello, Sylvia. The new intern is here. Would you send someone over to collect her?" After hanging up, she says, "Someone will be right along." And then she leaves the room through a side door.

I haven't been sitting for more than a few minutes when the door slams open and a man who looks to be in his early thirties stalks briskly into the office. He's dressed in dark trousers and a white button-up shirt that looks a bit rumpled, like he might've pulled an all-nighter. His short auburn hair looks a bit slept-in as well—there's a tuft sticking up in the back.

He walks to the counter and glowers when he sees there's no one there. "Mrs. Stewart?" He pounds his fist on the countertop and leans across the surface to bellow in a deep, resonant voice. "Hello! Is anyone there?"

God, his accent is divine.

Getting no response, he turns.

My stomach does a somersault when I get a look at his face. His eyes—they're green. He's tall, with sharp cheekbones, a perfectly aquiline nose, and a neatly-trimmed beard. He's... *riveting.*

My heart flutters when his gaze zeroes in on me, and I have to force myself to take a steadying breath. He stares intently, right at me, his jaw tightening as he looks me over from head to toe. He gives me a quizzical look, looking almost relieved.

Immediately, I feel underdressed.

I should have worn a suit.

He points at me. "You're late." And then he marches toward the door, waving for me to follow.

When I sit frozen, he snaps his fingers. "Well, come on. I don't have all day."

Flustered, I grab my purse and jump to my feet. "I'm not late! In fact, I'm fifteen minutes early. I wasn't supposed to be here until eight-thirty."

"Eight o'clock," he counters in the most swoon-worthy British accent I've ever heard.

He doesn't bother to slow down, and I find myself rushing out the door after him, my heart pounding. As his long legs eat up the distance, I myself racing to catch up.

I'm definitely not getting off to a good start.

4

Will

This is my new PA? So much for Dad's proclamations against attractive female PAs. She's gorgeous! Those long, coltish legs and that waterfall of honey-blonde hair? I'm fairly weak in the knees right now.

Dear God, I hope there's no boyfriend in the picture. Life couldn't be that cruel.

I was sure my father would pick Frankenstein's monster or The Hulk for my next assistant. But this goddess-like creature with big blue eyes and hair as shiny as spun-silk? I could eat her up for breakfast.

What in the hell was my father thinking?

As I head back to my office, my mind is reeling. I had a fucking awful weekend and drank way too much. I got absolutely no sleep, and I woke up this morning with a splitting headache. The week had started off like shit, but now *this*? It's a complete reversal. The gods are smiling down on me.

I stop to press the button for the lift. One quick glance down the hall assures me that my new PA is doing her best to keep pace.

I sneak a peek at myself in the large wall-mounted mirror hanging beside the lift and cringe. I look like death warmed over. I'm definitely not putting my best foot forward today. When I take the time to comb my hair and put on a freshly-pressed suit, I'm a pretty damn good-looking bloke, if I do say so myself. At the moment, though, I look like something the cat dragged in.

My eyes narrow on my reflection, and I shake my head. My eyes are bloodshot. My suit's horribly wrinkled, I'm in a shit mood, hung over, and I'm in serious need of caffeine. My cloak of superiority has been lifted, and today I'm just like everyone else. I'm a mere mortal.

I hear the *tap tap tap* of my new PA's sensible flats as she catches up.

What the fuck's her name, anyway?

I'm not sure if she said. "What's your name again?"

Her eyes widen in surprise, and I swear she must think me dense. "Skye Williams."

Sky, like the color of her eyes? How pretty.

And then I realize I just heard her speak for the first time. "You're American!"

What the fuck!

We don't have any sexy young British girls available to follow me around and do my bidding? We have to import them now?

"Yes, I'm American," she says, sounding a bit put out.

An American.

Actually, I find it a bit intriguing.

Aren't they supposed to be a bit promiscuous, or is that just wishful thinking on my part?

I admit to having seen a few too many American spring break films. Lots of booze and skimpy tops. "Hmm. Interesting."

There's a little scowl on her pretty face as she tries to make sense of my reply.

My shoes squeak on the polished floor as I pivot and step into the lift. I motion for her to follow suit before the doors close. "Hurry up, Miss America. I don't have all day."

She flinches, and I remind myself to tone it down.

Americans are so sensitive. I've worked with a few over the years, and they take offense at every little thing. I'll have to remember that. I sure as hell don't want to chase this one off.

Inside the lift, I punch the button for the fourth floor.

Just before the doors close, someone yells, "Hold the lift!"

Connor. Damn it.

Young Connor steps into the lift and gives me a tightlipped smile. Then he turns to the beauty standing beside me. "Hello there." He offers her his hand, and she takes it.

Damn it, why didn't I think of that?

"Connor Murphy," he says, sounding all posh. "Pleased to meet you."

She smiles warmly at the lad. "Skye Williams."

"*Williams?* You're Frank Williams' daughter, aren't you?" he says. "I heard you were starting today."

Suddenly, she looks much more at ease. "Yes."

"Wait a minute," I say. "As in Frank Williams, the managing director of finance?" Well, that explains how the American got a coveted spot as a PA in this firm. It was a fucking favor. A little bit of nepotism.

How very American.

She nods, giving me a bit of a glare. "He's my father, but I assure you, I earned this position on my own merit."

Oooh, she's a feisty one.

This is getting better and better.

The lift comes to a smooth stop and the doors open. I step out. Connor and Skye are right on my heels as we head to my office. We sail right past Lois, my administrative assistant, whose desk is located just outside my office. She glances up as we pass, but refrains from speaking. I'm sure she's curious as to the identify of this angel with me.

When we reach the door to my office, I pause and turn back to the lad. "Connor, don't you have something else you should be doing?"

"No, nothing at all," Connor says, not budging a centimeter. He's clearly not taking the hint.

Like a gentleman, I open the door for my new PA, but before I can follow her in, Connor steps in front of me.

The cockblocker!

He really does need to learn how to take cues better. "Connor, you'd better get to work."

He gives me an enigmatic smile. "I am."

I suppose I am being a bit of a prick. It's not that I want to belittle the boy; it's just that I'd like a few minutes alone with Miss Williams to establish the basis of our new working relationship.

I clap my hand on his shoulder. "Why don't you go do something useful, like make us some lattes?"

"Sure, boss, why not?" he says, winking at me as he walks out the door.

Finally, we're alone. I close my office door and motion for Miss Williams to take one of the chairs in front of my desk. "So, Skye, right?"

"Yes."

We chat for a few moments, getting the pleasantries out of the way.

How was her flight from America?

How was she finding London?

And so on.

"Let me be the first to welcome you to Carmichael & Son," I say. "I'm Will Carmichael, as in the *son* in Carmichael & Son."

My office door swings open, and Connor enters carrying three steaming lattes. He hands one to Skye, one to me, and keeps one for himself.

"So, boss, what did I miss?" he says as he takes the chair next to Skye.

I'm not sure why Connor keeps calling me *boss*. Frankly, I'm finding it a bit weird. "Not much. I was just going to tell Miss Williams what I expect of her whilst she's my PA."

Other than bringing me the occasional latte, maybe she'd like to join me for a five-star dinner after work, and then we could partake in a moonlit walk.

The kid snickers, and my heart stops cold.

Shit! I didn't say that aloud, did I?

I look to Skye for confirmation, and there's nothing more than an amused smile on her pretty face. She's clearly not offended, so I think I'm safe.

I ignore Connor and resume my conversation with Skye. Hopefully he'll get bored and go on his way. "So, Skye—is it okay that I call you that?"

Her amusement grows. "I'm sorry, but I think there's been some kind of misunderstanding."

"Misunderstanding? How so?"

Connor breaks into a fit of laughter, very undignified, and he nearly chokes on his coffee. I look from him to Skye and back again. Whatever the joke is, they're both in on it, whilst I seem to have lost the plot.

There's a huge, self-satisfied grin on Connor's face.

"I'm sorry, but what am I missing here?" I say to Skye.

She rises from her chair and smooths her skirt. Her cheeks are turning a pretty shade of pink. "I'm not your PA."

She's trying admirably hard not to laugh, and I find it sexy as hell.

"As much fun as this has been," she says, "I'm late for my actual job which—" she checks the time on her Apple watch "—started five minutes ago. Thanks for the latte, but I'll have to pass." She sets her coffee cup on my desk. "Now, if you'll excuse me, gentlemen, I need to find out where I should be."

She turns toward the door.

"Wait!" I say. "If you're not my PA, then what are you?" Now I'm really intrigued.

She turns back to me with a smile. "I'm here to complete a post-graduate internship in the risk assessment department. I'll just return to HR and get things sorted out. Sorry for the mix-up."

Connor races to the door ahead of her. "I'll show you the way, Skye." He's staring at her like a cat eyeing a bowl of cream.

"Thanks, but that won't be necessary," she says. "I'm sure I can find my own way."

And then she's gone, just like that, leaving us both shell-shocked.

Stunned, I stare at the spot where she'd been standing a moment ago. "What the fuck?"

Connor dissolves into laughter. "You idiot! *I'm* your new PA!"

"What!"

"Yes, your father promoted me to PA. Now I'll actually get paid to fetch and carry for you."

"What?" I know I sound like a broken record, but I can't help it. I'm reeling. With a growl, I point to the door. "Get out."

Most of the time I love this kid, but not right now. I could swing for him. He's just made me look like a total fool in front of Skye. Well actually, I did that all by myself. But he should have said right away he was my new PA. They say first impressions are everything, and after this little debacle, she'll never take me seriously.

Connor picks up a notepad lying on my desk. "But I'm your new PA. Don't you want to me to take notes? Maybe tell me how you like your lattes?"

I roll my eyes at the little fucker. Then I picture Skye scurrying through the building in search of the personnel office, likely to get lost.

I motion toward the door. "Oh, hell! Go after her. Make sure she gets to where she's going."

As soon as Connor's gone, a sinking feeling hits me in the gut.

Risk assessment department?

Well, fuck.

That means she'll be working for Spencer Sinclair, a notorious womanizer. He's been warned about sexual harassment more times than I care to count.

And Skye's going to be reporting to *him?*

5

Skye

As I breeze past the administrative assistant's desk, I step out into the corridor and look left and then right. *Darn it!*

I can't recall which direction we came from.

Where's the elevator?

I glance at my watch. I'm officially late now, thanks to a certain egotistical playboy who assumed I was his new office toy.

Hardly!

I don't know who this Fitzwilliam Carmichael, the second, thinks he is. Yes, he's ridiculously good-looking, and his accent is to die for, but still, that's no excuse to be so presumptuous. He just *assumed* I was his new PA because I'm a female.

When I hear someone running up behind me, I turn to look. It's the cute blond guy, Connor.

He grabs my shoulders and directs me to the left. "The lift is this way," he says.

He's blushing, if I'm not mistaken.

Connor reminds me of a young Brad Pitt, only much cuter, with blond hair and blue eyes. He's tall and built like a football player, with broad shoulders, a trim waist, and long, long legs. I'll bet there's a six-pack lurking beneath his white button-up shirt.

"You knew all along, didn't you?" I say as he escorts me down the hall.

"Of course I did. And it was hysterical. I've never seen him so flustered before." He stops me. "Here's the lift."

Connor presses the elevator call button, and we wait for the car to arrive. When the doors open, he follows me inside and bursts into laughter. "Oh, my God, that was classic."

"You did that on purpose," I say.

He nods readily as tears leak from the corners of his eyes. He brushes them aside. "I couldn't resist. I hope you're not mad. It was just a prank."

His amusement is infectious, and I find myself smiling. "I don't mind as long as you get me back to HR quickly." I check the time. "I'm ten minutes late now, and I hate to be late for anything."

"Right. On it."

As he shifts a bit closer, our arms brush, and I don't think it was an accident.

I take a discreet step away to put some space between us. "You and Mr. Carmichael seem to be on pretty friendly terms. Are you friends?"

"Mr.—" He frowns. "Oh, you mean Will. Yeah, we're mates. You threw me for a second. Around here, *Mr. Carmichael* is the old man—his father. Will's just... Will."

"Is he always so... abrupt... with people?"

Connor shrugs. "It's just his way. He's really a good bloke, once you get to know him."

"Well, as we won't be working together, I doubt I'll get the chance."

"Don't be too sure about that," Connor says, grinning. "I think he's smitten with you."

I feel an unexpected surge of heat at the thought of that man being interested in me. He's clearly older than I am, not to mention ridiculously out of my league. I'm sure women throw themselves at his feet. "Don't be silly."

Connor grins at me as the elevator doors open. He points to the left. "HR is that way, around the corner, second door on the right. You can't miss it. See you around, Skye."

"Thanks." I step out of the elevator and head down the hallway.

When I walk into the HR department for the second time that morning, a rather perturbed looking Mrs. Stewart glances at me from across her desk. "There you are! I wondered where you'd got to. Mr. Sinclair's executive assistant came to collect you, and I had no idea where you'd gone."

Mr. Sinclair?

Ah, my new boss.

My face heats. "I'm so sorry. There was a mix-up, and another gentleman thought I was his new PA. We cleared up the matter, and here I am."

"Another gentleman?" she says, sounding a bit baffled.

"Mr. Carmichael—the son, I mean. He thought I was his new PA."

"Mister—" She snickers. "You mean Will. Of course he did." She picks up her desk phone and punches a button. "Stella? I've found her. I'll make sure she stays put until you get here." She hangs up the phone and points at a chair in the waiting area. "Sit right there and don't move a muscle. Stella's coming to get you."

I take a seat, feeling like I just got a scolding from the principal. It's too bad I got off to a rough start on my first day here. I hope my new boss doesn't hold it against me.

It's not long before Stella breezes into the office. She's willowy thin, her hair a cloud of unruly white curls. She's dressed in a beige pantsuit with a white tailored blouse and black stiletto heels.

I'm definitely underdressed.

Mrs. Stewart points at me. "There she is. Good luck keeping track of her."

I laugh good-naturedly at Mrs. Stewart's retort; after all, it's in my best interest to be on good terms with the woman who appears to run the HR department. But she doesn't even crack a smile.

I follow Stella up one flight of stairs and down two corridors to an impressive office with double glass doors framed in mahogany. She opens one of the doors and ushers me inside.

"This is the risk assessment department," she informs me as she leads me through another set of doors to a large, open room filled with at least a dozen workstations. She takes me to one at the back of the room, near a wall of windows. "Here's where you'll be sitting. Make yourself at home. I'll tell Mr. Sinclair you're here. I'm sure he'll want to talk to you shortly."

There's a computer monitor on the desk, a keyboard, and a mouse. There's also a phone and a small metal trashcan beside the desk, but little else.

Stella opens the lap drawer, which is filled with pens, paperclips, and a stapler.

"That should get you started," she says, pointing to a printed sheet of paper lying next to the computer keyboard. "It has all your login details, username, password, and company e-mail address. I presume you know how to use a computer."

I nod. "Thank you, Mrs.—" I realize I don't know her last name.

"Stella's fine," she says. "My desk is at the front of the room, and Mr. Sinclair's office is right over there, through those glass doors." She points at a glass wall, through which I can see a middle-aged man with a brown comb-over seated at a large mahogany desk.

"Let me know if you need anything," she says, and then she leaves me to settle in.

I sit down and take a deep breath. Then I reach into my purse for my phone to check for messages. There are two.

Dad: Have a great day.

Mom: Miss you, sweetheart. Enjoy your first day at work.

So far, it's not looking all that good.

* * *

After logging into the computer and verifying that I can send and receive e-mail, I wait for my new boss to make an appearance. While I'm waiting, I make a concerted effort to put Fitzwilliam Carmichael *junior* and this morning's events out of my mind.

Unfortunately, the more I try not to think of him, the more he invades my thoughts. He's bossy, arrogant, egotistical… and sexy as hell. I hope I don't run into him often. I'm here to do a job, not moon over the CEO's son.

Finally, I spot my new boss heading my way. Every inch of him is polished and perfected, from the expensive cut of his Navy pin-striped suit to his carefully gelled hair. He's slick, in a smarmy way.

"Miss Williams," he says, offering me his hand with a grandiose flourish. He grips mine, cupping it with his other hand.

"Good morning, Mr. Sinclair."

"Please, call me Spencer," he says affably as he takes the seat beside my desk. "Well, it's actually *Sir Spencer*, you know," he adds, laughing. "Although I'm not one to stand on ceremony. Sir or Spencer will be fine."

I suspect the *sir* bit is a British thing, like some kind of title or special designation, like being knighted.

Aren't Paul McCartney and Elton John sirs, too?

I smile, trying not to act like this is painfully awkward. "Thank you—Spencer." Honestly, I don't think I could call him *sir* and keep a straight face.

He steeples his long fingers in front of him and leans closer. "So, Skye, tell me all about yourself. You're American—and unmarried, I take it. How fascinating."

6

Will

Despite a slight hiccup—that little case of mistaken identity called Skye—the morning has gone pleasantly well. With Lidia at hand, our Japanese translator, I had a lengthy conference call to a potential new client in Tokyo. We haven't had many prospects from Japan before, but I'm confident this company will be a great investment. As a senior account manager, my job is to oversee investment projects to make sure everything goes to plan and that the clients are living up to their side of the agreement.

Like the cat that got the cream, I sit with a smile on my face

as the client drones on and on about the breadth of their cus-
tomer portfolio and the meteoric rise in their market share over
the past two years. I've already studied their portfolio in depth,
so I'm already well aware of their potential. I'm confident it's a
great opportunity. This call is just a formality.

As I end the call, Connor walks into my office with a folder
clutched in his arms. "Here's the Cooperman file you asked for."
He drops the folder on my desk, and papers slide everywhere.

I shove my empty cup towards him, certainly not amused.
I'm sure I'm wearing the male equivalent of resting bitch face.
"Pick those up. And get me another latte, if you don't mind.
This time make sure it's palatable. The last one had way too
much sugar in it."

He arches a brow at me, mirroring my disdain. Connor reminds me of myself at that age... fearless, headstrong, and a bit
reckless.

"Haven't you had enough coffee this morning, Will? This
would be your third. Too much caffeine isn't good for your
heart."

"Don't give me any grief, kid," I warn. "Just do as you're told.
You wanted this job, so do it. Or I'll have you fired."

After replacing the papers neatly in the folder, Connor takes
a seat opposite me, folding his arms and crossing one leg over
the other. His eyes narrow on me, his lips forming a straight
line.

"You can't fire me," he says, sounding like a haughty, con-
temptuous little shit. "My grandfather plays golf with your dad.

Let's face it, you're stuck with me, mate. You'll drink your damn coffee the way it's made and be grateful."

The kid's got me by the balls, I have to admit. His grandfather and my dad are old school mates, so I can't fire him. Whatever foot he puts out of place, I've just got to put up and shut up.

I love my job, but what's always made it that little bit sweeter was the eye candy I had to look at every morning. Cindy, Jacinta, even Rachel—that back-stabbing bitch—were all great PAs, and all offered a little something extra. Now all I've got to look at is Connor.

"And don't even think of sexually harassing me," he says, again demonstrating an uncanny ability to read my mind. Or, maybe I'm just that predictable. His lips threaten to twitch into a grin. "I know you have trouble restraining yourself, but I warn you, I won't put up with it."

I laugh at his audacity. But it's got me thinking.

Is this how everyone in the office sees me? As a philanderer? Sex mad?

This isn't how I want my staff to see me. "Do me a favor, kid."

"That stops as well. I am not a *kid*. I'm eighteen years old. Call me Connor or Mr. Murphy, please."

"Okay, *Connor*, after you make me a coffee, will you kindly take Miss Williams one as well?"

His eyes widen. "Excuse me?"

"Tell her it's from me. Tell her it's an olive branch of sorts, to make up for this morning's fiasco—which was completely your fault by the way."

"*My* fault?"

"Yes, yours. You're the one who let me think she was my new PA. You should have spoken up right away. Instead, you let me go on and make a fool of myself. Of course it's your fault. And now I have to make things right with her."

"Aren't you forgetting something?" he says.

I frown, clueless as to what he's going on about now. "What?"

"Your manners, Will. It doesn't take any more effort to say *please*."

I bite the insides of my cheeks to keep from laughing. My God, this kid is priceless. At least he's entertaining. "*Please*, take Skye a latte. And make it a good one. Go easy on the sugar."

Connor stands, and he's valiantly trying to hide a smug grin. I know he's eager to see Skye again—as if he has a snowball's chance in hell with her.

"All right," he says, sighing as though I'm asking him to do some repugnant task. "If I must." Then he makes a face. "I just hope I don't run into Sinclair in the process. The man gives me the creeps."

Spencer Sinclair is the office scoundrel, and yes, I realize that's rich coming from me.

I'm a fine one to judge, right?

But at least I'm able to draw lines in the sand. He'll see Skye as fresh prey, and he'll be all over her. I can't let that happen.

"Keep an eye on her, will you?" I tell Connor. "I'll pay Spencer a visit this morning and set some boundaries where Skye is concerned."

Connor grins. "Staking your claim already?"

"Of course not." *Yes.* "I just don't want Spencer giving her any grief."

We both head out of my office and part ways in reception. He heads to the staff room to make Skye a latte, and I head to risk assessment.

Spencer keeps me waiting for five minutes, but we both know it's just for show.

Finally, he opens his door and waves me in. "Will, how good to see you. Sorry about that. I was composing an important e-mail."

More like he was closing the gambling app on his computer.

He and I both know he has a tiny gambling addiction, and I've caught him gaming online during work hours on more than one occasion after stopping at his office unannounced. He's been warned, and he's one misstep away from having his contract terminated. The irony is, he's the manager of risk assessment, when he's a huge fucking risk himself.

His office is huge, with fuck all inside, much like his head, I imagine. He's worked here for six years, and there's absolutely nothing in his office that is personalized—no photos on his desk, no quirky mugs, nothing.

He's a closed book. It's unfortunate for him his computer's search history isn't the same.

A floor-to-ceiling glass partition separates us from the staff in his department. I scan the view outside his office and quickly spot Skye seated at her desk, typing away on her computer.

A moment later, Connor appears at Skye's desk and offers her the latte, which she seems happy to accept. The little bugger probably won't bother telling her it's from me. No, he'll take all the credit as he tries to worm his way into her good graces.

"So, to what do I owe the privilege of this visit, Will?" Spencer says, directing my attention back to himself.

"I came to give you a friendly warning."

He scowls. "About what?"

I nod toward Skye's workstation. "Your new intern, Miss Williams."

"Ah, yes. The pretty American. What about her?"

"I want to make one thing very clear. She's off limits to you."

He sits up straighter. "Now, you see here—"

"Cut the crap, Spencer. Stay away from her. If I hear of you hitting on her, or treating her disrespectfully in any way, I'll—"

"What's it to you, Carmichael? You've already got your eye on her?"

He always uses my surname when he's pissed, but too bad. "She's Frank Williams' daughter. Show some respect."

A shrewd gleam enters his pale blue eyes. "Why such an intense interest in the new girl? She doesn't even work for you. How is she any of your business?"

I glance back at Skye, who's sipping her latte and laughing at something Connor's said. When I glance back at Spencer, he's eyeing me speculatively. For a cretin, he can be rather perceptive sometimes.

Rolling his tongue across his brilliantly white teeth, he says, "Care to tell me why Miss Williams was late this morning?"

There are a dozen answers I could give him, just to wipe that stupid smirk off his face, but I don't. I can't ruin her first day for her.

"Misunderstanding," is all I offer. "My fault, not hers."

His eyes challenge me, goading for more. "She's fairly attractive, isn't she? I love her accent. It's so American."

Who's he kidding? She's fucking gorgeous.

Looking past Spencer, I gaze out of the window and try to appear disinterested. The last thing I want to do is let Spencer Sinclair know I'm keenly interested in Skye. "Is she? I hadn't noticed."

"Oh, I rather think you noticed. Why else would you be in my office, beating your chest like an ape trying to stake his claim? If you don't mind, Will, I'll ask you to get out of my office and let me run my own department how I see fit." He sneers at me. "You're such a fucking hypocrite. Where's Rachel Whittingham? Funny, I haven't seen your PA all morning."

My blood starts boiling, and I can almost imagine steam bursting from my ears. I grit my teeth and struggle to keep my voice low when I say, "What I mind is management taking liberties with the staff. Your gambling problem is one thing, but sexually harassing your staff is another. There's taking liberties and then there's taking the piss. I won't stand for it."

Spencer's face turns from pasty white to bright red as he starts to sputter. "You can't tell me what to do." He's practically growling. "I'll do whatever the hell I want, with whomever I want. I don't have to answer to the likes of you!"

That's where he's wrong. I hate to pull rank on anyone and use my family name, but this is my family's company, and when my father retires, it will be my company. I'll be damned if I'll let a middle-aged letch like Spencer Sinclair poach on an innocent young woman. "Watch yourself, Spencer. If I hear of any unprofessional behavior on your part toward Miss Williams, you will answer directly to me—that's a promise."

His hand curls into a fist. "You can't talk to me like that, Will. I have seniority over you!" He's practically spitting now.

I try counting to ten slowly in my head, but I give up halfway. Oh, fuck it.

Just looking at this red-faced wanker is pissing me off. To think he has plans to try something with Skye! It's vile.

I lean across his desk and grab his tie, yanking him out of his chair so we're practically nose-to-nose over the desktop. I glare daggers at him, daring him to talk back to me. "You listen to me, Spencer. If you so much as touch one hair on Miss Williams' head, I'll have yours on a pike. Is that clear? She is off limits to you."

When I release him, Spencer falls back onto his chair, his mouth agape. Before he can get another word out, I walk out of his office, secretly hoping he'll continue talking crap so I have an excuse to go right back in there and do it all over again. But he doesn't.

Smart fellow.

I don't hear another sound out of him as I stride from his office and make my way across the floor to Skye's workstation. Connor is perched on the corner of her desk, regaling Skye with some stupid story about a school rugby match.

As soon as I approach, their laughter dies a quick death.

"Hello, Skye," I say, standing in front of her desk doing my best to look cordial. "I see you got the latte I asked Connor to bring you. Excellent. Consider it a peace offering after the fiasco this morning. I truly am sorry about the misunderstanding. I genuinely thought you were my new PA. It was my mistake, dreadfully sexist of me, wasn't it?"

I give her my best smile, and then I point at Connor. "Turns out this lout has been stuck with the job."

"Thank you for the latte," she says. "I could use a bit of caffeine this morning. And no harm done on the mix-up. Mr. Sinclair was very understanding."

"Was he, now?" I have to bite my tongue to keep from telling her what I actually think about her boss. I wave for Connor to get off her desk. "All right, back to work, Connor. Let Miss Williams get back to what she was doing before you so rudely interrupted her."

I wink at Skye, and she smiles back warmly.

As those lips curve up and her blue eyes twinkle prettily, I find myself a bit short of breath. She's really lovely, all wavy, dark blonde hair cascading over her shoulder and a fresh, sweet face. Other than a touch of mascara and a swipe of lip gloss, I don't think she's wearing any make-up. She's what they call a natural beauty.

"I'll see you around, Skye," I say as I take my leave, beckoning to Connor to follow. I'm not leaving him here alone with her a moment longer.

Practically pouting, Connor follows me out into the main corridor. "She's incredible," he says with a sigh as we step into the lift.

I press the button for our floor. He's right, of course, but I'm not about to encourage him. "She's too old for you, Connor."

He bristles. "She is not! She's twenty-four, and I'm eighteen. That's not such a huge difference. Besides, some girls dig younger guys. We have more stamina, you know."

I laugh, wondering how in the hell he knows her age. "Don't be ridiculous."

Twenty-four, eh?

She's a bit young for a jaded thirty-year-old like me, but I could make it work.

7

Skye

At noon, Connor reappears at my desk, his handsome face grinning down at me. It's a relief to see a friendly face. "Connor! To what do I owe the pleasure?"

He drops down onto the guest chair. "So, how's your first day been so far?"

"After a bit of a rocky start, I've settled in quite nicely." I motion toward my computer screen. "I'm reviewing the portfolio for my first assessment. It's a social media development firm here in the UK."

"Fascinating," Connor says, already sounding bored. "So, do

you have plans for lunch? I thought I'd show you around the neighborhood, if you'd like. There are tons of great restaurants within walking distance. How about it?"

"Perfect. I didn't bring anything with me for lunch today. I was hoping I could go out and do a little bit of sightseeing. And I can't wait to experience an authentic British restaurant."

"Well, that's exactly what you'll get." He stands and runs his hands down his trouser legs. "Let's go, then. I'm starving."

I grab my purse and follow Connor down the hall to the elevator. We ride down to the ground floor, and as we step out into the lobby, we encounter Will Carmichael at the front reception desk picking up a bag of food.

"Where the hell have you been?" he says to Connor, clearly peeved. "I've been looking everywhere for you."

Connor grins. "I'm sorry if you had to come all the way down here to collect your own food. I've got a lunch date with Skye."

Will's gaze bounces back and forth between me and Connor, looking dumbfounded.

"It's not really a date," I clarify, feeling my cheeks heat under the force of Will's scrutiny. I don't know why I have this need to explain myself; we're just going out for lunch. "Connor offered to show me around the neighborhood."

"And we're having lunch," Connor reiterates. "*Together*. Just the two of us, so that makes it a date."

Connor lays his hand on my lower back and gently nudges me towards the glass doors.

Will's brow furrows as he glares at Connor. But when his

gaze shifts to me, it softens. "I'd be happy to join you, Skye, if you'd like. I'd love to show you around Canary Wharf."

Connor nods to the bag of food in Will's hands. "Too bad, it looks like you've already sorted your lunch for today." He pats Will's arm. "Maybe another time, mate."

Leaving Will standing with his mouth open, Connor steers me through the lobby and out the front doors. I glance back to see Will still rooted to the spot, looking like he was just pole-axed. I think Connor got the jump on him.

Connor bursts out laughing as he takes my arm and propels me away from the building. "That was classic! Did you see the look on his face? He's not used to coming in second. So, what sounds good to you? Thai? Indian? Chinese?" He pats his lean stomach. "I could eat anything."

"Actually, I was hoping for something quintessentially British."

"Quinta—what? Oh, right. Well, a chippie it is, then. You can't get more British than that."

"Chippie?"

"Fish and chips. Come on, then. I know just the place. It's not far."

We walk three blocks, passing all sorts of interesting restaurants representing every cuisine imaginable, including Italian, Moroccan, Japanese, Chinese. I'm looking forward to trying them all over the coming year.

My gaze is pinging all over the place as I take in all the shops and cafés. I've never been in such a big city before. With a population of over three-hundred-thousand, Cincinnati isn't small by any means, but I grew up in a suburb with lots of open, green spaces. From what I've seen, it seems like every inch of London is jam packed with people, cars, buses, and buildings. It's a bit of a culture shock, to say the least.

The sidewalk foot traffic is brisk, with most people walking quickly as if on a mission, earbuds in their ears. I see a few women pushing strollers, but most of the folks out here are professionals on their lunch breaks, as we're in the financial district. I have to hustle to keep up with Connor's long strides. And every time a red, double-decker London bus passes me, I get a little thrill.

We pass expensive clothing and jewelry shops, bakeries, bookshops, and coffee houses.

Connor stops in front of a small corner shop, a little café with a fish and chips sign hanging above the door. "Here we are," he says.

Just as he reaches for the door handle, someone reaches around him and grabs it, shouldering his way between us.

I look up, shocked to see Will Carmichael standing between us. He's a bit winded, his cheeks flushed, as if he ran the entire way to catch us.

"Skye, fancy running into you here." Will gives me quick smile, and then he turns his attention to Connor. "Sorry, mate, but your granddad wants you."

"What?" Connor says.

"Your granddad. He's asking for you. I told him I'd fetch you.

I think it might be urgent."

Connor looks more than a little skeptical as he glares at Will and shakes his head. "You bloody wanker."

Will looks offended. "Language, Connor. There's a lady present." Will smiles apologetically at me. Then to Connor, he says, "You'd better run along. You don't want to keep the old man waiting."

Connor turns to me, looking dejected. "I guess I'll have to take a rain check, Skye. Will you be okay?"

Before I can answer, Will says, "She'll be fine." He nudges Connor back. "Don't worry. I'll see that she has a nice lunch."

"I'm sure you will," Connor mutters as Will ushers me into the restaurant and closes the door on Connor.

Aromas of fried food and the tang of malt vinegar make my mouth water.

Will steers me to a small corner table for two. "Have a seat, Skye. I'll get our food."

I grab hold of his sleeve. "Wait. Did you just make that up? About Connor's grandfather needing him?"

Will grins. "Of course I did. I'm not about to be outmaneuvered by a child."

I suppress a grin as Will leaves to order our food. He's an unusual mix of arrogance and charm, and I find myself liking him even when I think I shouldn't.

While Will's occupied at the food counter, conversing with the guy behind the counter who's dipping fish filets into batter and dropping them into hot oil, I spend my time people-watching, listening to snippets of the many conversations going on around me. The restaurant is crowded with a wide diversity of people speaking different languages. Not only do I hear British accents, but I detect a little French, Indian, and German.

When Will returns to our table, he's carrying two plates piled high with food. He sets them on the table, and then he goes back to get our drinks.

"Beer?" I say, when he returns with two large glasses of amber liquid.

He takes his seat. "Sure, why not?"

"Are we allowed to drink during work hours?"

"I do it all the time." He lifts his glass. "Cheers."

I raise my glass and touch it to his, still not convinced this is a good idea.

He takes a sip of his beer, then sets his glass down. "Tuck in," he says, picking up his fork and pointing it at my plate.

On my plate is a huge, fried battered filet of cod, a small mountain of thick French fries, a dollop of coleslaw, a wedge of lemon, and something bright green resembling mashed avocado.

I point at the green stuff. "What's that?"

"Mushy peas."

"What's it made from?"

He looks at me like I'm an idiot. "Peas."

"I know that! I mean, what else is in it? Garlic? Onions?"

He shrugs. "They're mushed up peas. Try it."

I reach for the bottle of Heinz ketchup on the table, and he slides it out of reach.

"What do you want that for?" He sounds thoroughly offended.

"For my fries."

"Your—oh, you mean chips. Good lord, no! You put vinegar on your chips, not ketchup." He hands me a bottle of malt vinegar. "You're in London, so do as the Londoners. Try it. It's delicious."

I drizzle some vinegar on my fries, then pick one up and take a hesitant bite. The tang of the vinegar, the salty crisp exterior of the fry, the tender fluffiness inside—it's delicious. I break off a piece of the battered cod, which is steaming hot, and blow on it, giving it a minute to cool before I pop it into my mouth. The batter is crunchy, and the fish is flaky and tender.

"I've had fish and chips in the US before, of course. It's actually pretty popular back home, but I have to say this is much better than anything I've ever had." I squirt some of the lemon juice on my fish and try the mushy peas.

Not bad.

"Skye."

I glance up. "Yes?"

Will pops a French fry in his mouth and chews. "I'm truly sorry about the mix-up this morning. I hope I didn't get you into too much trouble. I was expecting a new PA, and when I saw you, I thought—"

"Because I'm a female, you assumed I was a PA."

"Well, yes. My PAs are always female. Or, at least they have been in the past."

I shrug off his apology. "It was an honest mistake. It could have happened to anyone."

He nods. "To be honest, though, it wasn't just because you're a woman. It was also wishful thinking on my part. I'm keen to get to know you better. I was hoping you might feel the same."

I'm not sure, but I think he just made a pass at me. I focus my attention on my plate as he watches me closely, waiting for a reply. I don't even know what to say, or how to respond. I chew a bite of fish instead and swallow.

Out of the corner of my eye, I catch him watching me expectantly, clearly waiting for a reply. When I don't give him one, he takes a swig of his beer.

"Look, about your new boss," he says. "If Sinclair gives you any trouble at all, I want you to let me know straight away. All right?"

Surprised at the change of subject, I shrug. "He seems nice. I explained what happened this morning, and he thought it was funny."

"Sure he did." He rolls his eyes. "If he gives you any grief at all, for any reason, you let me know. I'll handle it."

As we eat, I try not to stare at him. He's undeniably handsome, with his dark auburn hair and green eyes. His shoulders fill out his suit jacket quite nicely. I find his hands mesmerizing, his fingers long. They look *strong*. I never realized hands could be so sexy. And truthfully, I could listen to him talk all day. His accent makes the most mundane of topics sound like foreplay.

Despite the expensive cut of his suit, there's a certain ruggedness about him. I'm so used to being around guys my age who are still trying to find their way in the world. Will is past all that. He radiates confidence and self-assuredness. That's quite attractive in a man.

"So, Skye," he says, as he picks up a fry. Very casually, he asks, "D'you have a boyfriend back home in America?"

My heart rate picks up, and I shake my head as I take a sip of my beer. "No. How about you? Do you have a girlfriend?"

He pops the fry in his mouth and shakes his head. After swallowing, he says, "I did have one until recently. We broke up just last week, in fact."

"Oh, I'm so sorry."

He shrugs. "It's the for best." He checks his Rolex. "Eat up. We should be heading back soon. I don't want to cause any further trouble for you on your first day."

After wiping my mouth on a napkin, I reach inside my purse for my wallet.

He lifts his hand. "Put your money away. I paid at the counter."

"Oh. I assumed we'd pay on our way out. Well, I can leave the tip."

He shakes his head. "This isn't America. We don't tip at places like this."

"Okay. How much was the meal? I'll pay you for my half."

Giving me an odd look, he closes his hand over mine and gently pushes my wallet back into my purse. "No need," he says dismissively. "It's taken care of."

I sit back in my seat feeling a bit awkward and unsure. I'm used to paying my own way or at the very least paying my fair share. The thought of someone paying for me makes me uncomfortable.

When we're both done eating, Will wipes his mouth on a napkin and scoots his chair back. "Shall we?"

As we head back to the office, Will walks beside me, his hand on my lower back, acting quite the gentleman. He skillfully steers me around construction barricades and caution signs.

"Next time, I'll take you somewhere nice for lunch," he says, his hand sliding gently up my back. "Not some shit-hole chippie."

At the mention of a next time, a shiver races down my spine. Or maybe that's from the presence of his hand on my back. Will Carmichael is a very appealing man. I'd be lying if I said I wasn't attracted to him.

When it comes to sex and dating, I'm not the adventurous kind. I'm certainly not interested in casual sex, or one-night stands, and Will doesn't strike me as the monogamous type. Besides, I'm only going to be in London for a year. After that, I'll be heading home to Cincinnati to get a permanent job. I'm here to work and learn, not to date.

I smile at him, not committing one way or the other to the suggestion of another lunch date. I think I'd be much better off with Connor as my lunch companion. Him, I can handle.

"I told Connor I wanted to try something quintessentially

British."

"Well, that's exactly what you got," he says. "But London has plenty of five-star restaurants. I want to show you the best we have to offer."

* * *

At five o'clock, my father comes to my office to get me, and we head out to his car. He's going to drive me to the flat I'll be sharing with another intern for the next year.

"Well, tell me all about it," he says as we pull into traffic.

"Where do I begin?" I say, shaking my head. "I got off to a rocky start this morning. There was some confusion in the personnel office, and I ended up in the wrong office. Someone thought I was his new PA."

"What?" He scoffs. "You're a little overqualified to be someone's PA. Whose office did you say?"

"Will Carmichael's."

My dad shoots me a stunned look. "You're kidding me."

"It took a little bit to get things sorted out. Eventually, I ended up in risk assessment, where I met my new boss—Spencer Sinclair."

My father frowns. "He's a pretentious one. Ignore all his bullshit, and don't let your guard down around him. He's a licentious bastard. His third wife recently divorced him when she caught him in a compromising position with his PA."

"Compromising? How so?"

"His pants were down around his ankles and the girl was on her knees when his wife walked into his office."

Just the image makes me shudder. "Wow. Thanks for the warning."

"And Will's not much better," he adds.

"Will seems nice enough. We had lunch together."

My father gives me a side glance. "He's a playboy, Skye. With all his money, he's got women falling at his feet."

My dad turns onto a street filled with apartment buildings and looks around. "Seems like a pretty nice neighborhood."

From what I've been told, Carmichael & Son leases a block of flats not too terribly far from the financial district. There's some off-street parking, and the bus stop is close by.

My father pulls up to the curb in front of one of the buildings. "Here you are."

I step out of the car and gaze up at the two-story building in front of me. Dad hauls my big suitcase out of the trunk of his car and lugs it up the steps to the front entrance.

My roommate doesn't seem to be home at the moment, so I use my key to let us inside the building. I'll be sharing the apartment with another female intern at Carmichael's.

Once we're inside the building, I unlock the door to my flat and switch on a few lights as we walk inside. It's pretty straightforward—a living room, a kitchen with a small table that seats two, two bedrooms, and a hallway bathroom.

There's a sticky note with a handwritten message stuck on one of the bedroom doors.

Welcome, Skye. This is your room.

Dad wheels my suitcase into my new room and places it on the bed. "Looks pretty cozy," he says, glancing around at the furnishings.

It's a pretty good-sized room with a large window overlooking the street. There's a double bed with a blue patchwork quilt and lots of pillows, two nightstands with lamps, an armchair positioned near the window, and a dresser. There's a flatscreen TV mounted on the wall opposite the bed. One door leads to a small closet.

I set my purse on the bed. "Looks like I'll be spending the evening unpacking."

"Hopefully you'll get a chance to meet your flat mate this evening. In the meanwhile, how about if I take you out for supper? My treat."

"What about Julia and the kids? Don't you need to get home to them?"

"It's your first night on your own in London, Skye. The least I can do is take you out on the town and buy you a good meal."

"If you're sure—thank you. I'd appreciate it. I'm going to have to go grocery shopping soon. I can't keep eating out."

"Let's go grab a bite to eat, and then I'll take you to the supermarket. How does that sound?"

"Perfect."

❦ 8

Skye

When I arrive back at my flat after a nice dinner and some grocery shopping, I knock on the door before opening it. If my roommate's home, I don't want to scare her by just barging in.

I open the door just a bit and pop my head through the opening. "Hello? It's me, Skye. I'm back."

A petite Asian girl dressed in red-plaid flannel shorts, a white tank top, and red fuzzy slippers greets me at the door. She's several inches shorter than me, with silky straight black hair just brushes her shoulders in a cute little bob. Her dark eyes are enhanced with kohl eyeliner.

She smiles brightly. "Welcome to London!" She steps back for me to enter. "I'm Kennedy Takahashi, New York City, twenty-three years old, post-graduate degree in global finance."

I smile, instantly liking her directness. "Skye Williams. Nice to meet you." I shake her hand. "Cincinnati, twenty-four, graduate degree with a double major in economics and finance."

"Ooh, you're a Midwesterner *and* an overachiever." She gives me the once-over. "*Both* economics and finance? Really? One wasn't enough?" She chuckles.

"My mom is an economics professor at University of Cincinnati, and my dad is in finance. I couldn't decide which field I was most interested in, so I majored in both."

"Skye *Williams*? Your dad is the managing director of finance, right?"

"Yep. That's why I applied for an internship. So I could spend some time here in London with my father and get to know his new family."

"But you're American," she clarifies.

"I was born and raised in the US. My mom met my dad in England, at Oxford, but ultimately, she didn't stay. She returned to the US when she found out she was pregnant with me."

Kennedy's eyes widen. "You'll have to tell me all about that." Then she glances down at her attire and gives me a bashful smile. "Sorry. I just got in and I'm exhausted. I couldn't wait to get into my PJs."

"I'll be right behind you on that, as soon as I settle in."

"How about an official flat tour first?" she suggests.

"I'd love that."

She motions me inside. "It's not big, so there's no risk of you getting lost. Here's the living room. The Brits call it the *lounge*."

It looks like a typical living room. The floors are dark polished wood. There's a sofa, a coffee table, and a fireplace with a large flat-screen TV hanging over it. At the front of the room is a large bay window seat overlooking the quaint residential street.

Kennedy opens a pair of French doors that divides the living room from the kitchen. "The kitchen's through here."

I follow her into a narrow galley kitchen with white cabinets, stainless steel appliances, and a wood floor. There are bright yellow, lacy curtains hanging in the window that overlooks the backyard.

I peer out the back door. "Nice yard." The lawn is lush green, and there are flowers planted along the perimeter of the brick walls.

"It's a *garden*," Kennedy says, correcting me. "First thing you need to do is learn the lingo."

I nod. "I see."

She points out a door that leads to a small laundry room, which has a washer and dryer and some storage shelves filled with canned goods.

We head back down the hall where the bedrooms are located.

"This room is mine," she says, pointing to the first bedroom. The door is partly open, and I see a glimpse of a bed covered in discarded clothing. The floor is littered with shoes, purses, more clothes, magazines, and stacks of books. "Yours is there." She points at the only other bedroom. "But you already know that. I saw you've brought your stuff in already."

"It seems like a nice place," I say.

"It is. Carmichael & Son doesn't skimp on the amenities. When you consider they're dealing in billions of pounds in investments each year, it kinda makes sense. They have a reputation to uphold, you know. Only the best for their employees." Kennedy claps her hands together. "You've had dinner, right?"

I nod.

"Then how about some ice cream?"

"I'd love some."

We head to the kitchen, and Kennedy pulls a brand-new pint of mint chocolate chip ice cream from the freezer. "Want to split this with me?"

"Yes. Thank you." I watch as she grabs two bowls from an overhead cupboard. "So, you're a New Yorker? You must feel pretty much at home here, since you come from a big city."

Kennedy shrugs. "It's still an adjustment. There's a lot to learn, as you'll soon discover. As much as we Americans have in common with the Brits, there's *so much* that's different."

"How long have you been here?" I say.

"Since January, so nearly nine months. I'd be happy to show you around, teach you the ropes, the do's and don'ts. London is a far cry from Cincinnati."

I laugh. "It certainly is."

"So, what's your specialty?" she asks as she digs two spoons out of a silverware drawer.

"Risk assessment."

Kennedy makes a face. "Ew. Spencer Sinclair, right? Good luck with that horndog. Just watch out for his hands. I work on the global operations team."

Kennedy spoons ice cream into both bowls and hands me one, along with a spoon. "Let's toast to your first day on the job."

We clink our bowls together, and then she motions for me to follow her through the French doors into the living room.

"Do you know my dad?" I say, as I settle down onto the sofa.

Seated beside me, Kennedy nods as she spoons ice cream into her mouth. Swallowing, she says, "Barely. I've been in a few meetings with him. He's a good guy. Very well respected and not grabby."

I laugh. "I'm relieved to hear that. What about Will Carmichael? I met him this morning, by accident."

Kennedy rolls her eyes, waving her hand negligently. "He's a man-ho."

I stifle my laughter. "Really?"

"Yes. The man has quite a reputation. He's lost two PAs in the nine months I've been here. His latest one just quit, on Friday. I give him a month before he gets his new PA in bed."

I try not to choke on a mouthful of ice cream. "His new PA is a guy."

Kennedy snickers. "Serves him right. He's loaded, like obscenely wealthy, you know—old family money. I'm sure his family rubs shoulders with royalty. He probably grew up in boarding schools and attended Eton College with all the other rich kids. He thinks he's God's gift to women. Watch yourself around him. I heard he prefers blondes."

I shake my head. "Definitely not interested. I'm here to work and learn, not to fraternize—especially not with the CEO's son. I don't care how good-looking he is."

Kennedy gives me a knowing look. "You do think he's uber hot, though, right?"

I shrug. "I'm not blind. But that's beside the point. I'm here to *work*, not date."

As the sun begins to set, the ornate streetlamps come on outside, adding to the quaintness of this residential urban neighborhood.

"So, Kennedy," I begin, wanting to change the subject, "tell me about you. Are you—"

"Japanese-American, third generation. My grandparents emigrated to the US back in the sixties. My parents were born in the US, as was I."

"I was going to ask if you're enjoying London?"

She laughs. "Oh, sorry. I'm just so used to getting questions like, *What are you? Where are you from? Do you speak English? Are you Chinese?*" She pauses and takes a deep breath, grounding herself. "Yes, I'm enjoying London. I love it, in fact. I'm hoping to get an offer of permanent employment after my internship is over."

As we eat, Kennedy fills me in on the company. She tells me all about the employee cafeteria, the fitness room, the swimming pool. "Like I said, only the best for their employees."

When we're done eating, we carry our bowls into the kitchen. Kennedy washes our dishes, and I dry and put them away.

"I'm heading to bed now," she says with a yawn. "I'll see you at breakfast, okay? We can go into work together in the morning. I'll show you where we catch the bus."

I head to my room and begin the arduous task of unpacking. I hang up my clothes in the closet and put my toiletries in the bathroom. I notice immediately that the bathroom is clean and tidy, which is a relief. I'm a bit of a neat freak, and I'd hate having to share a messy bathroom.

By the time I'm done, it's past ten, and I'm exhausted. I think my jet lag is still hanging in there.

After stowing my empty suitcase in the closet, I indulge in a hot shower and change into my PJs—a pair of flannel bottoms and a baggy t-shirt. I hop into bed and pull out my Kindle to read for a while, until my eyes are too heavy to keep open.

Then I snuggle down into cool white sheets and start dozing off.

It's too bad Will Carmichael is a *man-ho*, as Kennedy so eloquently put it. I kind of liked him.

* * *

The alarm on my phone wakes me up promptly at six-thirty,

giving me just enough time to take a quick shower, wash and dry my hair, and dress for work in a simple gray pantsuit with a white blouse. At the last second, I slip a silver chain around my neck that holds a tiny locket my maternal grandmother gave me when I completed my master's degree.

I head down to the kitchen just as Kennedy is pouring hot water in a teacup.

"There's plenty of hot water," she says. "Help yourself."

"What are you having?"

She dunks a tea bag into her cup. "English Breakfast tea," she says in a pretty convincing British accent.

"Is there any coffee?"

She gives me a look. "You're in England. Drink tea."

"All right, all right!" I pour myself a cup of hot water and drop in a tea bag.

"Toast?" Kennedy asks, as she pulls out a loaf of bread.

"Yes, please."

"I usually have tea and toast for breakfast," she says, as she drops two slices of bread into the toaster. "I'm saving myself for lunch. There are some amazing restaurants within walking distance of the office. I'll take you to some of my favorites."

"I'd love that, thank you."

The bread slices pop out of the toaster.

"We need to leave for the bus in twenty minutes," Kennedy says as she butters a slice of toast. "So be quick."

Will

My alarm wakes me from a deep sleep, and groaning, I stretch beneath the sheets. *I need coffee.* "Maggie!" A moment later, my housekeeper knocks before she cracks open my bedroom door and pops her head in. Maggie is a tall, sturdy woman with silver hair neatly coiled into a bun. She worked for my parents for years before she came to work for me after I completed my studies at Oxford and moved to London to work for my father in the family business. She's dressed in her light-gray uniform dress with a pristine white apron over top and flat, sensible shoes.

"Good morning, sir," she says, in her crisp, no-nonsense voice. "Ready for your coffee?"

"Yes, please. Strong and black."

"Right away, sir." And then she's gone as quietly as she came.

I toss back the bedding and stalk across the bedroom toward the *en-suite*. As I glance out the exterior wall of glass, I catch the sun just as it's beginning to rise, its golden rays glinting on the surface of the River Thames.

My penthouse apartment has an unimpeded view of the river, which is why I paid the overinflated asking price. Even this early, traffic over the bridge is already heavy as commuters scurry to their jobs. There aren't many boats out yet on the water, but there will be soon, by the time I'm dressed and having my first morning cup of coffee out on the balcony.

I switch on the light in the bathroom to a low setting—just enough that I can see where I'm walking. After a hot shower, I head into my dressing room and don a suit and tie, all bespoke, personalized titanium cufflinks, and my beloved Rolex that my grandfather gave me when I turned eighteen.

Just as I'm strolling out of my suite, Maggie is pushing a trolley onto the balcony.

"Perfect timing," I say, as I step outside.

"I took the liberty of preparing you a proper breakfast. Eggs sunny side up, sausages, and toast. Would you like anything else?"

"That's perfect, Maggie. Thank you."

I take a seat at the little outdoor bistro table, and Maggie pours my coffee.

"Hot and fresh, sir," she says, returning the pot to the warming plate. She lifts the silver lid off a heated breakfast plate. "Are you sure I can't get you anything else?"

"This is fine, thank you."

She leaves me to it, and I sip my coffee and eat my eggs and sausages as the sun rises in the sky.

I have a bit of a love-hate relationship with London. It's a magnificent city, but my heart lies in the countryside. As a kid, I spent summers with my nan at her country estate outside of Bibury. When she moved in with my parents, she passed the estate on to me because she knew I loved it as much as she did. It's a hundred and six acres of prime countryside, with pastures, woods, and a lovely little lake perfect for fishing and paddling around. But the real jewel is the beautiful early-eighteenth-century stone cottage surrounded by rose bushes. There's a barn to house the ponies, a chicken coop, a vegetable garden, and a small orchard.

I hardly get out there these days. My nan's old caretaker, Roy, and his wife still live there, managing the place for me. It's definitely my happy place, and I know I should spend more time there. Lately, I've been lucky to visit one weekend a month. Rachel hated the country and, whenever she went with me, she would complain the entire time.

This morning, I detect a heightened sense of anticipation at the thought of running into Miss Williams again. There's something about the American that appeals to me. Yes, she's lovely to look at with that glorious fall of sun-kissed hair and those clear blue eyes, no question of that.

But it's more than just her looks.

Gorgeous women are ten a penny. No, there's something about her I just can't put my finger on.

Oddly enough, I think it might be her practical, sensible nature that appeals to me so much. She's very down-to-earth, nothing like the women I've dated in the past. Certainly nothing like Rachel. And she doesn't seem to be the least bit impressed by me. Not by my wealth or my family connections. I find that rather refreshing.

With my breakfast nearly eaten, and two cups of coffee in me, I pick up my phone and text my driver, Hamish. I don't bother driving myself in the city because it's aggravating. I love to drive, and I often take my Aston Martin—my baby—out into the countryside when I go to visit my estate in Bibury or my parents in Surrey. But in the city, I let Hamish do the driving.

* * *

By the time I make it downstairs to the front entrance, Hamish has the Bentley idling out front. He opens the rear passenger door for me, and I slide into the backseat.

"To work, sir?" he says in his typical droll voice as he peers down at me.

"Yes, thank you."

"Very good, sir." And then he closes the door and climbs behind the wheel.

Hamish is a tall, sturdy fellow in his late sixties, with white hair cut close. I inherited him from my parents as well. After I left Eton College, Hamish came with me to Oxford, where I ended up with a graduate degree in financial economics. I then brought him with me to London, and he's been with me ever since. He and Maggie are like family to me.

With heavy morning traffic, it's a twenty-minute drive to the office. As Hamish pulls up to the front of the building to let me out, I gaze up at the name of the company carved into stone on the building—Carmichael & Son.

My family has owned this building for decades, since my father founded this company. But it doesn't seem to have made any impression on Skye. She treats me the same as she does Connor. Actually, I think she's more friendly with him than she is with me. I regret getting off on the wrong foot with her.

Hamish brings the car to a stop and jumps out to open the rear passenger door. I step out of the vehicle just as Skye and Kennedy from global operations walk past on their way to the front entrance, busily chatting away.

Kennedy notices me first, and she elbows Skye and nods in my direction. Skye glances my way, and when she lays eyes on me, her breath catches before she quickly looks away.

Ahh, so I'm not completely beneath her notice.

"Good morning, ladies," I say, dodging passersby to reach them. I give Skye a courteous nod.

Skye smiles cautiously in return. "Good morning, Will." She

glances back at the street as Hamish pulls out into traffic. "Was that an Uber?"

"Ah, no. That's my car, and Hamish is my driver."

Her eyes widen for a split second before her pretty pink lips flatten. "Oh," she says, as if the idea that I have a driver offends her.

I just can't seem to catch a break with her.

Remembering my manners, I rush forward to open the door for Skye and Kennedy. "After you, ladies."

"Thank you," Kennedy says, sashaying past me and into the front lobby.

As Skye follows her inside, I'm right on her heels.

The receptionist at the front desks asks the girls for their identification, and they present their badges. The woman simply nods at me, blushing slightly. "Good morning, Mr. Carmichael," she stammers, not bothering to ask me for ID.

I notice Skye's lips turning up in a tiny smirk as she watches the woman simpering a bit. I'm beginning to think I could be the King of England and Miss Williams wouldn't be the least bit impressed. Maybe it's an American thing. They're so very egalitarian and all that. Maybe they don't put much stock into social standing.

Connor races up to join us at the bank of lifts. "Good morning, ladies!" he says, nearly out of breath. "I saw you down the way and tried to catch up." Then he spares me a quick glance. "Hello, Will."

I hold the lift door for the girls to enter. Connor follows on their heels. Skye's wearing a light gray pantsuit today, with a very feminine white blouse. A tiny, silver locket hangs from a slender chain around her neck, resting just above a hint of cleavage.

My cock stirs at that innocent little hint of a shadow between her breasts, and I swallow hard as I shift my stance.

"Earth to Will."

Connor's voice disrupts my reverie, and I blink as he waves a hand in front of my face.

"Are you getting in the lift," he says, "or are you just going to stand there staring into bloody space?"

Shaking my head, I snap out of it and step inside the lift. I plant myself directly behind Skye. Connor places himself behind Kennedy. Kennedy pushes the button for the second floor.

Skye's standing mere inches away from me. I breathe deeply, taking in her scent. She smells faintly like roses. I'm guessing it's her shampoo and body wash. My new favorite scent. Forget expensive perfumes.

The lift walls are mirrored, and I watch her typing away on her phone, oblivious to the fact that she has an admirer. She's grinning as she types, her teeth biting on her bottom lip as she concentrates. I wonder who she could possibly be texting?

Her mother perhaps?

Or a friend back home? God, I hope it's not a male friend.

Thankfully, she's oblivious to the fact I'm sporting a growing erection just from watching her.

I turn my attention to Connor, who's standing resolute at

my side. He's trying to look very important, with his hands stuffed in the front pockets of his trousers. I glance at his face, expecting him to be smirking at me, but he isn't. He's too busy staring down at Kennedy's arse, which is encased in a rather tight-fitting black skirt.

I notice Kennedy observing Connor in the mirror.

"Stop staring," I hiss, nudging him. "The lift's mirrored, you tool. She can see what you're looking at."

Not missing anything, Skye snorts out a short laugh.

Fuck, that's hot.

I wonder what other noises she might make—maybe in a fit of passion. I'd love to hear the sounds she'd make in my arms.

Would she moan? Or sigh?

Great, now I'm sporting a boner that would give Eiffel Tower a run for its money.

"I don't care," Connor finally blurts out defiantly. "I've died and gone to heaven."

Kennedy's cheeks are splotched with red, and I'm not sure if she's blushing or simply pissed off. There's no time to find out, though, because once the lift door opens at the girls' floor, Kennedy steps out. With a small wave and a smile, Skye steps out too.

Like a love-sick puppy, Connor tries to follow Kennedy, but I grab his shirt collar and pull him back.

"I don't think so, mate," I tell him, bursting his bubble. "Don't be so obvious about it. Besides, it's time to get to work. The coffee machine has your name all over it. Latte. Try not to overdose me on sugar this time."

* * *

It's almost noon, and after two conference calls and a team meeting, my coffee mug remains empty. Has been all morning, and my PA is nowhere to been seen. Heads will be rolling if I don't get my caffeine fix soon.

I may drop in to see how Spencer is getting on. While I'm there, I'll have to check in on Skye, too. It'd be rude not to.

I head down to the second floor to visit risk assessment. Spencer's PA informs me that her boss is in a meeting and not to be disturbed.

Pity.

I didn't actually want to talk to him in the first place. Instead, I stroll over to Skye's desk and find her about to leave for lunch. She's just pulling her handbag out of the bottom desk drawer.

She looks up in surprise, seeming almost flustered when she sees me there. "Will."

"Have lunch with me." It's really more of a statement than a question.

A sardonic female voice from behind me crushes my hopes. "Sorry, pal, but she's having lunch with *me.*"

I don't look, but I can just make out Kennedy in my periphery. And she's not alone. Connor's standing at her side. That little shit's been spending time with Kennedy this morning.

I turn to face my elusive PA. "Where the hell have you been all morning? You had one job to do, and I'm still waiting. Where's my coffee?"

He shrugs. "I've been busy."

"Doing what?"

Connor nods toward Kennedy. "Helping Kennedy rearrange her office. She got a new desk today."

That explains his defection.

"No offense, Will," Kennedy interjects, "but we have some-where to be, and you're eating into our lunch break."

Skye gives me an apologetic smile. "Sorry."

Connor and I follow the girls out into the hallway and watch as they disappear into the lift.

I glance at Connor. "I guess we'll have to fend for ourselves."

"Let's you and I go get lunch, Will."

I shrug. "Sure, why not. You're not as pretty to look at as Skye, but you'll do."

As Connor and I exit the building, he steers us to the right, and we set off along the pavement.

"Where are we going?" I ask him, as he seems to be set on a definite course of action.

He picks up the pace. "Don't ask questions. Just keep up."

I follow Connor to a fried chicken establishment just around the corner. I'm definitely not a fan of greasy food. "Are you serious?"

But Connor isn't the least bit daunted. He opens the door and walks right in, leaving me to follow or not. Having nothing better to do, I follow him inside. Besides, I am rather hungry.

"Will ya look at that," Connor says slyly, nodding toward the booth where the girls are already seated with their food.

Now it all makes sense. He must have overhead Kennedy mentioning where they were going for lunch.

I smack him on the back of the head. "Stalker."

He grins as he strides over to their booth, leaving me to take up the rear.

"Fancy meeting you here," he says to the girls as he slides in beside Kennedy.

Kennedy glares at Connor. "You followed us."

He pretends to be affronted. "What? No! But since we're here, mind if we join you?"

Kennedy looks to Skye, who's busying herself folding and re-folding her napkin.

Is she nervous?

"Sure, they can join us." Skye scoots over to make room—for *me,* as I'm the only one still standing.

"We'll go order our food," Connor says, grabbing my sleeve and pulling me toward the counter so we can order.

As we stand in line, I say, "You're pathetic, you know that?"

Connor shrugs. "Hey, I'll be sitting next to a beautiful girl at lunch, as will you, so shut up and be grateful."

I have to admit the kid's right.

10

Skye

After lunch, the four of us walk back to work together. The sidewalk is too crowded for us all to walk abreast, so we fall into pairs, Kennedy and I in front and the guys right behind us.

I lean close to Kennedy so she can hear me whisper. "I think you have an admirer."

She rolls her eyes at me. "Oh, please."

Kennedy sounds like he's beneath her notice, but I detect a hint of a dimple in her cheek as she fights a smile.

When a bright-red double-decker bus comes barreling past

us, my heart does a little leap. There's just something about those buses...

When we're back at work, the guys ride with us in the elevator. Kennedy and I get off on the second floor, and Will and Connor continue on up to their floor.

"I'll stop by your desk at five," Kennedy says as we reach my department and go our separate ways.

* * *

That evening, as we're sitting on the sofa, eating turkey and cheese sandwiches and potato chips, watching a sit-com on Netflix, I gently elbow Kennedy. "You've made quite an impression on Connor."

She laughs. "How old is he, anyway?"

"Eighteen."

"He's just a baby! How is he old enough to work there?"

"His grandfather is a big shot in the company, and a friend of Fitzwilliam Carmichael Senior's."

"Well, that explains it."

"You have to admit he's very good looking," I say.

"Well, sure, if you're into blond hotties with piercing blue eyes, perfect skin, and great hair."

I laugh. "So, you have noticed him."

She pops a chip into her mouth and chews. "Of course. I'm not blind."

"Give him a few years to grow up," I tell her. "One day he's going to be a real stud."

Kennedy gives me a look that says *get real*. "What about Will? You seem to have made quite an impression on *him*."

I shrug off her comment. "I already told you, I'm not interested in dating while I'm here."

"You can still have fun, you know. You're living a year abroad. Enjoy it. Let loose a little."

"It would just complicate my life, and I want to keep things simple. I'm going home at the end of my internship, so I don't want to get attached to anyone, knowing I'll be leaving. My mom met my dad here, and when she discovered she was pregnant with me, she freaked out and ran back home. It broke her heart to leave my father, and I think it broke his too. I don't want to get my heart broken—or break someone else's heart."

Kennedy gives me a sad smile. Then, as our television programs comes to an end, she reaches for the remote. "How about a movie? Definitely one with a happy ending."

"Sure."

As the opening credits roll on a rom-com, Kennedy says, "There's a retirement party Friday after work for one of the guys in my department. Want to come?"

"I don't know him."

"His name's Terry, and it doesn't matter that you don't know him. Everyone will be there. You should come."

I shrug. "All right."

"Will might be there," she hints.

"No matchmaking, Kennedy. I mean it."

She grins. "Whatever you say."

* * *

It's Friday at five o'clock when Kennedy arrives at my desk, her small black purse slung over her shoulder. Her dark eyes are bright, practically glittering with anticipation.

"Time to knock off," she says, pointing at the very boring, utilitarian clock on the wall. "It's party time."

"I'll be right with you."

As my computer shuts down, I grab my purse from a desk drawer. I'm excited to go to an after-work party—London style—and meet new people. I don't know the guest of honor, but Kennedy will be there, and so will Connor. I wouldn't be surprised if I see Will there, too. Lately, he seems to be showing up wherever the rest of us are.

The pub is only three blocks away, so we decide to walk. On the way there, Kennedy points out several of her favorite restaurants, a vintage bookstore, and a clothing shop that caters to young professionals.

"That's where I do most of my shopping," she says. "Nice stuff, but not too pretentious. You should come with me sometime."

"I'd love to. I need to pick up a few new outfits for work since I didn't bring much from home."

"Maybe we'll go this weekend," she says.

"Hey, girls! Wait up!"

At the sound of a familiar voice, we both glance back to see

Connor jogging to catch up to us.

Breathing hard, he slips in between us, putting his arms around our shoulders. "Don't forget me!"

Kennedy looks back. "Where's Will? Did you leave him behind?"

Connor shrugs. "He wasn't in his office when I clocked out. Honestly, I don't know where he is. It's a Friday night, so I imagine he's out on the pull."

"On the *what*?" I say.

Connor grins. "You know. Out looking for ladies."

"Oh." My smile fades a bit at the reminder that Will is pretty much what I suspected all along—a player.

When we reach the pub, we have to wade through a small crowd standing out front on the sidewalk, many of them holding pints of beer and smoking.

Connor rushes ahead to open the door for us. "After you."

Inside, it's standing room only, and based on the business attire everyone is wearing, it looks like this is a Carmichaels crowd only. The company must have rented the place out for the evening.

It's warm, with so many bodies packed into a relatively small space. It smells like beer and fried foods, and immediately my stomach growls, establishing that I'm hungry. Several people pass by us as they carry their drinks outside, probably to avoid the crush inside the pub.

"That's Terry," Kennedy says, pointing to a balding man near the bar. He's talking animatedly to the group of people gathered around him, a huge smile on his face. He certainly looks happy to be retiring.

My gaze travels along the length of the bar until I spot Will standing with several women around a high-top table. He takes a sip of his beer and then sets his glass on the table. As he's talking, the women hang on his every word. He's got it all— looks, wealth, and plenty of charisma.

One of the women says something, touching his arm as she speaks, and Will laughs. I'm finding it difficult to look away.

Our paths didn't cross at work today, and I realize I missed seeing him. I missed talking to him.

"Don't fight it," Kennedy says as she leans playfully into me. "It's hard to resist his charm."

My gaze snaps to hers, and I pretend I don't know what she's talking about.

Am I that obvious?

"Don't fight what?" I say.

Kennedy arches a slender dark eyebrow. "You wouldn't be the first woman to fall for him. He leaves a trail of bodies behind him. It's his MO."

As we move closer to the bar, getting in the queue to order drinks, I shake my head. "I came here to work, not to—"

"Yeah, yeah. Keep telling yourself that," she says.

"Even if I wanted to—which I don't—I wouldn't get involved with someone like Will."

Kennedy gives me a skeptical look as she whispers, "Don't look, but he just spotted you and he's on his way over here right now."

My heart starts pounding. "You're kidding."

She shakes her head. "Like a man on a mission."

A moment later, I feel the presence of someone behind me. And then I hear a deep, husky voice that makes my belly clench tightly in anticipation.

"Hello, Skye. I didn't know you'd be here tonight."

Plastering a cordial smile on my face, I turn to face him and have to crane my neck up to meet his gaze.

Damn, he's tall.

I'm not particularly short myself, but he has to be at least six-two.

Will looks amazing this evening in a dark gray suit and white shirt. His hair is artfully tousled, as if he just came away from a make-out session, and it just adds to his blatant sexual appeal.

The bastard.

I give him a perfunctory smile. "Hello, Will."

His lips twitch into a grin. "You look lovely this evening." Then, he nods to Kennedy. "Kennedy." Turning back to me, he says, "Can I buy you a drink, Skye? What will you have? Beer? Wine?"

"Thanks, but you don't need to do that. I can get my own drink."

"I know you can," he says. "That's not the point." He lays his hand against the center of my back. "I want to."

By this time, we've made our way up to the bar. A guy with short, spiked black hair, every inch of him covered in tattoos, looks to me. "What can I get you, love?"

I stare at the sheer variety of beer taps on display, most of which I've never even heard of. I have no idea what to order.

"She'll have a Stella Artois," Will says, saving me from embarrassment. "And I'll have a Guinness."

The bartender hands me my pint, and then he pours Will's Guinness. "That'll be a tenner, mate," he says to Will.

Will hands over the money, and then he takes my arm and pulls me aside. "Let's find a table."

"Wait. I came with Kennedy. I—"

"She can join us." He waves Kennedy over, but she shakes her head and winks at me before joining a group of her co-workers.

Will's hand slides down my arm to capture my hand, and he draws me to an unoccupied high-top table in the corner of the pub. "I just wanted a chance to talk to you alone. Every time I get within a few feet of you, someone shows up to crash the party."

After taking a long pull on his beer, he sets his glass down on the scarred wooden tabletop. "So, how was your day?"

I don't like the way he's looking at me—like he's a hungry wolf and I'm a juicy steak. "Look, Will—"

"Sorry I'm late!" Connor sidles up beside me, throwing his arm over my shoulder. "What did I miss?" He glances from me to Will and back to me.

Will gives me a look that says, *See? What did I tell you?* Then he glares at Connor. "Who invited you?"

Connor laughs. "Didn't need an invitation. It's a work do. Everyone's invited to say goodbye and good luck to ol'—what's his name?"

Will scowls at Connor. "Terry Maynard."

"Right, ol' Terry. Great chap. I'll miss him terribly."

"You don't even know him, do you?" Will says.

Connor grins unapologetically. "Not a damn bit."

Will stares pointedly at Connor's arm. "Get your arm off Miss Williams right now, before I give you a warning for sexual harassment."

Connor chuckles. "Oh, that's rich coming from you." Still, Connor removes his arm. He gives me a disarming smile. "Sorry, Skye. I got carried away." Then he leans closer and whispers to me, "I spotted your very lovely flat mate across the bar."

Will perks up at that. "Why don't you go say hello to Kennedy? I think I caught her looking your way."

"Really?" Connor turns to look at Kennedy, who's facing away from us. "Good idea." And then he's gone, as quickly as he arrived.

"Now, where were we?" Will says as he locks his gaze on mine. "Do you have dinner plans this evening?"

"No. Nothing specific. I thought I'd go home with Kennedy and we'd order something in or maybe cook."

"Or," Will counters in a seductively enticing voice, "you could let me take you out to dinner tonight. I'll show you the best London has to offer. Just say the word and I'll wrangle us a reservation. How about it?"

At that moment, I'm saved from answering when Kennedy

and Connor arrive at our table.

"Connor and I are going out for pizza," Kennedy says to me, linking her arm through mine and tugging gently. "Come with us."

Will looks far from pleased by the interruption. "I'm afraid—"

But before he can complete his sentence, I blurt out, "Sure! I'd love to."

"Great," Kennedy says. "Finish your beer and let's go."

With an exasperated sigh, Will picks up his glass and downs the last of his Guinness. "We'd love to join you."

ᐇ **11**

Will

A fter the four of us finish our beers, we exit the pub. Outside, the warm breeze caresses my face, bringing with it the smell of the city—a cacophony of international foods mixed with car exhaust. I didn't bother with the pleasantries of saying goodbye to Terrence or anyone else at the retirement party. There was no time. Kennedy seemed bent on getting Skye as far away from me as possible, and I was determined to stay fast on that same young lady's heels. Skye has an uncanny way of slipping through my fingers.

Connor and I end up walking side by side, following the girls through the throng of pedestrians charging along the pavement. I take advantage of the opportunity to admire Skye's fine form from the rear as she walks ahead with Kennedy. Connor is beside me, his gaze locked onto Skye's flat mate.

When the girls are forced to stop at a traffic light, we catch up, and I plant myself directly behind Skye. I gaze down at her hair and wonder if it's as soft as it appears. The strands waft in the breeze, right in my face, and I detect the faintest scent of roses. What I wouldn't give to get closer and find out for myself.

She turns to Kennedy, and I catch myself staring at the curve of her cheek, which is softly flushed with exertion from walking. Her lips tilt up in a grin at something Kennedy's just said. I wonder what those pretty pink lips would taste like.

Strawberries and cream, I'd wager.

A surge of heat rushes through me at the thought of it, and I find myself needing to shift my stance to alleviate the pressure from my growing erection. Blue balls are a bitch, and I'm currently doomed to suffer in silence.

Skye intrigues me. She captivates me and beguiles me. No other woman has resisted my advances before. I've only had to suggest taking a woman out on a date, and *voila*, she was in my bed. But not Skye.

Connor always says I like the chase, and that once I bed a woman, her allure fades. I suppose it's true to an extent. But I'm beginning to suspect that Skye's the exception. I think if I had even just a taste of her, I'd only want more.

The light changes, and we walk on.

Connor jogs ahead and slips between the two girls. The pushy little bastard links arms with them both, like he's suddenly their best friend, while I'm stuck out in the cold.

I manage to move forward just as Skye falls back, and now she and I are walking side by side.

Perfect!

I oh-so-casually let my hand brush against hers. By the way she reacts, I know I'm affecting her more than she'd care to admit. Each time our fingers touch, her breath hitches a bit. She takes a small side-step away, and I match her so we're back to walking side-by-side, our fingers occasionally touching as our arms dangle at our sides.

This is almost as good as foreplay.

The next time our fingers brush, she manages to put some space between us. I'm itching to reach out and take her hand. I know it would feel damn good in mine, but I don't dare. I can't risk scaring her off.

I would happily walk the streets hand-in-hand with this woman. I'd gladly take her to visit every restaurant, café, and shop that interests her. All I need to do is find out what her weakness is.

Is it specialty coffees? Bookshops? Clothing boutiques? Jewelry?

Whatever it is, I'll give it to her.

When they said all good things must come to an end, they sure as hell weren't lying. We've reached the restaurant, but our anticipation is short-lived as there's a queue out the door and halfway down the street. It's not surprising, of course, for a Friday evening in the city.

"That's at least an hour's wait," Kennedy says, scowling as she removes her left shoe. "I've got a blister on my foot, and I'm hungry. Too hungry to wait that long. How about we go back to our place and order something? If we call it in now, it should arrive shortly after we do."

I'm more than keen to see Skye's living accommodations. "Sounds like a great idea," I say.

Connor nods, clearly happy to agree to anything that comes out of Kennedy's mouth.

"What about you, Skye?" I ask her.

She nods. "I am a bit tired, and my feet are killing me."

Kennedy slips her shoe back on. "This way to the bus stop," she says, starting off.

Public transport? Not in this lifetime.

"Kennedy, wait," I say as I pull out my phone. I punch a button, and my driver answers almost immediately. "Hamish, pick-up for four. At my location." As soon as I end the call, I say, "My driver is coming. He'll take us to your flat. In the meanwhile, call in the pizza order. We'll make it back in plenty of time."

Sure enough, not ten minutes later, Hamish pulls up to the pavement in the Bentley. He jumps out of the vehicle and opens the rear passenger door.

Connor sticks his head in the open doorway, his mouth agape as he takes in the interior.

"Step aside, Connor," I say, grabbing his arm and pulling him back. "Where are your manners? Let the girls in first."

I motion for Kennedy to duck in, and then Skye follows. Before Connor can barge his way in, I slide in after Skye. "You can sit up front with Hamish," I tell Connor.

Connor glares at me as he walks around to the front passenger seat and gets in.

Hamish sits behind the wheel and buckles his seatbelt. "Destination, sir?"

Kennedy leans forward and rattles off the address of their flat.

"This is much better than a smelly old bus," Connor says, leaning back in his seat and grinning like a fool.

I meet Skye's gaze, surprised to find her a bit wide-eyed.

Dare I think I've finally managed to impress her?

"Seriously, you have a chauffeur?" Kennedy says, her dark eyes narrowing on me.

"Guilty as charged," I say, winking at Skye.

She smiles at me as I reach for her hand.

* * *

We make it back to the girls' flat before the pizza arrives. Hamish lets us out in front of the building, and Kennedy unlocks the door and lets us inside.

Kennedy walks in first, flipping on lights. "Make yourselves at home." She checks the time on her phone. "The pizza should be here any minute."

Connor and I wander into the lounge while the girls disappear, presumably to freshen up. I take a seat on the sofa, while Connor walks over to the large bay window and peers outside.

It's a cozy little flat. Through a pair of French doors, I get a glimpse of a small kitchen.

A car pulls up outside, double parking in front of the building.

"Looks like our dinner has arrived," I say, rising from the sofa. "I'll get it."

Just then, the intercom buzzes, and I let the delivery driver into the building. When I open the flat door, he's standing there holding a huge pizza box. "Twenty quid, mate," he says.

I open my wallet and hand him the money. "Thanks."

As I carry the pizza into the lounge, the girls have rejoined us.

Kennedy takes the pizza box from me and sets it on a low coffee table in front of the sofa. "I'll grab some plates and napkins," she says. "Skye, why don't you help me? Do you guys want a beer?"

"I'd love one," I say.

Connor nods. "I can help."

Kennedy shakes her head as she heads toward the kitchen. "That's okay. We've got it. You sit."

A few moments later, we're digging into the pizza and sipping on beer. Skye sits on the sofa with me, whilst Kennedy chooses to sit on the floor, cross-legged. Connor joins her.

"So, how about a tour, Kennedy?" Connor says after he finishes off his third slice of pizza.

Kennedy rises to her feet and smooths her trousers. "Sure.

There's not much to see, but I'll give you the nickel tour." And then she winks at Skye just before she turns away, Connor hot on her heels.

"Young Connor is infatuated with your flat mate," I say to Skye.

She nods.

"How do you like the place?" I ask her, hoping to draw her out a bit.

She sets her beer on the coffee table. "It's perfect. And I'm grateful I have Kennedy to share it with. She's teaching me a lot about London."

I set my own bottle down on the table and lean back against the cushions. "So, what do you think of our fair capital?"

"It's beautiful. Amazing."

"You probably haven't had much chance yet to go sightseeing."

She shakes her head. "I hope to this weekend."

"What would you like to see?"

She smiles. "I know this will sound very touristy, but I want to see Buckingham Palace. And I want to ride a double-decker bus. And there's Big Ben, of course, and the London Eye."

My heart starts beating faster. Now's my opportunity. "I'd be happy to take you sightseeing, Skye. It would be a pleasure."

She meets my gaze, and I find myself lost in hers. Blushing, she grins.

"This is my city," I tell her. "Anything you want to see or do, I can make happen. If you'd like a private tour of Buckingham, I'm sure it can be arranged."

"Oh, no, just the regular tour would be fine. I just want to see the palace and the changing of the guard. I can't come all this way and not see it. There are so many things I want to see."

Abruptly, she stands. "I'll get you another beer." Then she walks briskly to the kitchen.

I follow her, not wanting to lose my momentum. She's so close to saying yes.

Skye opens the fridge and pulls out a bottle of beer. Then she grabs an opener and pops off the cap before handing it to me.

I'm pretty sure I'm making her nervous. "You're not having another one yourself?" I ask her.

She shakes her head. "I think one's enough. I don't want to overdo it and end up losing my head."

She looks so pretty standing there, gazing up at me with an intriguing mix of curiosity and unease on her face. I have to wonder if she's had many boyfriends. Knowing her, she probably spent most of her time focused on her studies, but surely the uni blokes were flocking around her. They'd have been idiots not to.

I take a step closer, and she takes a step back, until she bumps into the kitchen counter. The top of her head comes up to my chin.

"How about it, Skye?" I say, my voice low and even. "Let me take you sightseeing tomorrow, and afterward I'll take you out to dinner."

"She'd love to," Kennedy says as she strolls into the kitchen, Connor following close behind her.

She opens the fridge and grabs two bottles of beer, handing one to Connor. To me, she says, "Pick her up at nine in the morning and have her back before midnight." She gives me a wink. "We can't have her turning into a pumpkin, can we?"

"I believe it was the carriage that turned into a pumpkin," Connor says. "Not Cinderella."

I have no clue what they're rattling on about. All I care about is Skye's answer. "Is that a yes, then?" I ask her.

Skye lets out a heart-felt sigh. "All right, yes. I'd love to. Thank you, Will."

Hearing the sound of my name on her lips, in her soft voice, makes my chest tighten. It's just a sightseeing outing, for goodness sakes. So, why is my pulse racing at the prospect of spending an entire day with this girl?

12

Skye

I watch from the living room window as Will and Connor climb into the back of a silver Bentley and are driven away by Will's chauffeur. "I've never known anyone who has a chauffeur."

Kennedy pats my back as she laughs. "Your not-so-secret admirer is freakishly wealthy, Skye. He has his own *staff*."

I shake my head as I step away from the window. "He's not seriously interested in *me*. I'm just a novelty to him." It's after eleven already, and I'm exhausted. "I'm heading to bed."

"You'd better get some shut-eye. You have a full itinerary tomorrow with all the sightseeing and dinner. I'm sure he's going to take you to the fanciest restaurant he can think of. He's trying to *impress* you, Skye."

Kennedy follows me down the hall to our shared bathroom.

"No, he's not," I say, but I don't sound very convincing because I'm afraid she's right. And I don't want her to be right. I don't want him pursuing me or trying to impress me. He's not part of my plan.

I walk into the bathroom and grab my toothbrush and toothpaste.

Kennedy stops outside the bathroom, leaning against the door jamb while I brush my teeth. "He's crazy about you, Skye. Surely you've figured that out by now. It's no coincidence that he just happens to show up wherever you are. He's asked you *out*."

I pull back my hair as I rinse and spit, and then wipe my mouth on a tissue. "It's just not a good idea, Kennedy."

"Why the hell not? Will's hot, despite the fact that he's a stuffy aristocrat. Even I can see that."

"He's not stuffy. He's sweet." I swallow hard as my mother's parting words come back to me. *Guard yourself, Skye. Don't make the same mistake I made.* "I don't want any personal entanglements. No hurt feelings. No broken hearts."

"It's just a *date*, Skye. It's not a marriage proposal, for God's sake. Chillax."

My throat tightens when I think about the sadness I sometimes see on my mom's face when she thinks no one's looking. She gets this faraway look on her face, and I wonder where she's gone in her head. Sometimes I wonder if she's back here, in England.

I suspect she cared for my dad a whole lot more than she let on to me. They met at Oxford twenty-five years ago. They were crazy about each other, but his parents didn't approve of her, partially because she was a foreigner, and partially because she wasn't of the same social status as my dad's very wealthy family. Maybe they could have made it work, in time, but then she got pregnant and panicked.

But now we'll never know what might have been. My dad is happily married to someone else. As for my mom, she's remained single. Her focus has always been on me and her career.

Kennedy reaches out to touch a loose tendril of my hair. "Just have fun with him, Skye. It's only a date. If you don't have a good time, you don't have to go out with him again."

I let out a heavy sigh. "I suppose so. It's just sightseeing."

"There you go. Problem solved. Let him show you around London. Let him wine and dine you at the best restaurant this city has to offer. Let him drive you around in his fancy car. Just think of the stories you'll be able to tell your friends back home."

Kennedy disappears into her bedroom while I close the bathroom door and complete my nightly ritual—washing my face and putting my hair in braids to keep it from tangling while I sleep.

Once I'm in my bedroom, I change into my favorite pair of pink plaid pajama bottoms and a white cami top. I grab my Kindle and phone and climb into bed. I set my phone alarm for seven in the morning. That will give me two hours to get ready and eat breakfast before Will arrives.

I settle down to read for a while. It's late, but I'm too wired to fall asleep.

I can't believe I'm going out on a date tomorrow with Will Carmichael.

Part of me thinks this is really a bad idea, and another part of me has butterflies at the thought of spending an entire day alone with him—just the two of us.

I do find him very attractive. I have a thing for redheads, and his dark auburn hair and green eyes are irresistible. His short beard frames a strong jawline and beautiful lips. And I love to listen to him talk. His accent makes me weak in the knees. He's just... so... *everything.* And I find it astonishing that he's interested in a shy numbers geek like me.

When I think about all the women he's surely dated, I get a bit queasy.

What's he going to expect of me after our date?

It's probably not much different from what American men expect, right?

A kiss maybe?

I can handle a kiss, but I'm not looking for anything more.

I read for a while, hoping I'll grow sleepy, but my mind is still racing too much for me to settle down. Finally, I put on an economics audio textbook and stare out my window. Leafy branches from the tree outside wave in the breeze, casting shadows on the glass panes.

Lulled by the narrator's voice, I let my eyelids drift shut.

* * *

Saturday morning, I awake before my alarm goes off. As soon as my brain comes back online, reality hits me.

I'm spending the day with Will.

Why in the world did I agree to this? I should have at least insisted that Kennedy come along to act as a buffer.

I lie in bed for a few minutes, stretching and attempting to relax. When my phone starts buzzing, I shut off the alarm and hop out of bed.

After a shower, I get dressed and head to the kitchen. There's no sign of Kennedy, so I go through the motions just to give myself something to do… put some eggs in a pot to boil, put a kettle on the stove, check the news headlines on my phone. I'm full of nervous energy. When the eggs are ready, I pop a slice of bread into the toaster.

As I'm eating my breakfast, Kennedy comes shuffling into the kitchen—not quite fully awake—and plops down on one of the kitchen chairs. "I swear I didn't have that much to drink last night, but I sure feel hung over."

"Why don't you go back to bed?"

"And miss seeing you off on your date with Will? No way. What's for breakfast?"

"Two soft boiled eggs, toast, and tea. Want some? I made

extra."

She groans. "No thanks. Well, maybe some tea. The thought of food right now makes me want to hurl."

While I eat, Kennedy makes herself a cup of tea.

"What do you think about my outfit?" I ask Kennedy as she pours some milk into her tea. I stand and show her the twill slacks I'm wearing with a white blouse and a pair of short, comfy boots. "I've only ever seen Will in a suit. What do you think he'll wear today? I hope it's not a suit. I'll feel so underdressed."

Kennedy laughs. "I doubt the man owns a pair of jeans. And you look perfect, Skye. Stop worrying. Don't overthink it."

I laugh. "That's easier said than done. Maybe I should bring a sweater in case it gets chilly." I ask Siri what the temperature is, and she tells me the high today will be seventy-three degrees Fahrenheit.

Perfect.

Kennedy sips her tea. "Whatever you do, dress comfortably. You'll probably be doing a lot of walking."

After finishing her tea, Kennedy goes to take a shower while I clean up the kitchen. Then I go sit in the living room, in one of the chairs by the bay window, and read while I wait for Will to arrive.

At nine o'clock on the dot, a silver Bentley pulls up in front of our building and Hamish gets out and opens the rear passenger door for Will.

"Jesus, how many cars does he have?" Kennedy says as she peers over my shoulder and out the window. "I swear, men and their toys."

When Will steps out of the car, my breath catches.

Dear God.

"Wow," Kennedy breathes.

"No kidding," I say, unable to take my eyes off him.

Will is dressed in a pair of charcoal gray trousers, a cream-colored cable knit sweater, and a light-weight black leather jacket. Looking up at my building, he pulls off his sunglasses and hooks them on the neckline of his sweater.

"Holy shit," Kennedy says, sounding more than a bit awed as we watch him stride up our front walk. "He looks like something you'd see on Pinterest if you searched for *hot, sexy guy*."

"At least he didn't wear a suit."

At the sound of the buzzer, Kennedy nudges me. "What are you waiting for? Your date's here. Go let him in."

I buzz him into the building, and my stomach goes into a tailspin as I wait for him to arrive at our door. When he knocks, I take a deep breath before opening the door.

As he skims me from head to toe, his lips curve into a warm smile. "Good morning, Skye. You look lovely."

My cheeks heat as I return his smile. "Thank you. So do you."

Kennedy bumps me with her shoulder. "Where are your manners, Skye? Invite him in."

"I'm so sorry." I step back. "Please, come in."

As he steps through the door and stands before me, practically towering over me, my nerves get the best of me, and I'm starting to rethink the wisdom in agreeing to this outing. I'm not sure I'll survive a whole day with him.

"Do you have a jacket?" he says. "It's a bit cool out this morning. It'll warm up later, but right now you'll need a little something more than what you've got on." Will glances at the collection of sweaters and jackets hanging from hooks on the wall. "Are any of these yours?"

"Yes." I point to a gray knit sweater, one that will match my outfit.

Will holds my sweater for me as I slip my arms into the sleeves.

Kennedy hands me my purse. "Have fun, kids."

Will grins at her. "Don't worry, we will."

He walks me to the curb, where Hamish is poised to open the rear passenger door for us. I slide in first, then Will. We buckle up as Hamish gets behind the wheel. I'm still not used to the driver sitting on the right side.

I look up at Will. "How many cars do you own?"

He shrugs nonchalantly. "Just two. The Bentley and the Aston Martin."

I laugh. "Just two?" I'm finding it hard to relate. My mom drives a late-model minivan, and my car at home is what most would call just shy of being a clunker.

Will lays his hand on my thigh. "So, a tour of London. How about we start with Buckingham Palace?"

I try not to notice how warm and comforting his hand feels on my leg. "That sounds wonderful."

༄ 13

Will

As we head through traffic on our way to Buckingham Palace, Skye fidgets nervously with her bracelet. When she eventually looks up and realizes I'm watching her, she turns a charming shade of pink. She meets my gaze head on, holding her own against my scrutiny. I'm still trying to figure her out. She's quiet and reserved, yet I suspect there's a spine made of steel beneath her pretty exterior.

The car glides to a stop as we wait at a traffic light.

"What's that?" she says, pointing at a bus stop up ahead where several open-air, double-decker buses wait in a line.

There's a small crowd gathered around a kiosk.

"It's a hop on, hop off bus tour—very popular with the tourists. They visit many of the major landmarks."

Her eyes widen. "Let's do it. I've always wanted to ride on a double-decker bus."

"Why would you want to ride on a bus when Hamish can drive us anywhere we want?"

Fairly vibrating with excitement, she grasps my sleeve. "Because it'll be *fun*."

When she rolls down her window, we can make out the drone of the tour guide's voice over a loudspeaker. She glances at me hopefully.

Shit. I detest public transportation.

She tugs on my sleeve. "Come on, Will. Let's do it."

"Oh, all right." The words pop out of my mouth before I have time to reconsider. How can I resist? I sigh in resignation. "Hamish, let us out here. It looks like we'll be taking a tour bus."

Hamish swivels around, scrunching his nose a bit. "Are you quite sure, sir?"

No, I'm not.

"Of course," I reply, feigning a surety I don't feel.

Hamish pulls close to the pavement and hops out to open my door.

I climb out and offer a hand to Skye as she follows me out.

I give Hamish a look. "I'll text you when and where we need to be picked up."

Hamish looks like he just stepped in something unpleasant. "Best of luck, sir. I'll be ready to collect you when it's over, assuming you survive the ordeal." And then he's gone, having jumped back into the car and disappearing into the steady stream of traffic.

I pull out my phone to purchase two bus tour tickets online. "Just a moment," I tell Skye. "We can board here at this stop."

I study her out of the corner of my eye. I've never seen her so excited.

Once the transaction is complete, we get in the queue to board a bus. I force a tight-lipped smile as I gaze up at a bright red open-top bus idling at a stop.

Is there any bigger cliché in all of London?

I absolutely abhor public transportation, and yes, I suppose that makes me a bit of a snob. It's not the act of riding a bus that bothers me, *per se*. Rather, it's that I don't like being in such close proximity with hordes of strangers, sitting on seats that thousands have sat upon before me, touching railings that millions of grubby little fingers have touched. I take a deep breath and tell myself to calm down. I'm doing this for Skye—because this is what she wants.

She seems perfectly at ease as she snaps a selfie of herself with the giant red behemoth in the background.

"It's for my mom," she says, grinning bashfully. She pronounces it *mahm*.

Her American accent is adorable.

Who am I kidding? She's adorable.

Metaphorically speaking, I remove the stick from my ass and

bend down beside her—my cheek pressed against hers—and slip my arm around her shoulders. I smile as she takes a picture of the two of us.

"We look good together," I say. And as we move forward in the queue, I offer my arm to Skye. "My lady, your adventure awaits."

After hesitating for only a moment, Skye links her arm with mine.

Yes, we're about to go on one of those open-air bus tours of London. You buy a ticket and a bus takes you round to some popular sights. You can get off at certain spots to have a look around before you hop back on the bus to continue the tour. It's an all-day affair, finally ending with a cruise on the River Thames.

Skye bounces in her boots, practically bubbling over with excitement. None of the other women I've dated would be caught dead on a public tour bus.

Our bus pulls up, and we shuffle forward along with the crowd to board. As we step on, we're met with a deafening buzz from excited tourists.

Skye grabs my hand and pulls me toward the stairs. "Let's sit up on top."

I think this is the first time she's initiated touch, and strangely enough, my heart responds by beating double-time. I follow her up the narrow steps, and once we're on the top deck she pulls me toward the front. Just my luck, the front row is available.

I sit beside her, and it's not long before the bus doors down below close. A moment later, the bus lurches forward and our trek begins.

Almost immediately, once the bus picks up speed, Skye's long honey-blonde hair whips around her face in the morning breeze. She reaches into the handbag slung over her shoulder and withdraws a hair tie, which she uses to deftly tie her hair in a messy bun.

"Do you want to sit down below, out of the wind?" I ask her.

She laughs. "And miss this view? No way."

She has a point. Why ride an open-top bus if not to soak up sunshine and have the best view of the sights?

The tour guide greets the passengers over the speaker system. "Hello, ladies and gentlemen, boys and girls. I'm Marvin. I'll be your tour guide today. Our first stop will be Buckingham Palace."

As the bus takes a sweeping left turn, Skye wraps her arm around mine and holds me tightly. "I'm still not used to driving on the left side of the road," she says, speaking loud enough to be heard over the wind and the sound of our tour guide's booming voice.

I put my arm around her shoulders and draw her close to steady her. She doesn't seem to mind. In fact, she leans into me and rests against me. Her other hand is white-knuckling the metal railing in front of her.

"Are you nervous?" I ask her.

She shakes her head vigorously. "Just excited." She stares at the stone monuments and bronze statues that we pass. "You must love living here. Everything is so postcard perfect. I can see why my mom didn't want to leave England."

The little bit I recall is that Skye's father, Frank Williams, who's a Brit, has a wife and two young children. I raise a questioning brow. "Your mother is American, yes?"

She nods.

"Your parents are divorced, then?"

Skye shakes her head. "They never married. My mom was attending University of Oxford when she met my father. They were both working on their PhDs—my mom in economics, my dad in finance. That's where they met and fell in love."

"But you were born and raised in America?"

"My mother left England when she discovered she was pregnant with me."

"I see." Actually, I don't, but it would be uncouth to pry.

Skye's soft pink lips flatten, and I fear I've hit a nerve.

"Sorry, I didn't mean to be nosey," I say, tightening my arm around her shoulders.

She shrugs. "It's fine. It was a long time ago—and irrelevant now. They're both happy."

She turns her attention to the sights, and I sit quietly as she observes my city. I can't help but wonder... had Skye's mum stayed in England and married Frank, if Skye and I might have met sooner. We surely would have crossed paths over the years. She might have had a London accent, instead of an American one.

Though I have to say, it'd be a shame if she didn't have her American accent. I rather fancy it.

* * *

When the bus stops at Buckingham Palace, Skye jumps to her feet, grabbing my hand and pulling me to mine. "We have to get off here," she insists.

We head down the stairs and step off the bus into a crowd of tourists lining the street to get a closer look.

"Do you want to take an inside tour of the Palace?" I look at the long queue waiting to purchase tickets to go inside and hope she says no.

She shakes her head. "This is fine. I just wanted to see it with my own eyes."

Skye weaves her way through the crowd to get as close as she can to the gates, with me right behind her. I certainly don't want us getting separated in this crowd.

She gazes up at the Palace with wide eyes the same color as the clear sky overhead.

"It's huge," she says as she takes it all in, or at least the parts she can see from this vantage point. "I can't even imagine. Does the queen live here?"

"Well, part of the time, she does. She's usually in residence during the weekdays, along with a number of other royals. But they mostly disappear to their private homes on the weekends."

"I don't blame them. They're practically on display here. All these people standing and staring at their home. It must be unnerving."

We're here in time to see the Changing of the Guard. It's a long, stodgy process that takes three-quarters of a bloody hour. But Skye wants to see it, so I curb my impatience to move on, and we watch all the pomp and circumstance.

I position myself behind Skye, my arms itching to slip around her and draw her back against me. Instead, as a compromise, I rest my hands on her shoulders. She glances back in surprise, but she doesn't pull away.

The wind picks up a loose strand of her hair and whips it around. When I take the liberty of tucking it behind her ear, she smiles.

The changing of the guard takes quite a while, but Skye doesn't seem bored with it. I suppose if you've seen it a few times in your life, that's enough.

After the spectacle is over, we hop back on the bus and continue on our way. The next destination is Parliament Square, where we'll see Westminster Abbey and the House of Parliament.

Skye points at the clock tower, another quintessential London landmark. "That's Big Ben?"

I nod. "Sort of. The structure was renamed Elizabeth Tower in twenty-twelve. It's the actual bell inside that's called Big Ben. But, for all intents and purposes, it's close enough."

Next, our tour guide points out The Shard—the biggest skyscraper in the city—before we stop off at St Paul's Cathedral.

"Lady Diana and Prince Charles were married here," I tell her.

The tour continues. All in all, it's a busy day, with lots of hopping on and off the bus. The London Eye, Kensington Gardens... all the popular tourist spots.

A couple hours into our tour, Skye opens up her handbag and pulls out a bag of something—it looks like a mix of nuts and seeds and bits of dried fruit—and two bottles of water.

"You've been carrying all that in your handbag?" I say, stunned. "Why didn't you tell me? I would have carried it for you."

She practically rolls her eyes at me. "You would have carried my purse all day? I don't think so."

"Well, she has got a point."

She hands me a water bottle. Then she opens the bag of nuts and offers me some. "I thought we might get hungry, so I brought snacks."

Now that she mentions it, I am a bit famished. As the tour moves along, stopping here and there for us to gaze at the sights, we nibble on nuts and seeds and bits of fruit. There are even little bits of chocolate in the mix. Our snack is surprisingly filling.

After a while, though, my mind starts to wonder. Skye's is captivated by the sights, but I'm so bored I could doze off. I really could. The history of my city fascinates me, truly, it does; but I could look at all of these buildings on Google.

But Skye is taking it all in. I don't even know if she realizes she's holding my hand. The more excited she gets, the tighter her grip becomes. How easy she is to please. It makes me want to show her all my beautiful country has to offer.

I wonder what she'd think of my estate in Bibury. It's a lovely eighteenth-century country manor on a hundred and six acres of pristine countryside, with forests, pastures, and a pretty little lake behind the house and barn. I bet she'd like it.

The afternoon sun is beating down on us. The heat and a full belly is having its effect of me, and I feel a bit lethargic. I retrieve my sunglasses and slip them on, just to rest my eyes a bit.

I startle when I feel an elbow nudge my ribs.

"Will, wake up."

Removing my sunglasses, I sit up straighter. "What?"

"You fell asleep."

"I did *not*."

"Yes, you did. I think I heard you snore once."

Well, damn it. I did nod off.

She laughs, and I've never heard anything so endearing.

I lift my hands in surrender. "Okay, you got me. What did I miss?" I look around to see everyone gathering their personal belongings. That's when I realize the bus is parked alongside the curb.

I shake myself awake. "Shit, I'm sorry. How long was I out?"

"Not long. About fifteen minutes."

"And... that's it for the bus portion of the tour," our tour guide says over the speaker system. "Next up, a cruise on the River Thames. You can board the boat right over there." He points to another damn queue. "Just follow the signs."

* * *

We board a boat at Westminster Pier for even more sightseeing. Again, Skye heads for the front row of seats, and like a good lapdog, I'm close on her heels. I've never in my life followed a woman around. I've always led, yet here I am. I couldn't be happier about it, either.

It's three o'clock, and the day is still glorious. A beautiful pastel blue sky stretches overhead, as far as the eye can see, and there's not a cloud in sight.

I should have bought suntan lotion from one of the novelty shops. Now I wish I had as I can feel my forehead burning.

With my complexion, I tend to burn easily. I need to get some shade before I turn red. But like the bus, the boat also has an open top. Blue plastic chairs line the deck with a small walkway down the middle. And again, we're seated in the front row. Skye has a perfect view of the London Eye as it slowly rotates, and I have a perfect view of *her*.

She notices that my eyes are on her and not on the attractions. "Will you stop?" Laughing, she swats my arm.

"Stop what?" I tease, knowing full well what she's on about. I catch her hand in my own.

"Stop staring at me. You're making me paranoid."

"What have you got to be paranoid about? You're perfect."

She looks to our hands, our fingers entwined with each other's, and then to my eyes. Her gaze drifts up to my forehead, and her mouth forms an *O*. "You're starting to burn, Will."

Without another word she releases my hand and digs in her handbag for a travel-size bottle of sun cream. She squirts a small amount onto her fingertips and gently applies it to my forehead, the bridge of my nose, and the top edges of my cheeks.

Her touch is soft yet efficient as she anoints my face, and I can't bring myself to stop her.

"You're getting pretty pink, too," I say, touching the tip of her nose.

"I should reapply." And then she squirts out a bit more and dabs some on her face.

Catching her hand, I hold it aside and spread the dots of sun cream over her cheeks, nose, and forehead. "It's the least I can do, as you did mine."

Her cheeks pinken even more, but I think it's more from blushing than from the sun.

As the boat cruise proceeds, I reach for her hand, and she lets me have it. Occasionally, she gives me a curious look, but for the most part, her gaze is locked on the monuments and landmarks we pass.

When we float by *La Traviata*—a very exclusive floating Italian restaurant—she points. "A floating restaurant! That looks like fun."

At the mention of food, I realize I'm getting hungry. "Would you like to go? For dinner this evening?"

"Can we? I'd love to."

I nod. If she wants it, she shall have it. I'll get us a table. "Of course. It's formal dress, though, so you'll have to change. So will I. I can have Hamish bring me a suit. Have you got a dress at your flat?"

Her smile fades. "I didn't bring any dresses from home. I figured if I needed one here, I'd buy one."

"Well, then, when our tour is over, we'll go shopping and pick something up for you. My treat."

"You don't have to do that. I can pay for the dress myself. I need one anyway." She glances down at her brown boots, which are admittedly a bit worn. "I'm afraid I'll need shoes too. I only brought these and my sneakers."

I pull out my phone and text Hamish, telling him to return home and pick up one of my Armani suits. "Not a problem. I'll arrange everything. And I know of a nice dress shop where we can get you something. We can both change there, and then we'll pay a visit to *La Traviata*."

* * *

Hamish is waiting for us at the spot where the river cruise ends, dispersing its passengers. Sure enough, inside the car, he has one of my Armani suits in a garment bag, along with a shirt, tie, and a pair of Oxfords.

Once Skye and I are ensconced in the back seat, I give Hamish our destination. "To Francesca Rose, the dress shop."

And then we're off.

14

Skye

Hamish pulls up in front of a small dress shop in a ritzy shopping district. Will steps out of the car, and I follow him. He grabs his suit bag and follows me into the shop.

The Bentley pulls away from the curb, disappearing into the steady stream of traffic.

"He'll come back when I call him," Will says, as I watch the departing car. "Right this way." He takes my hand and leads me toward the shop's entrance.

In the shop windows are mannequins dressed in glittery, sequined cocktail dresses and ballgowns in bright jewel tones.

Holy crap. This is so not my style.

Will opens the door and ushers me inside. It smells heavenly in the shop—like fresh roses. That's not surprising as nearly every available surface holds a vase of freshly-cut roses in pinks and whites. It's truly lovely. It also looks more than a bit above my price range.

"This place looks rather expensive," I whisper to Will as a girl behind the sales counter eyes us curiously. "Can we go somewhere else?"

"Nonsense," he says, pulling me further into the shop. "And we don't have time."

"Can I help you?" the salesgirl offers, her voice surprisingly close.

I turn to find her standing right behind us. "Um, I need a dress. And stockings and shoes." I point to the shop windows. "Do you have anything a little less formal?"

Ignoring me, she bats her eyelashes at Will. "You've certainly come to the right place. Dresses are through here." She points at a curtained doorway. "You'll find all the necessary undergarments as well. Shoes are to your right. Please let me know if I can be of assistance."

"Thank you. We will," I say, as Will ushers me along with him.

In the back room, which is very stylishly decorated, there are numerous racks of dresses on display, containing everything from relatively casual day dresses to the more formal gowns I'd spotted in the windows.

Will points to a short, red-sequined cocktail gown with a plunging neckline. "You'd look stunning in that."

"Dear God, no." I laugh.

Typical man.

"That's definitely not my style," I say. "Besides, if I'm going to buy something, it has to be something practical that I can wear to work. How about something more like this?" I point toward a rack of more modest dresses that could possibly do for the office as well.

Will frowns. "Well, I suppose. If you insist."

"I do insist. I wouldn't be caught dead in a cocktail gown." I pull a dress off the rack. It's a simple yet pretty floral print on a cornflower blue background. The neckline is squared off, the sleeves short. "This is nice," I say. "Do you think it would be okay for the restaurant?"

"Sure, it's fine. If you like it, that's all that matters. Why don't you try it on while I change into my suit?"

I take the dress into a changing room, and Will occupies the one next to mine.

When I step out, he's already there, standing in front of a tall, gilded mirror as he adjusts his black tie.

OMG.

He looks amazing in a beautifully-cut black suit, white shirt, and Wedgewood blue cummerbund. There's a matching blue silk hankie in his breast pocket. The dark suit brings out the glints of red in his auburn hair. "Wow."

As he turns to me, his eyes widen and his mouth falls open. "You look lovely, Skye."

"Thank you. But after seeing what you're wearing, I'm afraid I'm clearly underdressed."

"No, you're fine." He steps closer, so that we're standing side-by-side in front of the mirror. "We look well together, don't we?"

It's true, we do. The blue of my dress matches his cummerbund. Still, next to him, I feel grossly underdressed. "Will—"

"Do you like it?" he says, nodding toward my dress.

"Yes, but—"

"Then we'll take it. Why don't you select some stockings and shoes to go with it?"

"Are you sure?"

"Absolutely. Now go on. Pick out some shoes to go with it."

It doesn't take me long at all to pick out sheer silk stockings and a pair of flat sandals.

He watches as I try on the sandals. "No heels?" He sounds surprised.

I laugh. "Not unless you want me to trip and break my neck."

He pulls me close with a side hug. "Good lord, no. Finish getting dressed. I'll summon Hamish to collect us and settle up with the sales assistant."

I look the dress over, searching for a price tag, but I don't find one. "There's no price tag."

"Don't worry. I'm sure she can figure it out. Go on, back to your dressing room."

* * *

After I finish getting dressed, I join Will at the sales counter. As the salesgirl hands me a shopping bag to put my clothes in, I pull my wallet out of my purse.

"Put your money away," Will says with a dismissive wave. "I've already taken care of it."

"Will." I give him a look. "You didn't have to do that. I told you I'd pay for my own dress. And the stockings and shoes."

"No time to worry about that now. Hamish will be here any moment."

After thanking the sales assistant, we head outside and wait on the sidewalk. Sure enough, the Bentley pulls up to the curb not a moment later. We slide into the backseat, and Hamish whisks us off to the restaurant.

Hamish pulls the car right up to a little wooden bridge that leads over the water to *La Traviata*. We cross over the bridge to a dock that takes us to the restaurant's entrance.

Once we're inside, we get in line behind a couple standing at the hostess's podium. The restaurant's pretty quiet, and I'm surprised there's not a long line waiting to be seated.

"Two, please," says the man standing in front of us. He has what sounds like an Australian accent. There's a camera slung around his neck, and he and the woman with him definitely look like tourists.

"I'm terribly sorry, sir," the hostess says. "It's reservation only, I'm afraid. We won't be able to seat you without prior arrangement."

The couple moans and groans a bit, clearly disappointed they can't get a table.

"We don't have a reservation either," I whisper to Will.

He winks at me as he takes my hand and leads me to the podium. "Fitzwilliam Carmichael. A table for two, if you don't mind."

The hostess gives him a blinding smile. "Yes, Mr. Carmichael." She picks up two menus and motions for us to follow. "Right this way, sir."

Will lays his hand on the small of my back and ushers me forward.

The hostess escorts us to a lovely table for two beside an open window, which lets in the warm evening breeze.

Will pulls out a chair for me, and I sit. He takes the other chair, opposite mine.

The hostess hands us each a menu. Then she smiles at Will. "Your waiter will be here momentarily to take your orders. In the meantime, would you like to see a wine list?"

"That won't be necessary. We'll have a bottle of the Masseto."

"A *bottle*, sir?"

"Yes, a bottle. Thank you."

"Yes, sir," she says.

I watch the hostess scurry off. "That certainly got her attention."

Will shrugs. "It's a lovely Merlot from Tuscany. Goes perfectly with Italian."

Not two minutes later, a young man dressed in black trousers and a crisp white shirt comes to our table holding a bottle of wine and two glasses. He sets the glasses down, then presents the bottle to Will, who nods. The young man opens the bottle and makes a big show of pouring for us.

Will takes a sip, savoring it. "Perfect, thank you."

I take a moment to glance around the restaurant, noticing the other patrons for the first time. All the men are wearing tuxedos, and the women are dressed in sequined cocktail dresses. "I'm woefully underdressed."

Will smiles as he shakes his head. "You look lovely, Skye. You put every woman in this room to shame."

I laugh. "Stop it." He's just being sweet. "Seriously, though, I had no idea this was a five-star restaurant or I never would have suggested we come here. I would have been just as happy at a pizza place."

Will points at my wine glass. "Try it."

"I'm not really much of a wine drinker," I say, but I take a sip, holding it in my mouth for a moment before swallowing. It tastes like any old red wine to me, but I have a feeling I'm missing something here. "It's good."

Will smiles. "Would you prefer something else?"

"Oh, no. I'll have some water, too, but this is fine."

I pick up my menu and begin to peruse the offerings. Then my gaze lights on the prices, and my stomach drops.

Oh, my God.

I quickly skim the single page of entrees. The least expensive meal on here is over one hundred pounds. I do a quick mental conversion. That's over a hundred-and-thirty US dollars. For pasta?

I lift my gaze to Will, who's watching me curiously. "Will."

"Yes?"

I lower my voice. "Look at the prices. I had no idea." I'm regretting the decision to come here more and more with each passing minute.

His smile widens. "Dinner is my treat. Please ignore the prices and choose what you'd like to have."

My stomach shrivels to the size of a walnut. "I think I've lost my appetite." This evening hasn't gone at all like I'd expected.

Will reaches across the table and takes my hand, squeezing it gently. "Sweetheart, please don't worry about the prices and just relax. I want you to enjoy yourself."

"I can't. This is all too much."

I turn the page of my menu, looking for some inexpensive sides I could order.

Maybe I'll just get a house salad and garlic bread. That can't be too expensive, can it?

I notice the wine list printed on the back of the menu. As I skim the list of offerings, my gaze lands on Masseto. It's six hundred pounds for a bottle.

I'm so in over my head.

"Skye? Is everything all right?"

I plaster a smile on my face and choke out a response, "Yes. Fine."

"Care to tell me what put that look on your face?"

I shake my head.

Will is prevented from questioning me further when our server returns to take our orders.

"What can I get you, miss?" the young man asks me.

I sit there staring at the menu. If I order a side salad and a piece of bread, I'll look stupid. If I order a pasta dish, it'll cost an arm and a leg. I'm screwed either way.

"Would you give us a few more minutes?" Will says to the server.

I look up. "No, that's okay. Why don't you order first?"

"All right." To our server, he says, "I'll have the pasta carbonara with Italian wedding soup and a salad."

That's one hundred and twenty-five pounds!

Will catches my gaze. "Skye? Do you know what you want?"

I smile apologetically at our server. "I'm not very hungry this evening. I'll just have a small salad."

Our server eyes me like I've grown two heads. "Yes, miss."

As soon as we're alone, Will reaches for my hand, and his thumb gently rubs the back of mine. "Skye."

I turn to the window overlooking the River Thames and stare at the huge stone monuments across the river.

"Skye, talk to me. Please. What's wrong?"

I finally face him. "I had no idea this place was so expensive. I never would have suggested we come here if I had."

He squeezes my hand. "You do realize I'm a man of means, don't you? I could *buy* this restaurant—right now—if I wanted to. I could simply write the owner a check for a sum he wouldn't refuse. I could buy *ten* such restaurants, a *thousand*. Money's not really an issue for me, and I wish you wouldn't worry so much about it."

I swallow against the knot in my throat. "I clip coupons, Will. I wear my shoes until they start to fall apart. I keep my clothes until they have holes in them. I *don't* eat pasta that costs over a hundred dollars a plate, and I certainly don't buy bottles of wine that cost a week's wages."

He sighs. "How about we compromise?"

"How so?"

"Let's split my meal. I'll ask for an extra plate, and we'll share it. It won't cost a penny more, and we'll both have a lovely supper. Is that okay with you?"

Tears prick my eyes as my vision turns watery. I swallow hard, not daring to speak. Instead, I nod.

He hears me. He's listening.

"Thank you," I say.

He gives my hand another squeeze. "Excellent."

15

Skye

The meal was delicious. And true to his word, Will asked the server to bring us an extra plate. He didn't seem the least bit embarrassed as we divided the pasta carbonara between the two of us. It was incredibly good, but I could never justify paying that kind of money for pasta. We each had a salad, and he insisted I eat the bowl of Italian wedding soup, which was wonderful as well.

After we leave the restaurant, Will's driver delivers me to my building and idles at the curb while Will walks me to the door. He even insists on carrying my shopping bag for me. He's such a gentleman, and he certainly looks the part.

When we reach my door, he turns to face me, his green eyes searching mine. I have to tilt my head up to meet his gaze.

There's an expression on his face I haven't seen before. He almost looks... nervous. But I'm sure that's impossible. He has nothing to be nervous about. He's one of the most confident people I've ever met.

Realization hits me hard.

Tonight was officially a first date.

I have no idea what his expectations are. My stomach takes a sudden tumble.

Is he going to kiss me? Should I invite him in?

"I had a lovely day today, Skye," he says in a low murmur as he reaches out to finger a length of my hair that's fallen over my shoulder. "I really enjoyed your company."

My face heats. "I had a wonderful time, too."

"Have you got plans for tomorrow?"

I nod. "My dad's picking me up in the morning. I'm going to spend the day with them."

"Ah, yes, Frank Williams. Good man. He's very well respected at work. I know my father values him highly. And, from what I hear, his daughter is quite clever too."

I jump when the living room light in my flat switches on. "That must be Kennedy's doing," I say.

He grins. "I imagine so. She's just being a good friend, looking out for you."

His hand slips around the back of my neck, his fingers and

palm warm against my skin. It feels good.

"It's late," he says. "I should let you get to bed."

He leans a fraction closer, and butterflies take wild flight in my belly as I'm sure he's going to kiss me. But then he straightens with a rueful smile on his face. He reaches for my hand and brings it to his lips to kiss. "It looks like I'll see you Monday, then."

I nod.

"Do you mind if I ring you up sometime, over the weekend?" he says. "Just to chat?"

"No. I mean, sure. I wouldn't mind."

He pulls his phone out of his back trouser pocket and unlocks the screen before handing it to me. "How about you program your number in?"

As soon as I key in my number, he sends me a text. My phone, which is in my purse, chimes.

"Excellent. Now you have my number as well. Don't hesitate to contact me should you need anything, all right?" He pockets his phone. "I'll see you Monday." Then, as if on impulse, he leans forward and presses a light kiss to my lips.

When he pulls back, I can still feel the residual gentle pressure of his mouth on mine.

He's halfway to the car when he pauses to look back. "How about lunch Monday?"

Completely tongue-tied, all I can do is nod.

"Great. I'll see you on Monday, Skye."

The front door of my building opens, and Kennedy is standing in the doorway. "Get in here," she says, grabbing my shoulder and pulling me into the building and into our apartment. She closes the door and turns the bolt.

"Oh, my God," I say, collapsing against the door. "What a day."

"He kissed you!" Kennedy steps back and scrutinizes my new outfit. "Nice dress and shoes, by the way. Where'd you get them?"

"We went shopping."

"Obviously. What for?"

"Because we were going to eat dinner at a floating restaurant called *La Traviata*, and their dress code—"

"*La Traviata*? Are you shitting me? Do you know how hard it is to get a table there?"

"Apparently, it's not hard if your surname is Carmichael. We walked into the place, he said his name, and they bent over backwards to seat us immediately."

Kennedy raises a brow. "Well, money talks."

I head to my bedroom to change and get ready for bed. Kennedy follows me in and sits on my bed, where she rifles through the shopping bag, pulling out my earlier outfit. "Um, Skye?"

"Yes?"

She's holding a slip of paper. "Who paid for your new outfit?"

"Oh, crap. Will did. I meant to pay him back when I got home, and I completely forgot."

She's staring at the slip of paper.

"What's that?" I say.

"The receipt." She lifts her eyes to mine with a telling intensity.

"What's wrong?" I take the receipt from her. As my gaze skims the printout, my heart jumps in my chest before taking off in triple time. "Holy shit!"

"Yeah. I'd say so." She glances at the embossed logo on the front of the shopping bag. "No wonder it cost a small fortune. Francesca Rose is very upscale—way too rich for my blood."

I drop down onto the mattress before I pass out. "Two thousand pounds?" My voice is little more than a croak. "How can a dress and shoes cost two thousand pounds?"

"That's around twenty-five hundred US dollars."

"Actually, it's closer to twenty-six hundred." I feel sick.

"Relax, Skye. Honestly, two thousand pounds is pocket change for him."

"It's not for me!" I'm trying desperately not to hyperventilate. "I wonder if I can return the dress. I can't return the shoes, since I wore them all evening." I turn my foot over to observe the slight, but obvious wear on the once pristine soles of the shoes. "But maybe the dress?"

"It's a nice dress," Kennedy says. "You should keep it. How did you spend that much money and not even realize it?"

"There wasn't a price tag on the dress. Will paid at the counter while I finished getting ready. I told him I'd pay him back when I got home."

"And what did he say to that?"

"He just shrugged and said not to worry about it."

"Well, there you go. Skye, honestly, he's not expecting you to pay him back."

I fall back on the bed, my fingers threading through my hair. "Two thousand pounds for the dress and shoes, plus the cost of the bus tour, plus half of a very expensive dinner. And he ordered a bottle of red wine that cost six hundred pounds!"

When Kennedy snickers, I give her a dirty look. "It's not funny, Kennedy."

"It kind of is. But honestly, Skye, it's a paltry sum to him. He'll never miss the money."

"But I can't let him buy me dresses and expensive dinners!"

"Why not? It's his money. If he wants to spend it on you, let him."

I close my eyes and groan. "I blew half my discretionary budget for the year in one day."

Kennedy pats my knee. "I'm sorry. Go to bed. I promise you, everything will look brighter in the morning."

"Math doesn't work like that. Oh, by the way, my dad is picking me up in the morning to take me back to his house for breakfast. I'm going to spend the day with him."

"You could ask him for some money. I'm sure he wouldn't mind."

"No way! I'm not asking my father for money."

Kennedy rises and heads for the door. "Hey, you have a boyfriend who has more money than he could possibly know what to do with. Don't sweat it."

* * *

That night, I can't sleep. Between the money spent and the memory of Will kissing me, my thoughts are racing.

There's nothing I can do about the money. It's water under the bridge now. I wouldn't be able to return the dress in good conscience, not after wearing it all evening.

My wages from interning at Carmichael & Son cover my half of the lease, utilities, food, and transportation. And there's some left over for incidentals. The five thousand dollars I brought with me from home is supposed to be my mad money for the year. That breaks down to four hundred and sixteen dollars per month that I can spend on whatever I want. And I just blew more than half of it in a single day.

It was a lesson learned the hard way, I guess. A very painful one.

Just as I turn off the bedside lamp, my phone buzzes with an incoming call. I check the caller ID. It's Will.

Reluctantly, I answer the call. "Hello?"

"Were you asleep? I hope I'm not calling too late."

"No, I just got into bed."

"I won't keep you then. I just wanted to thank you again for today."

"Thank you. I had a lovely time too."

"Skye? Is everything all right?"

My throat tightens painfully as I swallow. "Yes."

"It doesn't sound that way to me. I hope it's nothing I did or said."

I close my eyes and count to five. "I found the receipt for the dress and shoes in my shopping bag."

"Oh."

"I'll repay you for the clothes and for half of dinner when I see you on Monday."

"Skye." He sighs. "The evening was my treat, the dress and the dinner. Please, don't give it another thought."

I shake my head even though he can't see me. "I can't let you do that. It's too much."

"No, it's not. In fact, it's not nearly enough. I'd like to give you a lot more, if you'd let me."

"Will, no."

"Save your money, Skye. Today was my treat. And I won't hear another word about it, all right?"

I'm too tired and too emotionally drained to argue with him further, so I don't say more. But I will bring him the money I owe him on Monday, and he'll have to accept it. I always pull my own weight and do my share. Nothing less is acceptable.

"I should go now," I tell him, hoping to change the subject. "It's late, and I'm tired."

"All right, darling," he says in a hesitant voice, and I can almost picture him frowning. "Good night, then. Sleep well, Skye."

"You, too. Goodnight, Will."

↶ 16

Skye

My father picks me up Sunday morning at nine-thirty. We head to Mayfair, a rather nice suburb to the west of London.

"So, how'd your first week of work go?" he asks me.

"Pretty well, actually. I reviewed the portfolios of two potential new clients. One I approved, and the other I recommended against. Mr. Sinclair agreed with both of my assessments."

"Splendid! I'm not surprised, of course. You're so like your mum. You have a good head on your shoulders."

We chat more about work, the company, and my dad's wife

and kids. I'm looking forward to getting to know them.

The cityscape transforms gradually into a more residential neighborhood as we reach Mayfair. The homes here are beautiful, quite grand, with well-manicured front lawns and hedge rows.

My father pulls into the driveway and shuts off the engine. "Here we are." Then he turns to me, his eyes tearing up. "I'm really glad you're here, Skye. There's always a hole in my heart when I think of you half a world away."

I'm touched by the sincerity in his voice. "I know what you mean. I feel it too, when I'm at home, and *you're* half a world away."

He reaches for my hand and squeezes it. "Well, for right now at least, we're together. Let's go inside. Charlie and Rebecca are keen to spend time with you. They've talked about nothing else all week. Julia is looking forward to your visit, too. She doesn't expect you to think of her as your second mum, you know, but she'd love for the two of you to become friends."

As we reach the front door, it opens. Julia is standing there, an apron around her waist, looking radiant in a soft pink A-line dress. Her hair is pulled back in a ponytail.

"Skye, welcome!" She steps back and motions for me to enter. "I'm so glad you've come. I've just started making breakfast. Would you like to join me in the kitchen?"

"Sure."

From upstairs comes the sound of something hitting the floor, followed by a shrill cry of frustration.

My father points toward the stairs. "I'll go up and check on the kids."

I follow Julia to the open, spacious kitchen. She has several cast-iron skillets heating on the gas stove and a platter of ingredients laid out on the counter.

"I thought I'd make a Full English," she says. "Have you had one yet?"

I'm not even sure what she's talking about. "I don't believe I have."

"Well then, you must have one. It's the quintessential British breakfast—fried eggs, sausages, bacon, tomatoes, mushrooms, black pudding, hash browns, baked beans, and toast."

"That's a lot of food."

Julia waves the spatula in her hand. "I don't normally go to this much effort for breakfast, but sometimes on a weekend, when we have more time, I do. And since you're joining us this morning, it's a special day. Would you like to help me?"

"Yes, I'd love to."

"Wonderful! The oven's already preheated." She points to a baking tray filled with hash brown triangles. "First we'll pop the hash browns into the oven to bake." She slides the tray into the oven. "Next, we'll put the sausages in the pan to fry—they take the longest. Why don't you do that while I cut up the mushrooms and tomatoes?"

While Julia cuts tomatoes in half and slices mushrooms, I put the sausages in the pan. Immediately, they begin to sizzle, and the sound alone makes my stomach growl.

She laughs. "Are you hungry?"

"Apparently yes."

In a second pan, we lay out quite a bit of bacon. In the third frying pan, we place the tomato halves face down and add a little butter to fry the mushrooms in. Julia pours a can of baked beans into a saucepan to heat on the stove. Then she takes out a log of something solid and black and begins cutting it into slices.

"What's that?" I ask, watching her in fascination.

"It's black pudding. D'you know what that is?"

"Um, no." Frankly, it looks... odd.

"It's pig's blood, cooked with oats and seasonings."

Oh, my.

"It's actually not bad," she says. "You must try a bite."

Then, while I toast bread, Julia cracks some eggs in the third pan along with the tomatoes and mushrooms.

"I can't possibly eat this much," I say, watching her turn the tomatoes, mushrooms, and the blood pudding discs.

She nods. "It is a lot. Just eat what you like."

As she begins to plate the food, she says, "Would you mind getting the kids? Please remind them to wash their hands before they come down."

I head upstairs to find my little brother and sister. It doesn't take long; all I have to do is listen. I hear two little voices coming from one of the front bedrooms.

When I peek through an open bedroom doorway, I see a darling little girl's room—pink carpet, a single bed with four white posters, a pink dust ruffle, and a pink quilt. Lots of pink. There are dolls and stuffed animals all over the bed.

"Hello, there," I say softly as I enter the room.

Charlie and Rebecca are seated on a plush rug on the wood floor, playing with pink and purple Legos.

They both stop what they're doing to stare up at me.

"Remember me? I'm Skye."

Rebecca looks a bit unsure. As I get closer, I see that she's playing with a little female figurine in a pink convertible Lego car. I recognize the playset. It's the one I sent her for Christmas. Charlie is busy using the Lego bricks to build a house.

"Do you like Legos?" I ask them.

Wide-eyed, Rebecca nods.

"I love them," Charlie says. "But these are girl Legos. I'm just helping Rebecca. I have my own. Mine are for boys."

"I came up to get you for breakfast. Your mom said you need to wash your hands first."

Rebecca eyes me warily as she climbs to her feet. She leaves her bedroom, followed by Charlie. They disappear into a hall bathroom to wash their hands. I follow, watching them through the open doorway. Rebecca stands on a step-stool so she can reach the sink.

"Wash your hands, too," she says to me.

"Of course." I step forward and join them at the sink, and the three of us wash up with a bar of lavender-scented hand soap.

"If you're our sister, why don't you live with us?" Charlie asks as he lathers his hands.

"I live in America, with my mom."

"Why does your mum live in America?" he says.

"Because she's from America. So am I."

He rinses his hands and dries them on a hand towel. "Is that why you talk funny?"

Rebecca laughs as she dries her hands.

I laugh, too. "Yes, I suppose so."

Our dad appears in the hallway outside the bathroom. "Ready for breakfast?"

Charlie jumps down from the step stool. "I am! I'm starved."

Rebecca jumps down as well. "Me too!"

The kids race downstairs, and my father and I follow at a more sedate pace.

"It's good having all my kids under the same roof," he says in a wistful tone.

I glance back at him, touched by the smile on his face. And if I'm not mistaken, his eyes are a little misty.

* * *

Breakfast is a boisterous event. When we get to the table, Julia has already set out everyone's plate. We're eating at the formal dining room table, which seats six. Dad and Julia sit at each end, with Charlie and Rebecca on one side, and me on the other.

"Did you both wash your hands?" Julia asks the kids.

"Yes!" they chime.

"Skye washed her hands too," Charlie says.

Julia suppresses a grin. "I'm very glad to hear that."

I stare down at the mountain of food on my plate, not sure where to begin. At home, I might have an egg or two and a piece of toast on my way out the door. This is a feast. And I have to admit, I'm a bit wary of the black pudding.

I've eaten my fried eggs and a few bites of tomato, mushrooms, and beans, when Charlie says, "Eat your black pudding, Skye!" He demonstrates by taking a bite of his.

I cut off a small piece from one of the black rounds and stab it with my fork.

"Go on, take a bite," Charlie says.

I take a hesitant nibble, and Charlie laughs.

I take a second bite, this one larger, and actually, it's not that bad. It tastes a bit savory, a bit salty. I swallow it down with some orange juice.

"That's my girl," my father says proudly. "You're half-British, love, so I'm glad to see you embracing your heritage."

* * *

After we finish breakfast, Rebecca and Charlie run out back to play in the yard while I help Julia clean up. She rinses off the dishes, and I put them in the dishwasher.

"I'll finish up," she says. "Why don't you take a cup of tea to your father? He's in his office, just down the hall."

"All right. I will." I pour him a cup and carry it to his office.

The door is wide open, so I rap on the door frame. "Hi, Dad. Would you like some tea?"

He looks up from his desk. "I'd love some. Thank you, sweetheart."

I set the cup on his desk, and he leans back in his leather office chair. "Have a seat, Skye." He points to the chair in front of his desk.

He sips his tea. "So, tell me, how's it going with Spencer Sinclair?"

"Great. He's been very complimentary of my work."

"I'm glad to hear that." Then he frowns. "I don't mean to alarm you but just keep your wits about you when he's around. He's got a bit of a reputation for being hands on, if you know what I mean."

"I think I do. He doesn't seem to understand the concept of personal space."

My father laughs. "From what I've heard, no, he doesn't. How about your flat mate, Kennedy? How are you getting on with her?"

"Really well. She's been very helpful, teaching me the ropes."

"Have you made any other friends?"

"A couple. Will Carmichael for one, and his PA, Connor Murphy. Connor seems to have developed quite a crush on Kennedy."

My father's smile falls. "Will Carmichael? I thought I advised you to steer clear of him, sweetheart."

"Will's been nothing but a gentleman." I can't imagine him

trying to take advantage of me.

"Seriously, Skye. Stay away from him. He's not someone you want to get mixed up with."

* * *

Aside from my father's cryptic remarks about Will being a womanizer, it's a great visit. I really like Julia, and Charlie and Rebecca are adorable. Rebecca's really warming up to me, and before long she's talking my head off.

I spend a solid hour playing with her in her bedroom, as she shows me all her dolls and stuffed animals.

Late afternoon, just after tea, my dad drives me back to my flat.

He reaches for my hand and gives it a squeeze. "Please come see us again soon. I'm afraid this year's internship is going to fly by too quickly. I don't want us to lose track of time."

I promise him I'll come again soon. Then I'm out of the car and walking into my building.

I find Kennedy seated on the sofa in our flat watching *Bridget Jones's Diary* and eating ice cream. I join her.

"Hungry?" she says.

Laughing, I shake my head. "I'm still full from breakfast. We had a huge meal."

"A fry-up?" she says, nodding. "It is a lot of food. Did you try the black pudding?"

I make a face. "I did. Actually, it wasn't that bad."

"It's an acquired taste, and *very* British. We'll have to fry some up one weekend."

Halfway through the movie, I find that I am hungry after all. I make us some grilled cheese sandwiches, and we eat in the living room.

After the movie, I head to my room to relax and read for a while.

My phone chimes with an incoming call. I check the screen, seeing that it's Will. There's a flutter in my gut. "Hello?"

"Skye, good evening. I'm glad I caught you. How was your day?"

"It was good. My dad's kids are adorable. I think I like being a big sister."

"I'm sure they're even happier to have you as a big sister." He pauses for a moment. "Listen, the reason I called—"

"Yes?"

"Well, besides wanting to see how your day went, I wanted to ask if I could see you again."

Immediately, my dad's warning comes back to me, and suddenly I don't know what to say.

When I don't answer, he says, "Skye? Is everything all right?"

"Yes, sorry. I was just—I'm fine."

"Are we still on for lunch tomorrow?"

My pulse quickens at the thought of spending time with him again. I want to say yes, but I can't quite bring myself to do so. "I'll have to see," I say, knowing it's a lame response. "I'm not sure what my schedule is tomorrow."

He's silent for a moment. "Sure, of course. You can let me know tomorrow. I should let you go now," he says, sounding a bit subdued. "I don't want to monopolize all your time. I'm sure you have things to do."

"Goodnight, Will."

"Goodnight. I'll see you tomorrow."

⟿ 17

Will

I spend Monday morning at my desk reading through the Miller and Johnson contract, though I'm not retaining a single word of it. All I can think about is Skye and how upset she was about the money. I could kick myself for forgetting to take the receipt out of the shopping bag before giving it to her.

And when I spoke to her last night about lunch today, she seemed far from enthused. I'm fucking this up.

"What's put such a scowl on your face this morning?" Connor says as he walks into my office holding two lattes. He sets one on my desk and takes a sip from the other.

I take a sip. "Not bad. Close the door, will you?"

He bumps it shut with his arse before taking a seat on the corner of my desk.

I quickly fill him in on the dress and shoes fiasco, as well as the six-hundred-pound bottle of wine. "I'm such an idiot! I was trying to impress her, and instead I made her terribly uncomfortable. And now she's insistent on paying me back for the clothes and half the dinner, which is ridiculous. I never would have spent so much if I'd realized how she'd take it. I'm used to women *expecting* me to spend money on them."

Connor bites back a grin. "Dude, she probably thinks that you spending all that money on her meant she owed you something." He waggles his brows at me. "You know. A fuck."

I shake my head. "I didn't pay to get her into bed. I did it because I *wanted* to. She wanted to go to *La Traviata*, and I wanted to make her happy."

Connor whistles in appreciation. "That must have been a costly night out."

"I didn't think anything of it. She needed a dress and shoes to wear to the restaurant, so I took her to a dress shop. I thought, problem solved."

"You took her to the place you take all your expensive floozies?"

"They're not *floozies*. They just like nice things. But yes, I take your point. Crap. I never meant to make her feel uncomfortable."

Connor rolls his eyes at me. "Will, she works in risk assessment. I think it's fair to say she's risk-averse. She overanalyzes everything." Connor sets his mug down on my desk and lets out a heartfelt sigh. "Haven't you learnt anything about her? You're trying to impress her, but she's not the type of girl who's impressed by money."

I scoff. "What girl isn't impressed by money?"

"I just told you—Skye isn't. Are you even listening?"

"Then what's she impressed by, since you seem to know everything about women?"

"Simple things," he states, like it's obvious.

"Such as?"

He shrugs. "People who are kind. People who are fair. People who listen. Just *listen* to her. Hear her. Learn what makes her tick. Knowing Skye, I'd say she's into equality of the sexes and all that. She's independent. That means you can't do everything for her. She'll find it demeaning."

I toss a pen at Connor and it bounces off his chest. "Smart arse."

Connor takes a bow. "It's a gift. What can I say?" He grabs the document I'm holding and turns it upright. "I've watched you all morning staring at the same piece of paper. It's official—you're losing it over a girl."

Just then, Skye pushes my door open and pops her pretty head inside. "Excuse me, but the door was ajar. I hope I'm not interrupting."

Connor—the dickhead—must not have closed my door all the way.

"Skye!" I straighten in my chair. "Not at all. Please, come in."

Shit, how much did she overhear?

She looks gorgeous in a pair of light-gray pinstriped trousers and a cream-colored blouse with a feminine, ruffled collar. I can just make out her beloved charm bracelet peeking out from beneath her sleeve. Her hair is loose today, cascading over her shoulders. It shines like silk and looks just as smooth.

She comes into the room and plops a rather fat envelope on my desk. It's addressed to me—my name is written in ink in her neat handwriting. "Here's an installment of the money I owe you, Will—six hundred pounds. That's all the cash I could get from the ATM. There's an IOU in there for the remainder. I'll try to get to the bank on Saturday to withdraw the rest."

She looks so damn serious, like she's keeping a vow. But it's killing me to even consider accepting this money from her.

Connor stands there like an idiot, soaking in our every word.

"Thank you, Connor," I say dismissively. "You can go."

But he remains bloody rooted to the spot, his gaze ping-ponging between us.

I harden my voice, anxious to be alone with Skye. "Connor, I wasn't asking. Leave us—please."

Skye uses the tip of her index finger to slide the envelope toward me.

I push the envelope back in her direction. "I appreciate the gesture, I really do, but I don't want your money. The tour, the outfit, the dinner, it was all my treat."

Her cheeks flush hotly as her expression tightens. "We already talked about this, Will," she hisses. "You agreed you'd take it."

Unable to hold his silence a moment longer, Connor jumps into the conversation. "Skye, you really don't need to pay him back. He doesn't want to sleep with you."

For fuck's sake!

My mouth falls open in disbelief, just as the blood drains from Skye's face.

Undaunted, Connor continues. "Er, what I meant to say was—"

"That's enough, Connor!" I raise my hand to silence him. The lad really has no filter. "Skye, please ignore him. Of course I want to sleep with you."

Shit.

Fuck.

No.

"What I mean to say is, Connor's an idiot. Please ignore everything he says."

My tongue may as well be doing hurdles, it's tripping so much. Connor dug the hole for me, but I've made it even deeper, and currently I'm burying myself under a mountain of dirt, whilst Connor—the fuckwit—stands there reading my eulogy.

"Please, just take the money," she says. Her eyes are large and pleading, and she looks like she could burst into tears at any moment.

Connor butts in again. "If you don't want it, Will, I'll take it. I don't get paid enough for half the shit I do."

Skye, clearly at her wit's end, eyes Connor sternly. "Connor, would you mind giving us a moment alone?"

I like this sudden directness from Skye.

Hello, Miss Assertive.

Connor's cocky grin falls as he realizes he's clearly been dismissed. It's finally dawned on him that this isn't a joke. I've never seen the kid move so quick. He leaves and, this time, actually manages to close the door on his way out.

As Skye studies me, deadly serious, I realize this isn't about the money. It's about her pride and self-esteem. And if I keep fighting her on this, I risk causing irreputable damage to our budding relationship. She's backed me into a corner.

Skye makes the next move, once again sliding the envelope in my direction.

I don't like this one bit. When a gentleman takes a lady out, he'd damn well better pay the bill. But obviously Skye disagrees.

Swallowing *my* pride, I accept the envelope. "Fine, but you're not paying for half the bottle of wine. That was my choice—my expense—not yours. And to be fair, I'm the only one who ordered a meal—I don't consider a salad a proper meal—so the dinner is also on me."

She scowls as she considers my counteroffer, and I hate that we're even having this discussion.

"All right," she says. "But I'm reimbursing you for the dress and shoes."

I give it one last try. "Can we split the cost?"

She shakes her head adamantly. "No."

"Fine."

Her entire demeanor transforms instantly, and she gives me a genuine smile.

I don't get her at all. My ex—Rachel—didn't think twice about accepting a five-thousand-pound Prada handbag or a thirty-thousand-pound convertible sportscar. Shit, if girls paid me back for half the stuff I've bought them over the years, I'd be—well a lot richer than I already am.

I don't know what to say, so I say the only thing that comes to my mind. "Thank you."

"You're welcome." She stands slightly taller now, more at ease, her eyes bright, her confidence growing before my eyes.

The temptation to go to her and kiss the breath out of her is killing me.

"I should let you get back to work now," she says, smiling as she backs toward the door. She pauses with her hand on the door handle. "By the way, Will?"

"Yes?"

She gives me a cheeky grin. "I don't want to sleep with you either."

I clutch my chest and feign a direct blow. "Ouch. Those are harsh words, Miss Williams."

Her words say one thing, but the teasing glint in her eyes says something quite different. She's blushing.

Is she flirting with me?

My heart stutters as I return her grin. "You and me, lunch in my office at noon. I'll have something catered in. What would you like?"

She considers my invitation. "How about we go down to the cafeteria and get something? We could bring it up here to eat. That would be a lot cheaper."

And a lot less appetizing.

Again, with the bloody money.

But then I realize if I arrange for catering, she'll insist on paying for half, and that's no good. "All right. The canteen, then. I'll pop by your office at quarter to. How's that?"

"Canteen? Is that the cafeteria?"

"We call it a canteen, but yes."

She gives me a beaming smile that lights me up inside. "Perfect," she says. And then she's gone.

I stare at the spot where she stood not a moment ago, completely dumfounded. Nothing that's worked for me in the past is working with this woman, but I'm not giving up. After all, it was the tortoise that won the race in the end. I intend to take my time wooing this girl.

I'll do whatever it takes to convince Skye she wants to be mine.

* * *

The rest of the morning passes in a blur and I get absolutely nothing productive done. Finally, at half past eleven, I make my way down to Skye's floor. Right on time, I arrive at her department and take a moment to observe her from across the room. In a space with a dozen workstations, with people coming and going, conversations ebbing and flowing all around, she's deeply focused on reading something on her computer screen.

I watch her for a moment, admiring how she gives her work her full attention.

When I approach her desk, she catches sight of me and looks up, startled.

"Hello, Will." She looks at the clock on the wall. "It's that time already?" She reaches into a desk drawer and pulls out her small handbag, slipping it over her shoulder.

"Are you sure you wouldn't rather go out?" I say, giving it one last go. "There's a really nice little bistro just around the corner. You know, the canteen doesn't have a lot to offer."

"I'm sure." Then she frowns. "Unless you'd rather go out?" She looks to me, giving me the final say.

"No, no. The canteen is fine." It's certainly not my first choice, but it's hers. I want her to know that what she wants matters to me.

We head down the hall toward the lift, but she points to the stairs.

"Why don't we take the stairs?"

I laugh. "Are you implying I need to get more exercise?"

She grins. "Not you—me. I'm trying to get more steps in."

"Ah, I see. By all means, then. Let's get our steps in."

As we're halfway to the door, Spencer Sinclair steps out of his private office. The moment he sees me with Skye, he frowns. "Where are you two going?"

I slip my hand behind Skye's back. "I'm stealing your intern for a bit of lunch."

Sinclair doesn't miss the gesture. There's something about the man that makes me want to stake my claim on Skye.

He wags his finger at Skye. "Don't be late getting back. We've a lot of work to do this afternoon."

Skye nods, but before she can respond, I propel her forward, toward the stairs.

"What a wanker," I mutter as we enter the stairwell.

Skye suppresses a laugh, and I imagine she's far too ladylike to speak ill of her boss.

"Watch out for him, Skye," I warn her, my tone serious. "If he ever gets out of line with you, let me know."

We descend the stairs to the ground floor, where the canteen is located. The canteen offers a salad bar, hot entrees, pasta salads, fruit, and desserts—not to mention every type of beverage you could want—but still I'd much rather go out. The view is quite something, though. The back wall is all glass, and it overlooks an impressive garden with a three-tiered fountain as its focal point.

Skye and I part ways to grab our food. She heads to the salad bar, while I wait in line for one of the hot entrees. We meet in the queue to pay for our meals. Skye has a plate of greens and colorful veg, and I have a juicy cheeseburger and a mound of chips. When I offer her a chip, she lets me pop it into her mouth.

Kennedy and Connor appear out of thin air, waltzing into the canteen together.

"Fancy running into you two here," Connor says, sounding more than a little pleased with himself.

Kennedy eyes Skye's salad. "That looks good. I think I'll get one too."

As Kennedy heads off to the salad bar, Connor follows her.

Naturally, my first impulse is to pay for both my meal and Skye's, but Connor's words of advice come back to me.

When Skye reaches into her handbag for her purse, I bite my tongue and let her pay for her own meal.

This will take some getting used to.

Connor and Kennedy catch up to us in the queue. "Where are you sitting?" he asks us as he surveys the dining area.

"I thought we'd take our meals up to my office and eat there," I tell him.

Take a hint, Connor. Go away.

"Perfect!" Connor says. "We'll join you. Won't we, Kennedy?"

Kennedy bounces on her heels and gives Skye a cheeky grin. "Sure. We'd love to."

Lovely. Now our party of two has turned into a party of four.

As we ride up in the lift to my floor, Connor helps himself to one of my chips. "I should have gotten what you did," he grumbles.

I stare down at his salad. "Why didn't you?"

"Kennedy says I'll die of a heart attack if I keep eating like I do. She wouldn't even let me get a bag of crisps."

Kennedy reaches up to tease Connor's hair. "You're a growing boy, Connor. You need good nutrition."

I don't know what to make of Kennedy and Connor's odd relationship. Kennedy treats him like he's her little brother, but I'm sure that's not how Connor wants her to see him.

Connor gazes down at Kennedy dotingly. I don't think he realizes he's squarely in the friend zone, but it's understandable. He's just eighteen, and she's in her twenties. At their ages, that's a considerable gap.

* * *

As the week progresses, lunch in my office becomes a thing—our thing. And by *our*, I mean the four of us. Connor and Kennedy perch like two canaries at the little round table beside my window and whisper to each other as they eat.

Skye and I sit on either side of my desk, facing each other. She's taken to packing her own lunch to save money—usually bringing a sandwich, a piece of fresh fruit, and a yogurt. The rest of us run down to the canteen to buy our lunches and haul them back up to my office. I'm certainly not going to pack my lunch like a schoolboy.

I'm surprised at how much I'm enjoying the company of friends. Of course I want to spend time with Skye, but even Kennedy and Connor are growing on me. I've started looking forward to each day at work, mostly because I know I'll see Skye.

I've only known her for a couple of weeks, and yet I know this is something different—at least for me. I'm not sure how she feels.

But I hope to find out soon.

I want to take our budding friendship to the next level before she friend-zones me like Kennedy has done to poor Connor. And I have just the idea how to do it. I'll ask her tonight after work.

At half past four, I make a trip to Skye's office. The plan was to surprise her, but I'm the one who gets the surprise.

Spencer Sinclair is standing behind her chair—practically draped over her—with one hand on her shoulder as he points out something on her computer screen.

What the fuck?

His other hand is covering hers, guiding her mouse. "And the rating score goes right here," he says. "In this field."

Skye looks uncomfortable, and I swear she cringes when Spencer pats her on the back.

My hands contract into fists, and it takes all I have not to storm across the room and pummel Sinclair's weaselly face.

At my approach, Skye glances up and her harried expression instantly transforms into a relieved smile. "Will! Hi."

Sinclair straightens, putting some space between himself and Skye. "What are you doing here?" he says, clearly peeved at the interruption.

My blood is on fire. "I'd like to ask you the same thing."

He looks put out. "I'm mentoring my new intern. What does it look like?"

"I'll tell you exactly what it looks like." As I stalk toward him, he backs away, maintaining space between us.

"Look at the time," Sinclair says as he consults his watch. "I'd best be getting back to my office. "Good job, Skye. We'll revisit this Monday morning."

Spencer disappears into his office, closing the door behind him.

I stand staring at his door.

"Does he do that often?" I ask Skye. "Get in your personal space? *Touch* you?"

She winces. "It's been worse than usual today."

"Not acceptable. I'll have a talk with him." I sit in her guest chair beside her desk. "I came to ask you a question."

"Yes?"

"How about letting me take you out this evening? How about dinner and then maybe a film?"

She glances away for a moment, and I can almost see her thoughts racing.

Maybe Connor's right.

Maybe she does overthink everything.

"Skye?"

She turns back to me, her cheeks pink and her eyes bright. "I'd love to. But, I was just wondering... what if you came over to my place instead? We could eat in and watch a movie. It would be..."

I fill in the blank for her. "Cheaper."

Sheepishly, she nods.

To be honest, she could suggest we sit and watch the grass grow, and I'd be totally onboard with the idea. "How about seven o'clock?"

She smiles. "That sounds great."

↝ 18

Skye

At the end of the day, Kennedy and I take the bus home as usual. I'm a nervous wreck as I make a mental list of what needs to be done before Will comes over.

Vacuum the living room floor.

Wipe off the coffee table

Dust the TV screen and the mantle and the bookshelves.

Clean the bathroom.

What else?

"Relax, Skye," Kennedy says. "It's just a date—it's nothing to get worked up about."

"What should we watch tonight? An action movie? Superhe-roes? A mystery? Or maybe a thriller?"

She purses her lips in thought. "How about a rom-com? After all, it's a date. What's your favorite romantic movie?"

"*Pride and Prejudice.* The version with Colin Firth."

Kennedy makes a face. "Jane Austen? He'll be bored out of his mind. How about something more contemporary? How about *Fifty Shades of Grey*?"

"Dear God, no! He'll think I want him to tie me up."

"True. Okay, something a little tamer. *Twilight*?"

I shake my head. "Too YA."

"Yeah, you're right. How about *Notting Hill*? It's contempo-rary, relatively speaking, although it's a few years old. But it's a classic—timeless—and it takes place in Notting Hill in West London. That's a cool local connection."

That sounds like a good possibility. "Okay. I'll suggest that."

"What about food?" she asks me.

"Something easy," I say.

"Order pizza. That way I can have some too. I'll stay in my room all evening to give you two love birds some privacy, but my fee will be two slices of pizza and a bottle of beer."

I bump her shoulder. "We're just friends, Kennedy."

"He didn't ask you out because he wants to be your *friend*. He asked you out because he *likes* you."

I frown. "He has a reputation, though, and I'm not just look-ing to get laid."

"Maybe he wants more this time. You never know. And even

if he doesn't... have you seen the man? Like, really seen him? He's hot. I'd do him in a heartbeat, just for the thrill. I bet he's amazing in bed."

"If that's what he's expecting from me, then he's going to be disappointed. Look what happened when my mom hooked up with a guy when she was here."

Kennedy bumps me back. "Oh, come on! She got you, didn't she? I doubt she'd change that for anything."

"The last thing my mom said to me before I got on the plane was, 'Don't lose your head. Don't make the same mistakes I did.'"

As our bus pulls up to our stop, Kennedy stands and peers down at me. "You worry too much."

* * *

I'm home by five-thirty, so I have an hour-and-a-half to clean the apartment, take a shower, dry my hair, and change into comfortable clothes. I decide on a pair of faded jeans and a peach sweater. I pull my hair back in a ponytail and put silver hoop earrings on. I even go so far as to apply a touch of mascara and swipe on some strawberry-scented lip gloss.

When the intercom buzzes at seven on the dot, Kennedy disappears into her room, leaving me to let Will into the building. A moment later, there's a firm knock on our door.

Steeling my nerves, I open the door. And there stands Will Carmichael on my threshold, tall and impressive in a pair of charcoal gray slacks and a white button-up shirt, freshly pressed, sans tie. The top two buttons are undone—his version of casual, I guess—and I can't stop staring at the strong column of his throat.

"Good evening, Skye," he says in his perfectly cultured voice. "You look lovely."

I mentally shake myself. "Hi." I step back. "Come in, please."

He steps inside, and I gaze up to meet his eyes.

He hands me a bouquet of freshly-cut flowers. "These are for you." And then he leans close and kisses my cheek, his warm lips briefly lingering on my skin.

The scent of his cologne makes my insides quiver. My heart stutters. "They're beautiful. Thank you." I stare at him for a moment, feeling a bit flummoxed. He's just so... polished. Confident. Debonair. It seems to come naturally. "I'll go put these in a vase."

Will follows me into the kitchen, waiting patiently as I locate a glass vase in the cupboard under the sink.

I put the flowers in the vase with fresh water and set them on the windowsill. Suddenly, I feel nervous. "Shall we order pizza? I don't know about you, but I'm starved."

His lips quirk up in a grin. "Yes, let's."

I have a feeling pizza isn't quite what Will had in mind for our dinner tonight, but he seems agreeable. I suggest we order from a local pizza place that Kennedy and I really like. He makes the call, ordering a large pizza with the works.

"We have to share with Kennedy," I tell him after he ends the call.

"She's home?" He looks around. "Funny, it was so quiet I thought she must be out."

"She's in her bedroom. I'm sure we'll see her when the food arrives."

I take a seat on the living room sofa, and Will joins me.

When I catch myself fidgeting nervously with my bracelet, I still my hands, clasping them in my lap. "I thought we could watch a movie. How about *Notting Hill*? It's a rom-com."

"A rom *what*?"

"A rom-com. Romantic comedy. It takes place in Notting Hill, which is—"

"In West London, yes. It's quite a famous landmark and a big tourist attraction."

I bring up the movie on the flatscreen, but we decide to hold off watching it until the pizza arrives.

"Can I get you something to drink?" I ask him. "We have water, soft drinks, beer."

"I'd love a beer. Thank you."

Grateful for something to do, I hop up from the sofa and disappear back into the kitchen. A moment later, he joins me.

I hand him a cold bottle of beer from the fridge.

He seems perfectly at ease, sipping his beer, while I'm a wreck inside. Just to keep busy, I pour myself a glass of cold water.

"Skye?"

I take a gulp of my water. "Hm?"

"There's no need to be nervous." He sets his beer down on the counter. "We're just friends having a pint and some starters, right?"

"Right."

He reaches out to tuck an escaped tendril of my hair behind my ear. Then he gently skims his finger over my earring. "Very pretty."

"My earrings?"

His gaze meets mine. "No. You."

"I thought you we're just friends hanging out."

"We are. Can't one friend tell another friend she's pretty?"

My cheeks heat at the compliment.

Stepping closer, he snakes his arm around my waist and draws me closer. "Maybe I wasn't entirely straight with you."

I swallow hard as butterflies flutter in my belly. "How so?"

His gaze drops to my lips. "I don't usually have a burning need to kiss my friends."

And then, moving very slowly, as if to give me ample time to pull away, he lowers his mouth to mine.

But I don't want to pull away.

I want this.

Despite the warning from my dad. Despite what I've heard about his reputation. I want to know what it's like to be really kissed by Will Carmichael.

"We shouldn't," I murmur as his lips hover over mine.

He pauses. "Is that a no?" Then both his arms slip around my waist and he pulls me against his firm body. He grins as his lips find mine.

Surprised by the sudden contact, I gasp, and he takes advan-

tage of the moment and deepens the kiss. His lips mold themselves to mine, nudging mine open. His tongue slips inside,
stroking mine, lightly teasing me. His arms tighten around me,
and I'm pressed hard against his chest. The heat of his body,
and his scent—undeniably masculine—make my head spin.

I can count on one hand the number of guys who have kissed
me, and I can say unequivocally that none of those kisses were
anywhere near as good as this one. I guess it's not surprising—
given his reputation with women—that Will Carmichael is a
damn good kisser.

My breasts are pressed against his hard chest, and his hands
cradle my body. It's impossible to tell where he ends and I begin.
It's like we're sharing the same space, the same air.

When the intercom buzzes, I jump, and he releases me.

"The pizza's here," I say, quite unnecessarily.

He cups the side of my face and his thumb brushes across
my cheek. "I'll get it."

And then, he heads toward the door.

"Wait! The money." I have cash in my pocket—I made sure I
had enough cash to pay for the pizza. I catch up to him and hold
out the money.

He glances at the cash and gives me a restrained smile. "Since
you were kind enough to invite me for dinner, why don't you
allow me the honor of paying?"

The intercom buzzes a second time, making me jump. "All
right. Thank you." I hold out two one-pound coins. "I'll pay the
tip."

Will grins. "Darling, we don't tip the pizza delivery guy in the UK."

He opens the door and hands the young man cash, and then he takes the pizza box from him.

On impulse, I hand the guy the money anyway. "Surely there's no law against it."

The driver looks quizzically at Will. "What's this for, mate?"

Will shrugs. "It's a tip. She's American."

The delivery guy tucks the money into his pocket. "Excellent. Thanks!"

Will grins as he closes the door.

"What?" I say.

He leans forward and kisses my forehead. "Nothing." And then he carries the pizza box into the kitchen.

I hear Kennedy's bedroom door open. "Was that the pizza? I smell pizza."

"Yes, come get some," I call to her.

Kennedy peeks around the corner, into the kitchen. "Is it safe to come out?"

I laugh. "Get your butt in here."

When Kennedy joins us, I hand her a plate. "Help yourself."

As Will grabs another beer from the fridge, Kennedy whispers to me, "How's it going?"

But before I can answer, Will closes the fridge door and turns to us. "Hello, Kennedy."

"Hi, Will." She looks from him to me, a knowing smile on her face. "I'll just grab some pie and a beer and get out of your hair."

"Pie?" he says.

Kennedy laughs at the look of bewilderment on his face. "Pizza," she says, helping herself to two slices and grabbing a beer from the fridge. Then she disappears down the hallway.

"It's a New York thing," I explain.

Will collects the pizza box and carries it to the living room, setting it on the coffee table. I bring our drinks, two plates, and napkins.

I start the movie then, and we sit together on the sofa.

The film begins with Hugh Grant's character walking down a street crowded with vendors selling everything from fruits and vegetables, to clothing, to antiques and collectibles.

"That's Portobello Road Market," Will notes, pointing at the screen. "I don't suppose you've been to see it yet." He leans forward to grab a slice of pizza.

I grab a slice, too. "No, I haven't."

"Would you like to?"

He catches me just as I'm biting into my pizza. After I finish chewing and swallowing, I dab my mouth with a napkin. "Yes, I'd love to."

"How about tomorrow, then? It's a perfect outing for a Saturday afternoon. The weather should be good. What do you say?"

I swallow a bite of pizza. "I say yes."

"Excellent. I'll pick you up tomorrow at one. We'll walk around Notting Hill, do a little sightseeing, and then grab some dinner afterward."

My heart rate picks up.

Three dates in one week?

Everything's moving so quickly.

Is he really interested in me, or am I just a novelty to him?

The American.

Either way, I don't see anything serious coming of it, and I'm not one to mess around just for the sake of messing around. I should put an end to this now before I get my heart broken. I've only known the man a few weeks, and already I'm in too deep to just walk away.

Will Carmichael is a real-life Prince Charming, but more importantly, he's a good person. He's kind and thoughtful and compassionate, and I'm finding it hard not to swoon over him.

After we're done eating, we pause the movie to put the rest of the pizza in the fridge. I run to the bathroom to brush my teeth and freshen up.

When we meet up again on the sofa, he holds his arm out to me. I sink down beside him on the cushions, and he tucks me against his side. My heart feels heavy from the knowledge that I shouldn't let this go any further, but I can't help allowing myself to take comfort in his embrace.

He smells so good. Besides his cologne, which I imagine costs a fortune, I detect a whiff of laundry starch. His white shirt is crisp and bright. I spot a hint of auburn chest hair at the opening, and that makes me wonder what he looks like without a shirt.

I start the movie back up again and force myself to pay attention to the screen. When his fingers skim across my shoulder a few minutes later, my brain short circuits and I lose all ability to pay attention to the movie.

He starts kneading my shoulder—I'm not even sure he's aware he's doing it—and my body lights up like the Fourth of July. Shivers race down my spine, and it's all I can do not to melt into him.

Before long, the movie ends and the credits roll. I glance out the front window, noticing it's dark out and the streetlights are on. The apartment is quiet—we haven't heard a peep out of Kennedy since she got her dinner. Suddenly, I realize we're alone—just the two of us. My stomach drops, and I'm even more nervous wondering what comes next.

"How'd you like the film?" he says.

But it does nothing to ease my growing tension. I wonder if he feels it too.

"I loved the ending. I'm a sucker for happy endings."

He chuckles softly. "I'm not one bit surprised you're a romantic." He reaches for my hand. "So am I." And then he raises my hand and kisses the back of it. Then he slips his hand around my waist and draws me closer. "Is this okay?"

"Is what okay?" I'm having trouble catching my breath.

Is it okay that he kissed my hand? Or that his hand is curling around my waist?

He looks like he wants to do a whole lot more.

Yes, please. To all of it.

"Is *this* okay?" His voice is so low I can barely make out the words. And then he kisses me, only this time, much deeper and with so much more heat.

His strong arms encase me, and he lifts me, pulling me onto his lap. Heat emanates from his body, so warm and enticing. My body starts trembling with need.

His lips are soft on mine, yet firm, as he nudges mine open. His tongue slips into my mouth and strokes mine. Both of us are breathing hard now, and I am fully in danger of losing my head.

"Will," I murmur against his lips.

When I press my hands to his chest, he loosens his hold and leans back.

"What's wrong?" he says.

"I—" My hands flutter nervously. "I need to be upfront with you."

He bites back a grin. "All right."

"I'm not one—I mean, I don't—casual sex isn't my thing. I don't just hop into bed with the first guy I—"

He smiles. "I know you don't, but I appreciate you telling me." His hand strokes my hips soothingly. "Does this mean you *don't* want me to kiss you?" He's still fighting a grin.

"No! That's not what I meant. It's just that I don't want to give you the wrong impression. I don't do—"

"Casual sex. Right. I understand."

I let out a heavy sigh. "As long as we're clear on that."

"Skye?"

"Yes?"

"I'm not asking you for casual sex."

"Oh." *Oh.* "Okay. Good."

His hands come up to cradle my face. "When we have sex, there won't be anything casual about it, I promise."

When.

He said *when*, not *if*.

My stomach is in a freefall, my head spinning madly. I didn't have one drop of alcohol this evening so I can't blame it on booze. No, I'm drunk on *Will*.

I'm so screwed.

❧ 19

Will

Hamish picked me up from Skye's flat at midnight. I didn't want my Cinderella to stay up past her bedtime and risk turning into a pumpkin.

Isn't that how the story goes?

I wanted her to get a good night's sleep and rest up for our outing to Notting Hill.

So far, on the entire drive home, I haven't been able to stop thinking about that kiss, or the feel of her sitting on my lap. Even now my cock is hard.

My phone lights up in my hand, and I see she's texted me. I

open it to find an emoji of an eggplant.

Hmm... okay.

I'm not sure what that's supposed to mean. Then another text comes in, and another. Next is a poo emoji, followed by a winking emoji.

What the hell?

Skye only had water tonight. She can't be drunk.

I get one more text after that.

Skye: OMG, Will! I'm so sorry. That was Kennedy on my phone. She said I should text you.

I laugh. This is more like it. It figures it was Kennedy up to her antics. She's a wild one.

I send Skye a text of my own.

Will: Can't wait to kiss you again

There's a bit of a lull in the conversation, and I'm starting to think I've scared her off. But then I receive another text.

Skye: Who said there will be a next time?

Ahh, now she's just being cheeky.

I reply.

Will: I assure you, there will be

I find myself grinning like an idiot at our little exchange. Skye isn't a one-night-stand kind of girl. She's not even a casual fling—she's the kind of girl you take home to meet your mum.

My mum would love her. I know my nan would. It's a shame she doesn't fit my father's expectations of the type of girl I should be courting. He envisions me with a carbon copy of Kate Middleton—someone with connections in high places. Someone socially desirable.

My father thinks the flings with my PAs were merely me sowing my wild oats, but that wasn't the case. With each one of them, I'd hoped for the best. I don't care much for the stuck-up princesses my father would have me marry for the sake of producing two fine boys to take over the company after me—an heir and a spare, so to speak. I want to choose my own future wife, and I just want to be happy. And yet all the women I've dated turned out to be gold diggers.

But not Skye. I don't think she could care less about my bank balance. As cliché as it sounds, could she be the one I've been looking for? Dare I think she could like me for *me*?

"Sir."

I glance up at my building. Ah, we're home. "Right. See you in the morning, Hamish."

"Indeed, Sir. Cheerio."

Once upstairs, I take a quick shower and climb into bed. Hoping it's not too late, I send Skye last text.

Will: See you tomorrow, beautiful

* * *

The next afternoon, I'm seated in the backseat of my car, Hamish behind the wheel. Just as I'm getting out of the car to walk up to the front door of Skye's building, Kennedy rushes out and snaps a photo. She's a regular paparazzi.

"So, this is how the other half lives," she muses, bending over to peer through the rear passenger window. "Hello, Hamish!" She waves at my driver, who gives her an awkward wave back.

"Haven't you got something more important you could be doing?" I ask her.

She shakes her head and gives me a quirky smile. "Not really."

I glance inside the open doorway to see if Skye's on her way out.

"Relax, pal," Kennedy says. "She'll be out in a sec. Sheesh. Impatient much?"

I keep my eye on the doorway, and as if on cue, Skye appears. She looks sexy as hell in a pair of ripped skinny jeans, an oversized pale blue sweater, and short boots. Her long hair is pulled up into a messy bun, a few tempting tendrils left hanging down the sides of her face.

Smiling, she waves at me.

I take one look at her, and my breath catches in my chest.

"Sorry I'm late," she says, a bit breathless as though she'd been in a mad rush.

"Not at all. Your timing is perfect. I was just chatting with Kennedy."

Kennedy winks at Skye. "Have fun, kids. Don't do anything I wouldn't do."

Skye blushes, and I have to wonder what these girls have been talking about. Kennedy's probably been teasing Skye all morning. Reaching forward I open the passenger side door

Kennedy snickers behind me. "How chivalrous."

I reach behind my back and flip her the finger.

Skye slides into the back seat, and I follow her in. Leaning close, I kiss her lightly on the lips.

"Oh my God, will you two get a room?" Kennedy grouses.

Skye blushes again, this time at Kennedy's insinuation, whilst I, on the other hand, think it's not a bad idea. I could have Hamish drop us off at a five-star hotel—the best in the city. The thought lingers for a moment before I reluctantly dismiss it.

Skye isn't interested in extravagance, you tool.

I could throw thousands at this girl and get nowhere.

I can't fuck this up. She wants to go to Notting Hill, so that's where we'll go.

Kennedy lingers by my open car window.

"Take care of her, Will," she says, practically glaring at me. "You hear me?"

I nod. "I will."

She leans down to whisper, "If you hurt her, I'll personally castrate you. Capeesh?"

I laugh, but she doesn't even crack a smile. She's dead serious, and I realize I'm walking a very fine line here. We've all become good friends—Connor included. If I fuck up, I risk throwing a massive spanner in the works.

I reach out the car window and take Kennedy's hand, looking at her with a hundred percent sincerity. "You have my word as a gentleman. I promise I'll treat her like a queen."

Kennedy's tense expression melts into a genuine smile. "You *like* her," she mouths. "Get out of here," she says aloud, laughing as she shoos us away. "Go have fun."

Skye jumps when I squeeze her knee.

"Miss Williams, you look lovely today."

"So do you," she says, grinning.

She reaches into her handbag and pulls out an envelope. I know what's in it before she even speaks.

"Here's the rest of the money I owe you," she whispers.

She hands me the envelope, and I have no choice but to accept it. There's a lot more at stake here than a mere fourteen hundred pounds.

"Thank you," I say, nearly choking on the words. I tuck the envelop in the seat pocket in front of me, wishing I could give it back.

* * *

Hamish drops us off on Portobello Road, only a few streets from the market. As is typical of a weekend, the market is fairly overrun with people, most of whom are tourists.

People squashed together like sardines isn't my idea of a fun time, but Skye's face is transformed by utter jubilation. She stops at nearly every stall, looking over the wares, pointing out this oddity or that. Portobello Road Market is like a treasure trove, offering just about everything—jewelry, vintage books, clothing, toys, antiques.

She glosses over the expensive stuff with little interest, but she stops to admire little quirky things, like old vintage toys and used books. I follow her closely, looming over her like I'm her own personal bodyguard. It's very crowded and there's a lot of jostling bodies. I don't want someone accidentally bumping into her.

Most of the trinkets are crap, but something has definitely caught her eye. Leaning down I rest my chin on her shoulder to see what has her so fascinated. It's a small antique display case filled with carefully arranged silver charms pinned to a silk back. The charms vary in price, the cheapest being 90p, to the most expensive being twenty-two pounds.

"I could buy them all for you, if you'd like," I whisper in her ear.

She shivers as my breath tickles her ear, and when she turns to me, our noses brush gently.

"I only have four spaces left," she says, lifting her wrist to show me her bracelet. The charms are spaced equally, and there's a bit of room left to be filled. "Every one of these charms means something special to me. I don't want to buy any old charm for the sake of it."

Straightening up, I rub my jaw and watch as she methodically scans the rows of charms.

I point to two charms on the bottom row. "How about those?" One is a Big Ben charm, and the other a Buckingham Palace guard. I bet she'd like both of those.

Skye reaches for my hand and squeezes it. "They're perfect."

"Excuse me?" I say to the elderly lady on the other side of the table. "We'll take these two charms, please. Big Ben and the guard."

The lady unlocks the glass case, unclips the charms, and pops them into a small paper bag. "That'll be five pounds fifteen."

Just as Skye starts to open her handbag, I hold out my hand, three two-pound coins in my palm.

"I can pay," she says distractedly as her gaze focuses on the coins. She picks up one of the coins and looks it over. "What's this?"

"A two-pound coin."

"I don't think I've ever seen one before. I used to collect coins when I was a kid."

I pull another two-pound coin from my pocket and pay the woman. "Keep that one," I say to Skye. "I have plenty."

It's so damn cute how she inspects the coin. If she likes it that much, I'll gift her a million of them. And that's just for starters. Hell, I'd gladly give her anything she wanted.

"Where would you like to go now?" I inquire, once she has the little bag in her grasp.

She looks up and, with her index finger, taps her chin. "Let's go find the door from the movie."

"Ah, yes. The blue door. Of course." I pull out my phone and do a quick search for the exact location of that iconic symbol of modern romance. A simple query brings up the exact address. "Got it. Let's go."

With my arm tightly around her, to protect her from the throng of eager shoppers, we weave in and out of the crowd. We're not official, *yet*, but I want the world to know she's off the market.

As we approach our destination, it's painfully clear we're not the only ones having this idea. There's a horde of people standing in front of the iconic *Notting Hill* blue door, all talking excitedly and taking selfies.

Personally, I don't see what all the fuss is about. It's just a bloody door that was once in a film. But when I glance down at Skye, I can't miss the excitement in her eyes.

There's a sort of a queue formed, as people wait their turns to shuffle closer to the door. We wait our turn. I never thought I'd be here doing something so touristy, but I am for her, because I've learned it's the little things that make her happy. And if this is what it takes to impress her, then so be it.

Finally, we're at the front of the queue. Skye snaps several selfies of us. I smile and bend down so our faces are at the same level. Laughing, she turns toward me, and I take advantage of the moment to plant one on her. As our lips touch, she gasps and pulls back, her eyes wide.

I caught her by surprise. When she smiles, I move in again, more slowly this time, and touch my lips to hers, gently increasing the pressure.

"Where to next?" I murmur against her lips.

I catch a lock of her hair that has escaped her bun and finger the silky strands. I know where I'd like to go—straight home.

"How about the travel bookstore?" she says.

I pull out my phone and search for the location of the famous Notting Hill travel bookshop that Hugh Grant's character supposedly owns. I find the location, which isn't far, and we head off in that direction.

Unfortunately, it turns out the bookshop isn't a bookshop anymore, but rather a shoe shop. Skye frowns as she snaps a photo. "That's too bad. I was going to buy a book to commemorate our visit."

"Come on," I say, taking her elbow. "I'll find you a bloody bookshop. There's got to be other ones around here."

Sure enough, we do come across a second-hand bookshop. I open the door for Skye, and she walks inside. I follow her as she browses from one section to another, paying special attention to the classics—the Jane Austens and the Brontes. She fondles a few old copies of *Pride and Prejudice, Emma,* and *Jane Eyre.*

Then she moves on to a section of travel guides. She picks up a book filled with color photographs of quaint English villages and zeroes in on some late eighteenth century country houses, complete with crumbling stone borders and wild roses.

She sighs. "I love these old houses. They look like they're right out of a Jane Austen novel."

I point at the caption of the photo she's admiring. "That was taken in Bibury. Would you like to see it?"

Surprised, she glances up at me. "Really?"

"Of course. I own an estate just outside of Bibury."

Her blue eyes light up. "I'd love to see it."

I don't think I've ever seen her so excited. "How about next Friday? We'll make a weekend of it, if you like. Just the two of us."

She swallows hard, and I force myself to keep a straight face. She looks a bit scandalized, as if I've just propositioned her for sex right here on the pavement. Although to be honest, I'm rather intrigued by the idea of the two of us spending the weekend in a quiet country house. It would be romantic as hell. I can just picture her in my bed there, in that big, antique four-poster.

"Come on, it'll be fun," I say, secretly hoping she'll agree. "There's plenty of room. You'd have your pick of four guest bedrooms. And you can meet Roy and Alice, the caretakers. I know they'd love to meet you."

At the mention of guest bedrooms and other people, she relaxes visibly. "Oh. Well, I'd have to think about it. I'm not sure what I'm doing next weekend."

I tuck a wayward strand of her hair behind her ear. "You do that." Then I glance down at the well-loved copy of *Romantic English Cottages* in her hand. "D'you want the book?"

She nods, so we make our way to the sales counter, and Skye hands her book to the balding man behind the register. While she's chatting with the old guy, I pull out my wallet and withdraw a crisp twenty-pound note, which I hand to him.

Skye looks at me. "What are you doing?"

"Paying for your book."

"You can't."

"Of course, I can. I just did."

"Let him, lass," the man says. "When a handsome bloke wants to buy you something, just smile and look pretty." Then he winks at Skye. "Looks like you've caught yourself a keeper."

The salesclerk hands me my change, which I pocket. He wraps up Skye's book and puts it in a paper shopping bag. I steer Skye out of the bookshop as she sputters on about me paying.

Out on the pavement, I glance up at the dark clouds gathering overhead. "Looks like rain." I check my Rolex. "I don't know about you, but I'm famished. What do you say we summon the car and head to my apartment for some dinner?"

Skye frowns as a drop of rain hits her cheek. "Good idea."

I call Hamish and give him our location. It's spitting with rain now, so I buy the biggest brolly I can find from one of the street vendors. As we walk to the location where Hamish will collect us, I hold the brolly over the both of us. I've got my arm around her, tucking her close to my side to keep her dry.

As we wait for the car, I kiss the top of her head. "Hungry?"

She nods. "Starving."

I love how she's resting her weight against me. "Fancy a nice hot meal and a cozy fire in the hearth? Maybe a film?"

"You've read my mind." And then she slips her arm around my waist to get closer, probably just wanting more of my body warmth. Still, I can't help the stupid smile on my face.

For the first time in my adult life, I feel like I'm in the right place with the right girl. The question is... how do I keep her here?

20

Skye

The rain is pouring by the time Hamish arrives to pick us up. Will opens the rear passenger door and holds the umbrella while I slide in. He follows right after me, stowing the wet umbrella on the floor.

I'm exhausted from so much walking and only too happy to collapse on the seat of the car. I buckle my seatbelt and lean back with an exaggerated sigh. "My feet are killing me."

Will laughs as he buckles his seatbelt. Then he pulls out his phone and presses a key. "Maggie, would you be a dear and prepare supper for me and Miss Williams? We're on our way." He pauses a moment to listen. "Thank you, love. That sounds perfect." And then he ends the call and pockets his phone. "There. Dinner is sorted."

"Who's Maggie?"

"My housekeeper."

"You have a housekeeper?"

"Of course. She's also a brilliant cook. I promise you'll be impressed. How about filet mignon and steamed baby potatoes? Sound good?"

"Yes, thank you. But please, I'd hate for her to go to any trouble on my account. Honestly, I'd be happy with a grilled cheese sandwich."

"It's no trouble."

The early evening traffic is heavy, and we move slowly, but Hamish skillfully navigates the crowded streets of London.

Will reaches for my hand and places it palm down on his thigh, covering my hand with his. When his thigh muscles flex firmly beneath my hand, my stomach clenches.

Hamish approaches the front of a towering apartment building, pulling to a stop in front of a pair of gold-trimmed glass doors. An older gentleman in a suit opens the rear passenger door, and Will steps out of the vehicle and offers me his hand.

"Good evenin', sir," the doorman says. He opens one of the doors for us and tips his hat. "Evenin', miss."

My first glimpse of the foyer in Will's building is a bit of a shock. It's sleek and modern with its shiny, black marble floors and soaring ceiling made of glass. The evening sky is already starting to darken to a muted gray-blue.

Behind a sprawling mahogany desk sit two young men, also in uniform. And behind them is a double bank of elevators.

"Good evening, Mr. Carmichael," one of them says, straightening in his chair.

The other guy looks me over curiously, about as subtle as a sports announcer.

Will cups my elbow and steers me around the desk to the hallway lined with elevators. We stop at the last one on the left, which is marked **PRIVATE**. After Will punches in a code, the door opens promptly.

"After you," he says, motioning me inside the roomy car.

He follows me inside and pushes the single button labeled **PENTHOUSE**.

"You live in the penthouse?" That must cost a small fortune.

He nods. "I do."

"How many apartments are on the top floor?"

"Just the one. Mine." And now the price tag has grown considerably.

The elevator zips up to the top floor, slowing to a graceful stop when we arrive at our destination. The doors slide open and we step out into a spacious apartment that looks like something you'd see on an episode of *Lives of the Rich and Famous*.

"This is your apartment?" The words slip out before my brain-to-mouth filter engages.

His lips quirk up in a smile. "The code worked, so it must still be mine. Come, I'll show you around."

The penthouse's foyer is nearly the size of my entire apartment, the walls lined with gorgeous oil paintings depicting quaint, old English houses made of stone, just like the ones pictured in the book he bought me.

That reminds me!

"Will, I left my book in your car."

"That's okay. I'll have Hamish bring it up with him."

"He lives here too?"

"Yes, he and Maggie both live here with me. They have their own living quarters attached to the penthouse."

We walk through an arched doorway into a huge living room. The outer wall is solid glass, and even from here I can see the view overlooking the River Thames. There's a balcony beyond the glass walls.

My gaze skims the living room, lighting on a fireplace, two sofas, numerous upholstered chairs scattered throughout the space, and end tables.

"The kitchen is through there, the dining room that way, and the bedrooms are down this hallway."

He takes me on a whirlwind tour of the apartment, pointing out five bedrooms, a home office, a work-out room, and a home theater that includes the largest TV I've ever seen. Lastly, back in the main room, he opens the sliding glass doors and we walk out onto the balcony.

I stand at the railing and stare out at the river. Darkness is falling, and the city lights are flickering on. We have an unimpeded view of the setting sun.

"I like to take my morning coffee and breakfast out here before I head off to work," he says. "I never get tired of watching the river."

He joins me at the railing and puts his arm around me, pulling me close. Then he drops a kiss on the top of my head. "It's nice having you here."

"Excuse me, sir?" a female voice says, from behind us.

We turn to see a middle-aged woman dressed in a light gray uniform dress with a spotless white apron. She nods to me with a smile. "Good evening, miss." And then to Will, she says, "Dinner is ready. Shall I serve it out here?"

"Thank you, Maggie, yes," he says. Then he turns to me and makes introductions. "This is Maggie, my housekeeper. Maggie, this is Skye Williams."

"Pleased to meet you, Miss Williams," Maggie says. And then to Will, she says, "I'll bring your meals right out."

Will pulls out a chair at a small round bistro table for two. He takes the other chair, opposite mine. We watch contentedly as boats meander up and down the river.

A moment later, Will's housekeeper rolls a silver cart out on the balcony. On the cart are two plates covered with silver domes. There's also an ice bucket holding a bottle of red wine, two crystal wine glasses, napkins, and silverware.

Without a word, Maggie places the plates on the table, the glasses—everything. She hands Will the bottle of wine, already opened, and he pours for us while she removes the domes from each of our plates which hold filet mignon, tiny steamed potatoes under a buttered herb sauce, and grilled veggies. Then she sets a cloth-covered basket of warm rolls in the center of the table. Lastly, she gives us each our own little dishes of butter and sour cream. She moves quietly and efficiently, like she's done this a thousand times before, and for much more impressive guests than me.

"Enjoy your meals," Maggie says, giving me a warm smile.

Will picks up his glass of wine and takes a sip, savoring it. He nods toward my glass. "Have a taste."

I sip the wine, but I'm much too overwhelmed by the meal to register the taste. "This is like something out of a five-star restaurant."

He smiles, looking comfortable and confident. "Maggie is an amazing cook. Try the food. Is it to your liking?"

I take a bite of everything, moaning in appreciation. Everything is simply perfect—flavorful and tender. "It's delicious. Does she spoil you like this every night?"

He laughs. "I'm afraid so. I'm glad you like it."

He has a cook *and* a chauffeur. I knew Will was wealthy, but I'm just now realizing it goes much beyond anything I had imagined. He's not just wealthy. He's *loaded.*

It all makes sense now. The dress and shoes. The expensive dinner and six-hundred-pound bottle of wine. This penthouse. He'd never bat an eye at the expense, because it *is* immaterial to him. It really is all pocket change, just as Kennedy said.

I glance at the bottle of wine sitting in what I imagine is a sterling silver bucket, and my appetite evaporates. I lay my fork down.

"Is something wrong?" he asks, after swallowing a bite of his filet mignon.

I shake my head.

He sets his fork and knife down and wipes his mouth on a pristine white linen napkin. "Skye, what is it?"

I turn to look at the river as the sun dips below the horizon, streaks of orange and pink visible in the fading light.

How much does it cost to own a front-row seat to the Thames?

Suddenly, I feel dizzy, and it's not from the height. "You're very wealthy." I realize my words sound more like an accusation than a simple observation.

He doesn't laugh or make a joke of it. Instead, he nods. "Guilty as charged, I'm afraid. I hope you won't hold it against me. It's not my fault. I was born into it."

I swallow hard, comprehending the immense gulf that exists between us, much wider than the timeless river we overlook. It's more like an ocean's worth of divide.

I was raised by a single mom. We never went hungry or had to go without, but it wasn't always easy. I glance through the glass wall at the luxurious designer place he calls *home*. There's a real wood fire in the hearth. I can smell wood burning. Maggie must have lit a fire.

I'm so out of my element.

Oh, my God, I fed him pizza last night. Delivery, no less.

I close my eyes, trying to hide my mortification.

"Please tell me what you're thinking. Something's going on

up there—" he points toward my head with his fork, "and I'll bet it's not looking good for me."

I don't know what to say.

I don't belong here?

I'm not your type?

"Skye, please. You're making me nervous."

I laugh, although it sounds a little bitter. Maybe melancholy is a better way to describe it. "Will, I—" I take in a deep breath and let it out slowly. "I don't belong here. With you. I'm sure you're used to a very different type of woman—certainly not my type. Not the kind of girl who shops in used clothing stores and buys second-hand things."

As Will reaches across the table for my hand, his gaze lights on my charm bracelet. "How about a girl who collects charms that represent the most meaningful moments in her life? Can't I like a girl like that? How about a girl who doesn't look down her nose at anybody? Not the doorman, not the bin man, nor the road cleaners? Can't I like a girl like that?"

My face heats and a knot forms in my throat. He sounds so earnest.

He squeezes my hand and gives me a heartbreakingly beautiful smile. "Please eat your supper before it gets cold. Then, I promise you, we'll do something a girl like you might enjoy."

He releases my hand so we can eat our food, which is delectable.

I sip my wine slowly, not accustomed to drinking alcohol and not wanting it to go to my head and make me do something stupid.

After our meal, we each have a second glass of wine—just a half-glass for me because I'm already feeling a bit of a buzz.

When we're both done, Will stands and pulls me to my feet. "Let's have some dessert."

"I'm so full, I don't think I can eat another bite."

"It's not much. Just a bit. Come with me."

He leads me by the hand into a gourmet kitchen that looks like something you'd see featured in an interior design magazine. Maggie is putting dishes in the dishwasher.

"Can I get you something?" she says, looking a bit perplexed at seeing us there.

"Maggie, have we got any ice cream?" Will says.

"Sure. There are several cartons in the freezer."

"Great." And then he gets down two bowls from the cupboard, grabs two spoons from the silverware drawer, and opens the freezer to retrieve a brand-new carton of chocolate ice cream.

"D'you like hot fudge?" he asks me.

I nod.

"And whipped cream?"

I can't help smiling. "Yes."

"And how about chocolate sprinkles?"

"Of course."

We end up making hot fudge sundaes together, and then we carry them out to the living room and sit together on a small sofa in front of the fire. It's just big enough for the two of us, very cozy, and we eat our ice cream.

"It doesn't always have to be filet mignon and expensive bottles of wine, you know," he says, as he scoops up some ice cream. "I want you to feel comfortable. I'm happy to adjust. When I was at Eton, we boys would happily exist on pizza, crisps, and sweets. I don't need filet mignon to be happy, Skye." He leans close and kisses me, his lips cold from the ice cream. "But I think I do need *you*."

* * *

Later that night, Will accompanies me as Hamish drives me home. It's started raining again, and the streets are shiny wet. Will walks me up to the door of my building, holding a giant umbrella over the both of us. The porch light is on, and I can see Kennedy spying on us through the front window.

I turn to face Will. "Thank you for a wonderful day."

His warm hands feel good on my face as he cups my cheeks.

"I had a lovely time," he says. "Thank you for spending the day with me. It's late, and I know you're tired, so I'll just say goodnight." And then he leans close and kisses me. It's a gentle kiss, not demanding at all, almost hesitant as if he's not sure how I'll react.

His lips feel so good against mine, and as they nudge mine open, I feel a warmth spreading low in my belly. A moan slips out without warning.

He cups the back of my head and holds me close as he deepens the kiss. "I hate to say goodnight, Skye, but I know I must. Until Monday, then."

I reach up and grip his muscular forearm. "Until Monday."

The building's outer door opens, and Kennedy pokes her head outside. "Say goodnight, Will, and let the poor girl come inside. It's wet out."

Once I'm inside the flat, I head to my room and lay my book on the bed. Then I head to the bathroom to get ready for bed. It is late, and I am truly exhausted.

Kennedy loiters outside the bathroom door. "So? How'd it go?"

"We had a wonderful day."

"And...? Why was it wonderful? What happened?"

After finishing my nightly routine, I open the bathroom door and step out. "We walked all over Notting Hill, saw the door and Hugh Grant's bookshop, which is now a shoe store. I bought two charms for my bracelet. We went to a used bookshop, and I bought a book on gorgeous English country cottages, and then we had a gourmet meal in Will's million-dollar penthouse apartment."

Kennedy whistles.

"Oh, and then we made ice cream sundaes for dessert and ate them in front of a blazing fire."

"Million-dollar apartment, eh?"

"It has to be. He lives on the penthouse floor, and he has a balcony overlooking the Thames."

"Fancy."

"Oh, and he has Maggie—his housekeeper-slash-gourmet-chef. And, of course, you've met Hamish, his chauffeur. Kennedy, the man is loaded."

"Lucky for you, Prince Charming has taken a liking to you."

"I don't see why. I'm not even close to being in his league—not by any stretch of the imagination."

"Girl, have you looked in a mirror lately? You're gorgeous, and he's a man. Of course, he's interested."

I dismiss her comment. "He invited me to go away with him next weekend, to see his house in Bibury. Apparently, it's one of those gorgeous old Jane Austen type houses."

Kennedy's eyes widen. "Seriously? The whole weekend? What did you say?"

"I said I'd think about it."

"What's there to think about? Go! Dazzle him with your charm. Wow him in bed. Give him the best blow job he's ever had, and he'll be putty in your hands."

"Kennedy!"

"What?"

"I don't know if I'm ready for any of that."

She flaps her hand dismissively. "Of course you are. You're two consenting adults. Go for it. Don't you *want* to go?"

"I do. I'd love to see a quaint English village in person, and I'd love to see Will's country house."

"Then tell him yes, for God's sake."

When Kennedy goes to get ready for bed, I get out my jewelry tools and attach my two new charms to my bracelet. Then

I pick up my copy of *Romantic English Villages* and climb into bed to leaf through the pages and stare at the fairy tale pictures. These country houses—and these villages—are so picturesque, they look like something out of a British period film.

Finally, exhaustion kicks in and I'm having trouble keeping my eyes open. I set down my book and turn off the bedside lamp. I relax into my comfy bed and relive the day's outing, remembering the feel of Will's arms around me. The feel of his lips on mine.

Oh, I'm in so much trouble.

✑ 21

Skye

Monday morning, I ride the bus to work with Kennedy. After I stow my purse in the bottom drawer of my desk and pull out my chair to sit, I notice a small, hand-written sticky note attached to my computer monitor.

Thinking of you,
Will

He even drew a little happy face on the note. Warmth rushes through me, and my chest constricts. We had an amazing weekend together, both Friday evening and all of Saturday. After sharing a few kisses, I'd say we've definitely gone past the *just friends* stage. Now, I don't know what to do. Falling for him was never part of my plan, and yet I can't bear the thought of not seeing him again.

My dad shows up unexpectedly at my desk and sits in my guest chair. "Hello, sweetheart. I thought I'd pop in to say hi and see how your weekend went."

"Hi, Dad. It was good." My heart starts pounding, as if my dad has X-ray vision and can see Will's note through my computer monitor.

"Glad to hear it. How about lunch today? Do you have plans?"

"No, I don't. I'd love to."

"Great. I'll stop by and get you at noon. We can go downstairs to the canteen."

My dad leaves, and I boot up my PC and check my e-mails. There's one from my boss, one from Connor, and one from Kennedy. I open Connor's first, as I can't imagine what he needs to e-mail me about.

> *I see Will's in a damn fine mood this morning. What's that all about? I know you two went out this weekend. Details! Or do I have to ask Kennedy? – Connor*

Then I check Kennedy's e-mail. She's going on about Connor pestering her for details about my date Saturday with Will.

Lastly, I read Spencer Sinclair's e-mail.

> *Skye, when you get a chance this morning, come see me in my office. – S. Sinclair*

My stomach drops at the idea of going to Spencer's office. Though the man gives me the creeps, I figure I'd better get this over with.

I cross the room and knock on his office door.

"Come in!" he calls.

I take a deep breath and hope for the best before opening the door and popping my head in. "Mr. Sinclair? You asked to see me?"

"Skye!" He waves me inside. "Come in, please, and close the door, will you?"

I do as he says and take a seat in front of his desk.

He steeples his fingers in front of him, resting his elbows on his desk. "I wanted to talk to you about the Hoffman Enterprises portfolio you reviewed last week."

"Yes?" It was a pretty straight-forward assessment, and the client didn't fare well. I marked them high-risk.

He consults his computer screen. "I see that you advised against them."

I nod. "Yes. They lack the technical expertise, and they don't have any plans to bring in outside help. They have some good ideas and their marketing plan is strong, but they don't seem to understand what's required from a technical standpoint to implement their vision. It just wouldn't be a sound investment."

Mr. Sinclair smiles as he folds his hands in front of him. "You see, Skye, if you rate them high-risk, they'll have no chance of securing investment funding. They're dead in the water. However, if you rate them a bit more favorably, they'll have a chance

of getting funding. I'm sure once they get their project un-
derway, they'll realize the types of capabilities they'll need to
acquire."

"I understand that, sir. But they really are high-risk at this
time. I couldn't in good conscience rate them any higher than I
did. It would be too risky for Carmichael & Son."

"Skye." He sighs as he rises from his chair and walks around
to where I'm seated. Sitting on the corner of the desk, he crosses his arms and looks down at me. "Sometimes, in the course
of doing our jobs, we have to think outside the box. We have to
be a little *creative* in how we state our conclusions. Sometimes
a gentler approach is warranted. Do you understand what I'm
saying?"

A chill runs down my spine because I understand perfectly
well what he's saying. And I won't do it. "Are you asking me to
lie?"

He snorts out a short laugh. "Of course not. Don't be silly.
I'm simply suggesting that you reconsider your assessment.
Hoffman Enterprises is a start-up and in need of funding. They
have great ideas and incredible potential and—"

"But Carmichael & Son isn't in the business of funding *potential*. We fund organizations that show strong promise for a
good return on our investment. Hoffman Enterprises has no
track record at all, and already they're underestimating what it
would take to bring their ideas to market. No matter how you
look at it, they're a huge risk, and I can't in good faith—"

I halt mid-sentence when there's a knock at the door.

Mr. Sinclair glares at the door before he yells, "What is it?"

The door cracks open and Mrs. Farmer, his executive assistant, pokes her head inside. "Mr. Carmichael is requesting to see you, sir, in his office. He said straight away."

Mr. Sinclair swallows hard, his Adam's apple bobbing. "Tell him I'll be right there."

As soon as Mrs. Farmer is gone, Mr. Sinclair looks me in the eye. "We'll continue this discussion later, Miss Williams." His expression tightens. "I'm sure you'll see things differently once you've had time to think about it. After all, you wouldn't want anyone getting the impression that you're difficult to work with."

And then my boss shoos me out his office door, closing it behind himself as he heads down the hallway toward the elevator.

I stand outside his door frozen in shock.

Did he really just try to pressure me into giving a good assessment to an organization that clearly is a bad risk?

That sure sounded to me like a loosely veiled threat.

A bit dazed, I head back to my office and find Kennedy sitting in my office chair, spinning in circles.

"Hey, Kennedy," I say, taking a seat in the guest chair.

She stops spinning. "Where were you?"

"In Sinclair's office."

She sneers. "Ew. My condolences."

"I think he tried to pressure me into changing my assessment of a client portfolio I ranked as high risk," I tell her, my voice lowered.

She stops spinning the chair. "You're kidding."

"No. He was in the middle of explaining to me why I should change my assessment when he got called away to Mr. Carmichael's office."

Kennedy grins. "Maybe he'll get sacked." She starts spinning the chair once more. "What have you decided about Will's invitation?"

"Nothing yet."

She makes a face. "Stop overthinking and tell him yes."

"My dad wouldn't be happy. He's already warned me about Will." My mom wouldn't be happy either.

Kennedy hops up from my chair. "I've got to get back to work. I'll see you at lunch?"

"I'm having lunch with my dad in the cafeteria, but you're welcome to join us."

"Okay. I'll see you then."

The rest of the day progresses normally. I start working on a new assessment report for an Internet start-up company. Lunch with my dad and Kennedy is a lot of fun, and then I'm back to my desk.

As I'm reading a new potential client's portfolio, my mind keeps going back to the strange conversation I had with Mr. Sinclair this morning. I don't think I'm overthinking it. I'm pretty sure he tried to talk me into giving Hoffman Enterprises a pass they don't deserve. But I can't do that. My original decision was a no-brainer, and I'm not changing it. It simply wouldn't be ethical.

Near the end of the day, I hear footsteps approaching my workstation.

I glance up to see Will leaning against the partition. I stop what I'm doing and smile up at him. I can't help it. Seeing his face makes me happy. "Hey."

"Hey to you, too." He nods to my guest chair. "May I?"

"Sure. Have a seat."

He sits. "How's your day going?"

"Fine. Well, mostly fine."

"Something happened?"

"I'm not sure. Maybe I'm overreacting."

He frowns. "Tell me."

I sigh. "Spencer Sinclair called me into his office this morning to talk about an assessment I turned in last week. I gave a potential client a high-risk rating, and he questioned me on it. My rating is accurate; I stand by that. But he hinted that I should revise it to something more *agreeable*."

"What did you tell him?"

"I told him I couldn't do it. Not in good conscience. And, he told me not to tell anyone. Don't you think that's weird?"

He nods. "It is indeed."

"Then he got called away—to your father's office, actually. I haven't seen him since. But I don't care what he says—I'm not going to revise my assessment. It was pretty cut and dry. It would be a mistake to change the rating."

Will nods. "You stick to your guns. Don't let Spencer, or anyone else for that matter, try to force you to change your mind.

Since you're young—and an intern—people might think they have a right to influence your judgment. Don't let them."

"Thanks for saying that. I appreciate it."

He smiles at me. "You have a damn fine head on your shoulders. I trust your opinion, and Spencer should too." He shifts in his chair, leaning closer. "Speaking of opinions, have you formed one about this coming weekend?"

I chuckle at his sly segue to the topic of this weekend. "Not yet." I grin at him. "Kennedy says I should go."

"By all means, listen to Kennedy." He reaches for my hand. "No pressure, but I'm hoping you'll say yes. I'd love to show you the countryside where I spent my childhood summers. And I know you'd love Bibury."

As he rubs the back of my hand with his thumb, he heats up more than just my hand.

Liquid heat pools low in my belly, and the butterflies return with a vengeance. "I'll think about it."

He kisses the back of my hand. "Fair enough." He notices my charm bracelet. "I see you added the new charms."

I lift my wrist to show off my bracelet. "Yes."

"Looks like you've got space for at least a couple more. There are car boots in Bibury on the weekend and several vintage shops. I imagine you might find some trinkets to your liking."

"Are you trying to bribe me, Mr. Carmichael?"

He grins. "Absolutely."

* * *

The rest of the week passes productively. I get my current report completed and turned in to Mr. Sinclair, and then I start on a new one. Mr. Sinclair hasn't said another word about Hoffman Enterprises, and I'm hoping he won't bring it up again. He praises my work on my newest assessment and gives me a more challenging portfolio to review next.

I have dinner with my dad and his family Tuesday evening, and on Wednesday, I go out to lunch with Will, Kennedy, and Connor for sushi.

By Thursday, I know I need to give Will an answer about the weekend. He hasn't said another word about it, which I appreciate. He's not trying to pressure me, at least not openly. He calls me mid-morning and invites me to have lunch with him in his office. I accept.

When I arrive at his office at noon, there's an impressive spread of Chinese take-out on a table by the window. He went all out, ordering a number of entrees and side dishes.

"This is quite a spread," I say.

"I wasn't sure what you liked, so I ordered a few things." He points out the main dishes, spring rolls, steamed rice, and fried rice.

We both end up eating a little bit of everything, and we share the rolls and the rice. He has tea to drink, and I have my trusty water bottle with me.

As we eat, we have a perfect view of the street below and The River Thames beyond that. It's mesmerizing to watch the boats puttering up and down the river.

"Please come with me this weekend," he says, eyeing me over the pair of chopsticks in his hand. "I really want to show you the countryside. I think you'll love it. The River Coln runs right through Bibury."

I take a bite of my entree and chew slowly in an effort to stall. Finally, after I've swallowed and have no excuse not to talk, I tell him the truth. "I want to come."

He listens carefully, reading between the lines. "And yet?"

"Everything's just moving so fast. I wasn't expecting this at all. I came here to get to know my dad's family and to gain professional experience. I never envisioned—" I stop mid-sentence.

"You never envisioned what? Dating?"

I nod as I sip my water. "I just keep thinking about my mom and what she went through while she was here. If she knew I was seeing someone, she'd be worried."

He nods. "That's understandable."

I stifle a laugh. "I'm really tempted to go."

"Say yes, Skye. London is amazing, but I want to show you the beauty of the countryside. I want to amaze you, show you a bit more of what England has to offer."

He reaches for my hand and begins fingering the charms on my bracelet. "Let's add some more charms to your bracelet, shall we? Maybe a quaint English cottage? A sheep, or a horse?"

I smile. "I'm holding out for a double-decker bus."

"I think that can be arranged." He brings my hand to his mouth and kisses the back of it, his lips warm and gentle. "No pressure, love. Absolutely no expectations, I swear. Just a couple days alone, the two of us, so we can get to know each other better."

I sigh. "Okay."

"Really?" He squeezes my hand. "You won't regret it, I promise."

ꙮ 22

Skye

W ill picks me up in his sleek, black Aston Martin Friday after work. It's odd seeing him behind the wheel for a change. I'm so used to Hamish driving us. He looks relaxed, very much in his element, with one hand gripping the leather steering wheel and the other on the gear shift. He drives confidently, the powerful car engine purring under his touch, and I find myself watching his hands.

The drive from London to Bibury is quite picturesque once we get out of the city and into the countryside. When we leave the main highway, we travel along some smaller roads bordered by fields and pastures, stone walls, and an abundance of wildflowers. The road narrows as we approach Bibury, which is where Will's country house is located.

We pass through the center of town and drive a ways out into the countryside, where the properties are spaced farther apart.

He slows the car and turns right into a charming little lane bordered on both sides by a well-maintained, low stone wall. Soon we come to a gate, and Will pulls up to a keypad and enters a code. The gate swings open, and we drive through. Apparently, there's a bit of technology lurking in this quaint countryside.

He follows a long lane, bordered with shrubs and bursts of wildflowers on both sides, with pastures spreading out as far as the eye can see. Then he rounds a curve, and right there ahead of us is the most beautiful house I've ever seen. It's a large, stone structure, two stories tall, and it looks like something right out of a Jane Austen novel. There are rose bushes and creeping ivy everywhere, and a three-tier fountain in the center of the circular drive.

"It's beautiful," I breathe.

Will shoots me a grin. "I'm glad you approve." He pulls up toward the front of the house.

I look up and I'm mesmerized. It's something right out of a fairytale. The front door is in the center of the structure, with two pairs of windows on each side. There are corresponding windows on the second floor, and then the little attic windows higher up.

To the right of the house is a separate garage with a small shed attached. And beyond the garage, I can see part of a barn.

A white-haired man wearing a blue flannel shirt under a pair of denim overalls ambles up to the driver's door and raps on the roof.

Will lowers the window. "Hello, Roy."

Roy bends at the waist and peers through the open window at me, studying me curiously. Then he turns his attention to Will. "The missus is inside preparing tea for you and your lady friend. Go on in, lad, and I'll carry up your luggage."

Will pops open the trunk, and Roy walks around to the back and pulls out our bags.

"Roy and his wife, Alice, are the caretakers here," Will says. "They live in a little cottage around back. Roy takes care of the land and the structures, and Alice manages the household." He reaches for my hand and gives it a light squeeze. "Shall we go inside?"

Will opens his door and steps out.

As I follow suit, I notice a wooden fence to the left. Three little ponies stick their fuzzy noses between the railings and observe us.

"Ah, yes. Alice's ponies," Will says. "They're more like oversized dogs if you ask me, and spoiled rotten."

Roy clears his throat. He turns his attention to Will. "Where *exactly* shall I take your bags, sir?"

Will pauses a moment, considering. "Take mine up to my room, if you don't mind, and take Miss Williams' bags to the blue room."

Roy tips his head. "Aye, sir. Just wanted to be sure."

My face heats. Was that Roy's subtle way of asking if we're sleeping together?

Oh, God.

My mouth goes dry. We've haven't discussed the sleeping arrangements this weekend. To be honest, I've thought about hardly anything else since he asked me to spend the weekend with him.

Does Will expect us to sleep together?

Obviously not, if he told Roy to take my bags to a guest room. I've gone over and over this in my head.

Should the opportunity arise, do I want to sleep with Will? Have sex with him?

Yes, I do.

But the idea also makes me a nervous wreck. I've come pre-pared, just in case. It was the only sensible thing to do.

Will walks over to my side of the car and stands directly in front of me. His warm hands cradle my face, and he makes me look up into his eyes. "I'm glad you're here with me." And then he leans down and gives me a light kiss on the lips.

"I am, too. Now, how about a tour? I'm dying to see everything."

"And you shall. But first, let's go say hello to Alice and take some refreshments. Knowing Alice, she's been planning our tea all day long. It's sure to be superb."

Will wasn't wrong, of course. "Skye, this is Alice. Alice, this is

Miss Skye Williams."

Alice, a petite older woman with long, silver hair is dressed in a simple blue cotton dress and white apron. Smiling, she curtsies.

She actually curtsies.

"Pleased to meet you, Miss Williams."

"Thank you, Alice. But please, call me Skye."

She's standing next to a rather round table with two chairs, set in front of a large picture window overlooking the fountain. I glance out the window and notice that the Aston Martin has been moved.

The table has been set with fancy china with matching tea-cups and silver flatware. In the center of the table is a two-tiered plate containing tiny crustless sandwiches, scones, cookies, and tiny petit-fours. There's also a pot of what looks like strawberry jam and a little dish of butter. Of course, there's a kettle of water on a hot plate and an assortment of tea bags arranged in a fancy wooden box. No proper English refreshment would be complete without tea.

"Thank you," I tell Alice, truly impressed. "It's very kind of you."

Alice's expression transforms as she smiles widely. "Thank ye, miss." Her accent differs from what I'm used to hearing in London.

"Just Skye, please."

"Yes, miss." Another curtsy. "Certainly."

Will pulls a chair out for me, and I sit. As he takes the other chair, Alice disappears.

"Roy and Alice are like family to me," he says. "I inherited them, so to speak, when my nan gave me this house." Will motions toward the food. "Help yourself." He pours hot water into both cups. "There's a wide assortment of tea here. I'm sure you'll find something you like."

After taking a quick peek, I select a bag of Lavender Honey Citrus and dunk it into my cup. Will selects Tetley. We sip our tea and nibble on the delicious treats Alice has prepared for us. The view out the front bay window is breathtaking.

I pick up a shortbread cookie. "If I lived here, I'd never want to leave."

"It is idyllic. You should see the village. Bibury is lauded as one of the most beautiful villages in England. We can go there tomorrow. You might like all the quaint shops and cafés."

After we've had a bit to eat and drink, Will takes me on a tour of the house.

"Like many of the homes in this area, this one dates back to the late eighteenth century. It's been updated, of course, with running water, electricity, and gas. It's even got Internet."

The ground floor has a small parlor, a larger living room, kitchen, formal dining room, and a library. We walk up the narrow stairs to the second floor, which has five bedrooms and nearly as many bathrooms. The master bedroom is the biggest, and it's at one end. Next to the master bedroom is the blue bedroom—aptly named for its pale blue walls. There's a white quilt covering the bed.

My bags are in the blue room, sitting on a wooden bench at the foot of the bed. Besides a pair of nightstands and a matching antique dresser, there's an upholstered armchair by the window. There's a small closet and a private bath.

We peek in at the other three bedrooms, and Will shows me the narrow little staircase that leads up to an attic. "There's nothing up there except cobwebs."

After the house tour, he takes me through the kitchen and out the back door. There's a lovely gated flower and herb garden just out back.

Will points at the small white cottage a few hundred yards behind the house. "That's where Alice and Roy live."

We follow a well-worn stone path to the barn, which is currently occupied by three little ponies in their stalls, all happily munching on fresh hay.

We pass a chicken coop, where all the chickens have gone to roost, as it's nearing sundown, and continue down the gradual slope to a small lake.

A wooden rowboat rests on the grassy bank, with two oars sticking out of it. A dock stretches out into the water, and plenty of ducks and geese paddle around, squawking noisily at our approach.

The property is pristine countryside—part pasture, part woods. Will points out a tiny little babbling brook that meanders through the farm. The back of the property is wooded, and he assures me it's home to all sorts of wildlife, including deer and foxes.

When we get back to the house, Alice is in the kitchen putting a kettle of water on to boil. "Any special requests for supper?" she asks.

I'm not very hungry after the amazing spread we had for tea earlier. "How about sandwiches?" I suggest.

"Of course, miss," she says. She looks to Will.

He nods. "Sandwiches sound perfect, thank you."

After a supper of sandwiches, potato chips, and an apple pie, we head into the living room to relax. The house is quiet.

Will lights a wood fire in the hearth, and then he turns off the lights and joins me on the sofa, putting his arm around my shoulders. The flickering firelight is magical, casting shadows in the room.

"Alice and Roy have turned in for the night," he says. "It's just us now. We have the place to ourselves."

"This house really is beautiful, Will. I feel like I'm in a Jane Austen novel. It's almost as if I could look out the window and see Mr. Darcy riding his horse up the lane as he comes to pay his respects."

He laughs. "If it would impress you, I could ask to borrow one of the neighbor's horses. I'm afraid Alice's ponies are too small for me to ride."

"I confess I would be impressed."

"How about a glass of wine instead?"

A little wine might help mellow me out and put a damper on my nerves, so I accept his offer.

While he's in the kitchen getting the wine, I sit alone on the sofa, my mind racing, feeling more and more nervous. I finally get up, too anxious to sit still, and pace the room.

Am I ready for this?

For tonight?

I have no doubt that Will wants to sleep with me. And the truth is, I want to be with him too.

I've never felt like this before. I never dated much in school—I was too focused on my studies. I went out with a few guys, but those relationships never amounted to much.

I'm just not sure I'm ready for this.

Kennedy was right. I need to let go for a change and take a chance. I need to listen to my heart and not let myself get tied up in knots.

A few minutes later, Will returns with a bottle of red wine and two glasses, which he sets on the coffee table.

I watch him pour for us both. "This isn't another six-hundred-pound bottle of wine, is it?" I tease.

He glances at me, his expression clearly guilty.

I laugh. "Are you serious?"

After setting the bottle down, he picks up both glasses and hands me one. "Not *quite* six hundred." He raises his glass. "To us. To a memorable weekend."

I touch my glass to his, and then we both take a sip of wine. If I end up getting naked with him tonight, it will be memorable all right.

I gaze up into his mesmerizing green eyes, flecked with bits of gold and gray. "To us."

He smiles as he reaches out to brush my bottom lip with his thumb. "You are so beautiful."

My face betrays me, warming as I fight a grin.

"But do you know what I admire even more than your beauty?" he says.

"What?"

He gently taps my chest with his index finger. "Who you are in here." And then he taps my skull. "And what you've got going on up here."

I laugh. "You mean overthinking everything?"

"No. I don't mind your very analytical nature. I think it's endearing. I like that you know your own mind. You're not swayed by money or prestige—things that others aspire to. You're an original."

"You mean I'm boring and unimaginative."

He takes hold of my wrist and lifts it so that we're both looking at my charm bracelet. "This isn't unimaginative at all. These symbols mean the world to you. They capture all the magic you see in the world. I love that about you. Other women want expensive handbags and jewelry, and designer this and that. When I try to buy you something expensive—or even suggest it—you have a small fit."

"Do you know what I like about you?" I ask him. "Besides your beautiful hair and hypnotic eyes?"

"What?"

"You make an effort to understand me. Most guys don't."

"Most chaps are fools then." He sets our wine glasses on the coffee table. "And I strive never to be a fool, if I can help it." And then he draws me to him and kisses me. I can taste the wine on his lips.

One of his hands cradles the back of my head, and the other is at my back, gently urging me closer. When my breasts come into contact with his chest, he groans.

His fingers are in my hair, kneading my scalp and making me shiver as pleasure streaks down my spine.

"I love having you here."

He pulls me onto his lap.

"My boots!" I say, scrambling to remove them before they get the sofa cushions dirty.

He pulls off one boot, then the other, and sets them on the floor. Then he tucks my feet close and wraps his arms around me, holding me securely to him.

I wrap my arms around his neck and lean in to kiss him. For a few moments, he lets me have control, but before long he deepens the contact, using his lips to coax mine apart.

"It's getting late," he says. "I thought tomorrow we'd have a big breakfast, then go into the village and look around. I meant what I said about having absolutely no expectations this weekend, Skye. It's all up to you. You have your own bedroom, your own space. But I want to make it very clear to you that my bed is yours, if you are so inclined to share it with me."

I appreciate the fact he's being a gentleman, but the truth is I'm really tempted to take him up on his offer.

ॐ **23**

Skye

We walk up the stairs to the second floor, and like the gentleman he is, Will walks me to the blue bedroom—my bedroom.

"Here you go," he says. "Make yourself at home, and sleep well. If you need anything during the night, just call for me."

He gazes down at me for the longest moment, almost hesitant. His hands cup my face, and he studies me. Then he tucks my hair behind my ear.

Neither one of us speaks. This silence says everything.

He swallows hard and then opens his mouth as if to speak,

but all that comes out is a heavy sigh. "Good night, love." Then he leans forward and kisses my forehead. "I'll leave you to your rest."

And then he turns and heads across the hall to his own bedroom.

I stand in place, watching as he disappears into his room. Oddly enough, I feel bereft, already missing him. Other than kissing me downstairs, he didn't even make a pass at me. The kiss on the forehead was purely platonic. He meant what he said—he has no expectations. It's up to me.

I close my door quietly. Then I gather my pajamas and toiletries and head into the bathroom to take a quick shower and get ready for bed.

After brushing my hair, I change into the pink silk nightgown I brought.

As I turn off the light and climb into bed, it occurs to me that my room is located directly across the hall from his. I don't think that's a coincidence.

Wide awake, I read a while on my phone. I'm far too wired to fall asleep. On top of that, the romance novel I'm reading is giving me ideas.

Can I really do this?

Can I walk across the hall and climb into his bed?

I blow out a frustrated sigh. I almost wish he had made a move on me. But then I remember what he said earlier. I guess if someone's going to make a move, it has to be me.

I climb out of bed and walk barefoot across the smooth wood

floors to the window overlooking the front lawn. The moon is bright tonight, and I can see the water from the fountain spraying high up into the air.

The setting is so serene, it reminds me of the best romantic literature the British have to offer. They certainly have cornered the market there. Jane Austen, Charlotte Bronte and her sisters...

But enough stalling.

It's now or never, before I lose my nerve completely.

In that split second, I decide.

I cross the hall to his bedroom. The hallway is dark, but I can make out that his bedroom door is ajar. And I see a faint glow of light coming from under the door.

He left his bedroom door open.

For me?

I feel hot and dizzy and queasy all at the same time. But then Kennedy's words ring in my head.

Live a little, Skye. You don't always have to be so careful. Don't overthink. Just act.

So I knock, softly, in case he's asleep.

"Come in, sweetheart."

His low voice rumbles through me as I open the door and walk inside.

Will is sitting up on his four-poster bed, leaning against pillows propped up against the headboard. He's shirtless, and the bedding comes up to his waist. He has a book in his hands. The lamp on his bedside table is on.

Will marks his place with a bookmark and puts the book on the nightstand. When he meets my gaze, he looks perfectly calm and relaxed while I, on the other hand, am shaking.

"Do you need something?" he asks.

I almost laugh aloud.

You.

"Skye?"

"I—" And then my throat seizes up on me.

Biting back a smile, he tosses his covers aside and climbs out of bed. He's wearing a pair of gray boxers and nothing else.

I stare at his bare chest, seeing it for the first time, completely unprepared for the ridges and muscles that define his abs. Light and shadows play across the contours of his chest, and my mouth goes dry.

Oh, my God.

Suddenly I feel self-conscious about my own body.

He comes to stand in front of me, his hands on my shoulders. "Everything okay?"

I nod. "Fine."

He studies me for a long moment before he says, "What do you need, Skye?"

As I meet his curious gaze, I realize there's no point in drawing this out. It's going to get harder the longer I delay the inevitable. "You. I need you."

His expression tightens as he pulls me into his arms and kisses me, his mouth hot and hungry. I gasp, taken by surprise at the abrupt change. It's like he's been holding back for so long, and now he doesn't have to.

His hands are everywhere, gripping my arms, then sliding up to my shoulders. One hand clasps a fist full of my hair while the other one pulls me hard against his chest.

Our kiss deepens, his tongue seeking mine and stroking me. His lips are soft, and yet firm, and my head is spinning.

Suddenly, he steps back and reaches for the hem of my nightgown. "You won't need this." He pulls it up slowly, exposing one inch of my body after another.

When he's exposed my bare body, he sucks in a breath. Then he sweeps me up into his arms and lays me in the center of the bed, my head on a pillow, and crawls onto the bed.

What happens next is a bit of a blur. I'm trying to pay attention, but my emotions are quickly swept away by a slew of new sensations and experiences.

His body fairly radiates heat as he looms over me. His hands are in my hair as his mouth devours mine. His lips coax mine apart, and his tongue slips inside. Our breaths mingle as our bodies strain closer together.

He slides his knee between my legs, nudging them apart, and works his thigh between mine until it's up against me. There's so much aching heat between my legs, I moan when he presses closer, harder. I'm throbbing down there now and helpless to stop the breathy cries escaping me.

But I'm not the only one who seems to be losing control. He's breathing hard, and when I press my aching sex against his thigh, animalistic sounds tear out of him.

Instinctively, I rock against him, and I realize that was his intention all along. He wants me to rub against him—to pleasure myself.

"That's it, sweetheart," he says in a low, guttural voice. "Ride me."

It feels so good, I don't want to stop. I rock against him, so close to coming that my legs are shaking, my belly quivering. I may not be experienced when it comes to sex, but I'm no stranger to orgasms. I know how to make myself come.

He kisses me hotly, drinking in the high-pitched sounds I'm making. But before I reach my peak, he shifts position without warning, sliding down the bed and pushing the bedding aside.

I gasp when he settles himself between my thighs. Before I can utter any sort of protest, he pries the lips of my sex apart and licks my clitoris.

Dear God!

My garbled cry of surprise is quickly lost as my chest rises and falls with frantic breaths. "Will, no!"

He pauses, lifting his head. I can see the glint from my arousal on his trim beard. "Why not?" He seems perplexed.

Mortified, I cover my eyes with a shaking hand. "Because!"

He chuckles. "Oh, if that's all." And then he resumes what he was doing before, only with far more gusto.

I'm absolutely horrified, but my thighs are shaking uncontrollably. I've never in my life felt anything like this. I'm so completely overwhelmed with sensation, with pleasure so sharp and piercing it steals my breath.

He devours me without hesitation. Pleasure zings down my nerve endings, culminating in a firestorm of sensation. My body is quaking, shaking, rocking.

I'm right on the precipice of something life-altering, and then I feel a sucking sensation on my over-stimulated, tortured clitoris, and I find myself grasping at the sheets, then at his hair, grabbing and pulling desperately.

And then a bomb goes off deep in my core, waves of pleasure radiating outward, stealing my breath and my sanity. I gasp, I cry, I wail. I have no shame. He's turned me into a quivering, wet mess.

Will shoots up to his knees and shoves down his boxers. He reaches for a condom packet that I hadn't even noticed was there. He rips open the wrapper and sheaths his cock with faultless expertise. And then he's kneeling between my quaking thighs, angling himself toward me, lowering his body. And before I can utter a word, he sinks inside me, so deep and so far I feel like I've been impaled.

I cry out sharply, my back arching off the mattress, caught completely off guard and unprepared. I claw at his thighs, my nails digging into him.

"Jesus!" He freezes, holding himself completely still. Rising up on one hand, supporting his weight above me, he glances down between our bodies at the spot where we are joined. He pulls out a bit and bites out a glorious curse. "Why the bloody fuck didn't you tell me you're a virgin?"

"I—"

"Christ! Are you okay?" He pulls the rest of the way out, his hand gripping a blood-stained erection. "Did I hurt you? Of course I fucking hurt you! I had no idea."

"I know. I'm sorry I didn't tell you." I grasp his shoulders and pull him closer. "Don't stop now. Please. I'm sure it will get better soon."

His chest heaves as he sucks in lungfuls of air. "Skye." He rocks back on his haunches, kneeling between my open thighs. He runs the fingers of his free hand violently through his hair. "You should have told me, love."

I lay my palms on his hard thighs and rub gently. "Don't stop. I want this."

He looks torn. Filled with regret. "Skye—"

I reach for him. "Please."

Gently, he lowers himself between my thighs, careful to keep his weight off me. He fists his sheathed cock, wet with my arousal and hints of blood, and gingerly guides himself to my throbbing opening. He sinks inside me, slowly, just an inch at a time.

I suck in a breath, noticing the burn. I bite my lip to keep from moaning, this time in discomfort.

"Try to relax, sweetheart," he says. "Your body will adjust to me. Just give it some time."

Sure enough, as he sinks slowly inside me, an inch at a time, my body softens for him, letting him in. Soon, the stinging pain has receded, leaving behind a bit of a burning sensation.

Once he's fully seated, he pulls out carefully, and then sinks slowly back in. He repeats this a few times until my body has caught on and the discomfort ends.

"Better?" he asks, as he sinks in once more.

I nod, gasping a response. "Yes."

"We're going to talk about this later."

I laugh despite myself. "I figured we might."

He starts moving, slowly, his body now gliding easily through my wetness. "Oh, yes, we're going to talk about this."

My hands follow the contours of his chest, moving over his pectorals, to his biceps, and up to his broad, muscled shoulders.

He's the sexiest man I've ever seen naked. To be fair, he's the only man I've ever seen naked.

As he strokes slowly inside me, my body softens, growing warm and liquid. I love the feel of his steely erection sliding through my body, creating delicious heat and friction. The residual ache is still there, the slight burn, but the trembling of my thighs and quiver in my belly are welcome sensations.

Will stiffens between my legs, his back arching as he cries out. His arms stiffen as he holds himself above me, careful not to crush me with his weight. His hoarse cry rises to the ceiling and shakes the rafters, and I smile, more than content with the outcome. As he comes, I'm still throbbing inside from my own orgasm earlier.

After gingerly pulling out, gritting his teeth either in pleasure or pain, I'm not quite sure, he excuses himself and walks naked to his own private bathroom. I hear the water running. A moment later, he returns with a warm, wet washcloth.

He washes me, removing every trace of blood and stickiness from the lubricated condom. Then after disposing of the cloth, he turns off the bedside lamp and crawls into bed, drawing me close and covering us both.

I feel his lips move in my hair, but I can't make out what he's saying. "What was that?"

He sighs heavily. "I wish you had told me, Skye. It would have gone so differently. I'm sorry I hurt you."

I press a kiss to his chest, right over his sternum. "I didn't want to make a big deal out of it."

"A woman's first time is a big deal." He rolls me to my side and slides up close behind me, his arm going securely around my waist. When he kisses the back of my neck, I shiver.

And then I yawn.

He laughs softly. "Go to sleep, my American virgin."

"Not anymore, I'm not."

24

Will

As daylight peeks through a small opening in the curtains, I lie wide awake and watch Skye sleep. She's lying on her side, her back to me, her long hair sprawled everywhere. She looks so damn perfect, so innocent. Well, perhaps not so innocent anymore, thanks to yours truly.

A virgin.

Fuck.

I feel so at odds knowing I took her virginity. I feel guilty for plowing into her with such force. I've wanted Skye from the moment I first met her, and finally having her beneath me, wanting me to take her, it went to my head. I might have gotten carried away. I only hope she isn't too sore today, and that her first time—*our* first time together—hasn't put her off sex completely.

She groans as she stretches her limbs.

I brush hair back from her face. "Good morning, love."

She presses her round ass against me, making my cock twitch to attention. As I rock against her, she presses her face into her pillow and moans. My cock hardens even more at that sweet sound. She's getting me off, and all we're doing is dry humping. If I keep this up, I'll come.

I turn her to face me, taking in her swollen lips and her messy hair. "God, you're beautiful."

She grins. "You're such a liar. I'm a complete mess."

The girl really has no idea how attractive she is. Her skin is soft and lush, and the bridge of her nose is dusted with tiny freckles. *It's adorable.* There are faint smudges under her eyes from last night's mascara. And her dark blonde hair is wild this morning. She looks well fucked.

I turn her face toward me so I can plant my lips on hers.

She rises up to meet my kiss. It starts slow and little by little she relaxes, allowing me access. I slip my tongue into her mouth and deepen our kiss.

I reach down to slip my hand between her legs, and she flinches. I pull my hand back. "You're sore."

"No, it's okay," she murmurs against my lips. Reaching for my hand, she places it back where it was. "I want you to touch me."

I feel the heat and wetness through the folds of her sex. I slide a finger into her lushness and gently rub slow circles on her clit.

Obediently, she spreads her legs and squirms as soft plaintive sounds escape her lips.

God, I love hearing her pleasure. And better yet, I love hearing her come.

Breaking our kiss, my eyes lock on hers as I press my finger against her clit. Then I slide my finger down and dip into her opening, relieved to find her deliciously wet. When I press deeper, she stiffens with a soft, plaintive cry.

I withdraw my finger, not wanting to press my luck, and I go back to teasing her clit, which she seems to like just fine. "Is this okay?"

Biting her lip, she nods as she sinks back down onto the bed with a gasp. "Yes."

I'm desperate to be balls deep inside her, but I know it's too soon. However, I can make her come.

I circle her clit with the tip of a slippery finger, faster and faster until she's making high-pitched, desperate sounds. Her thigh muscles tighten, clamping down on my hand, and she's panting for breath. Her entire body stiffens, and she clings to me as she cries out.

I slow my motions, easing her down from the high of her climax. When she finally relaxes once more, I pop my finger in my mouth, tasting her and making her blush.

"I should go take a shower before I get any more carried away," I say. With one last, lingering kiss, I roll off the bed and head to the *en suite*. My balls are throbbing, and I need a cold shower and possibly some serious hand time.

My *en suite* is spacious as befitting the master suite. Matching gray slate tiles line the floor and wall, and recessed spotlights run equidistantly along the ceiling. Upon reaching the wall-mounted shower, I turn it to cold and quickly jump under the spray. Squeezing my eyes shut, I endure the cold water as it cascades over me.

Suddenly, I feel an arm wrap around my waist. And then there's a female shriek.

"Shit, Will! That water is ice cold!"

"I believe that's the first time I've heard you cuss, Miss Williams. I rather like it."

"Don't get used to it." She reaches around me and turns the water temperature up.

The whole purpose of having a cold shower was to cool off and lose this damn erection.

Fuck it.

I'd much rather suffer in silence to have her with me. I turn to face her, my arms going around her wet body.

I take a moment to fully appreciate her naked form. With fascination, I watch the water travel down the valley between her breasts, to her navel and beyond, disappearing between her supple thighs. My gaze eats up the lush curves of her body.

Reaching for the soap, I lather my hands and then turn Skye

away from me as I massage her back in slow, deep circles. I press my body to hers, my cock against her back. Then I wrap my arms around her and begin soaping the front of her body—her waist and hips, her breasts, her neck, and lastly I drop a dollop of lather on the top of her pert little nose.

There's a mischievous glint in her eyes as she takes the soap from me. She motions for me to turn around, and then she begins lathering my shoulders and back. But I soon turn back to face her, as I'd much rather have her slippery hands on my chest and cock.

Her hands work their way down my body until her gaze locks onto the broad crown of my cock, which is straining upward, begging for attention. She stares at it a moment, looking a bit uncertain. I guess she's unsure of what she should do with the ruddy head that's staring up at her. As she was a virgin until last night, chances are she hasn't encountered a lot of cocks.

"Take hold of it," I tell her in a firm, no-nonsense tone, hoping to quell any hesitation on her part.

She hesitates a moment before wrapping her fingers around my length. Her touch is soft, gentle. Not quite what I had in mind.

"Squeeze harder." I demonstrate. "You're not going to hurt me."

Her soft blue eyes lift to mine, gauging my reaction as she tightens her grip on me.

"Better," I say, nodding encouragement. "Go on. It won't bite or break."

She grins as she tightens her grip.

I cover her hand with mine and show her how to stroke me from base to tip. Once she has the basics down, I release her hand. As she strokes me, she observes me closely, watching my reaction.

Damn, she's a fast learner.

It's not long before I'm panting like I've run a marathon, and a groan rumbles through my chest. "That's right, love. Just like that."

Already my balls are drawing up. "God, Skye. I'm so close."

I cover her hand once more, speeding up her movements and tightening her hold on me. Her grip feels so damn good. I squirt some bodywash into the process for added lubricant, and her hand slides briskly up and down my cock.

My heart is hammering in my chest, and my lungs are burning for air. "I'm coming," I warn her, attempting to brush her hand away and taking a step back. But she's having none of that, and despite the warning, I come in a heated rush, my spunk hitting her belly. "Fuck, I'm sorry!" I'm afraid I've traumatized the poor girl.

Quite the opposite, she laughs, her eyes bright as she goes up on her toes to kiss me.

* * *

Once dried off and dressed, we head downstairs for breakfast. As soon as I open the door to the kitchen, I'm met with the scent of fried bacon and freshly-baked bread. Alice has laid out a magnificent spread on the sideboard.

"Thank you, Alice," I say. "This looks wonderful."

Skye squeezes my hand as her stomach growls in approval. I guess we both worked up quite the appetite and are more than ready for a Full English.

Alice points toward the hall. "Have a seat in the dining room, and I'll bring in your plates."

I'm glad to see Roy standing just inside the kitchen, kicking off his muddy work boots. Yesterday, I'd asked both Alice and Roy to join us for breakfast this morning, as I want Skye to get to know them. And I want them to get to know her. Roy and Alice aren't just employees, they're part of my family. I have very fond memories fishing with Roy when I was a boy, and it's a tradition I hope to carry on when I have a boy of my own one day.

Once we're seated in the formal dining room, Alice and Roy join us, each carrying in two large plates filled with food. They set ours at our places, and Skye stares at her plate. Fried eggs, hash browns, toast, bacon, sausages, baked beans, black pudding—the whole thing.

As we tuck into our meals, Roy and Alice entertain Skye with stories of my family's history, from my parents, to my grandparents, and all the aunts and uncles and cousins. Then they both start telling embarrassing stories of me growing up—including the time when I was ten years old and fell off my pony, here at this estate, and broke my leg.

Roy tells Skye about the time I fell out of the fishing boat and got myself tangled in the line, and how he had to jump in to save me.

They go on to talk about their own children and grandchildren, who now live in Edinburgh. I let their family stay here at the house when they come for a visit. It's really no bother; it's my way of thanking them for their hard work and dedication.

Skye dabs the corner of her mouth with a serviette. "Thank you so much for breakfast, Alice. It was delicious."

Finished with her own meal, Alice stands and picks up her plate.

"I'll do that," Skye offers. "I'll clear the table and do the dishes."

Alice's mouth drops open. "What? No, miss! Thank you, but I—"

Skye lifts her hand. "You cooked us such a beautiful breakfast, the least I can do is clean up. Please, I insist." Then she winks at me. "Will can help me."

Alice is speechless, and she looks at me for instruction.

I nod. "I agree. You've really outdone yourself this morning. Take the rest of the morning off. Skye and I will clean up here before we head into the village."

Alice waits a few beats, looking around at the amount of cutlery that needs washing up. "Only if you're sure?"

"Yes, I'm sure." I walk Alice and her husband to the back door.

Just before she takes her leave, Alice squeezes my hand and whispers, "Look after her, Will. She's a keeper."

I smile. "I know, Alice. I know."

◡◞ 25

Will

We spend the morning walking hand-in-hand around Bibury. As my nan lived here when I was a child, I'm well acquainted with the village. Most of the shop owners remember me as a kid, running in and out of their shops, playing with the local kids, running errands for my nan. But seeing it through Skye's perspective is quite eye-opening.

It's a picture-perfect, quaint English village where cobble-stone pavements are lined with rustic shops housed in centu-ries-old stone buildings. Flower boxes hang beneath every window, and emerald green ivy and honeysuckle creep up their exterior walls. The village pub seems to be the main attraction; its pristine gardens are hugged by lavender bushes trimmed to perfection.

It's apparent that the locals take pride in their village. And unlike London, Bibury isn't overshadowed by concrete high-rises, but instead completely enveloped by lush greenery and architecture that has withstood the test of time. Majestic trees stand tall, their leaves in varying shades of green forming the perfect backdrop to this lovely spot.

Breathing in the fresh air loosens a lingering tension in my chest.

Whilst Skye's attention is on the local scenery, mine is on her. She looks so damn cute today. Her long hair is neatly secured in a French plait, and she's wearing denim shorts and a feminine pink top with a scooped neckline that almost reveals a bit of cleavage. It's that *almost* that keeps me on my toes.

I decided to dress down today, to coordinate better with her outfit. Instead of my usual dress trousers, I've donned a pair of stone-washed jeans and a long-sleeved gray t-shirt.

"That's a good look on you," Skye said earlier when she saw what I was wearing. "You look like a *GQ* farmer."

I mocked offence, but inside, I was beaming.

Now I watch in fascination as she snaps pictures of the shops and cafes and uploads them to Instagram.

"It's magical here," she muses. "Like something you'd see on a postcard." She pockets her phone. "Speaking of postcards. I'd like to send one to my mom. She'd love it."

"This way." I point her in the direction of the village shop, which doubles as the post office. It most assuredly sells postcards.

Draping my arm around her shoulders, I walk with her down the cobbled pavement and we go inside.

The bell above the door rings, and the old guy behind the counter looks up from his fishing magazine. "Well, look who it is. Will Carmichael."

I wave. "Hello, Bill. It's good to see you."

Skye makes a beeline for a rack of postcards standing in the corner. She wastes no time spinning it around, looking over the assortment they offer before finally selecting one featuring a photo of a stone house sitting just beyond the banks of the River Coln. At the counter, she writes a long note on the back of the card, addresses it to her mum, and then pays the postage to send it overseas.

Once that business is concluded, we stop next in a vintage dress shop. Skye tries on a number of hats, the kind you'd expect to see on ladies' heads at Royal Ascot. I offer to buy one for her, but after checking the price tag, she declines. She does, however, let me buy her a pink ribbon badge costing one pound to support a local breast cancer charity.

As we're on our way out, I realize I've lost her. After a quick scan of the shop, I locate her peering into a tall glass cabinet.

"What have you found?" I ask as I join her. I peer into the cabinet, where there's an array of trinkets, including thimbles, buttons, crystal animals, and even silver charms. The bits and bobs are all jumbled together on a silver tray. Her gaze skims over the items.

The girl turns down a three-hundred-pound hat, but she can't resist cheap little trinkets.

When I spot something I know she'll like, I point it out.

She follows the trajectory of my finger and it takes her a minute to spot what I'm looking at.

When she sees it, her face lights up. "A bus!"

It's not the best quality charm in the world, obviously cheap and mass-produced, but it fits the bill. We call the clerk over, and she opens the cabinet and retrieves the double-decker bus charm.

Wonder of wonders, Skye agrees to let me pay the one pound fifteen for the charm, and the clerk slips it into a little paper bag, which she hands to Skye.

"Thank you, Will," Skye says as we step out into the sunshine. She peeks into the bag. "It's perfect."

Seeing her smile is the only thanks I need. That, and knowing how pretty the new charm will look dangling from her wrist.

By twelve o'clock we find a bakery, and I purchase two Cornish pasties and two lemonades. We sit on the grassy bank of The River Coln and alternately feed ourselves and the ducks.

"It's funny," I mumble between bites.

Skye meets my gaze, but doesn't reply as her mouth is full. Chewing, she raises her brows with intrigue.

Wrapping her in my arms I gaze at the water below. At the

ducks and geese who have grouped together waiting for us to throw them some more crumbs. At the little fish that occasionally swim to the surface in search of tiny insects to devour. At the father and son a few yards away skimming pebbles into the water, watching them take flight and bounce.

"This feels more like home to me than anywhere on the planet. I'd spend summers here with my nan and extended family, and it was perfect. I felt free. Free to ride my bike, play with my cousins, to run and just be a kid."

I gaze up at the clear sky and all around me. "No skyscrapers, no bustling traffic, hardly any people. It's not a rat race here, unlike in the city."

Skye relaxes into me as she sips her drink. "You don't like London?"

I think for a moment, pondering all the things I love about it. "I love London. I just don't love living there all the time. Sometimes I feel smothered there, trapped within the glass and steel. I usually try to get out here at least one weekend a month, just to recharge."

My words have silenced her, and she studies me thoughtfully.

The squawking from the geese and ducks die down when we have nothing left to throw them. They tire of us and move on. Their ruckus is soon replaced by the soft sound of bird song, the rustling of leaves and children's laughter in the distance.

I draw her close. "This is my idea of heaven."

Skye lays her head against my shoulder. "Mine too."

* * *

Back at the house, we chill out for the afternoon. Alice has left us a tin of homemade biscuits—still warm from the oven— and we have them with tea. I pull an old photo album off a shelf in the bookcase beside the hearth to show Skye some pictures from my childhood.

I point to a photograph of children playing in a treehouse. "That's me with two of my cousins, Esme and Louisa."

As I flip through the pages, I point out more of my cousins— John, Kelley, Marie, Darcie, Nadine, Thomas.

Skye laughs. "I hope there's not going to be a test. Just how big is your family?"

I turn the page and spot a photo of Esme sitting on the lawn, playing dolls with Rachel.

"Who's that?" Skye asks, pointing at the red-haired girl.

"That's Rachel. She's the daughter of close friends of my parents."

"Is she your ex?"

"I guess you could say that. We've known each other since we were kids, but we only dated recently. Our parents have always wanted us to get married, since we were kids. When we started dating earlier in the summer, they started to think they'd get their wish, but it didn't work out."

I quickly flip the page. Rachel's betrayal is still a sore spot, but in hindsight I'm glad she left. I now realize I wasn't in love with her. I never felt for her one-tenth of what I feel for Skye.

"My mother and father were both one of six. I have a lot of cousins—thirty-two to be precise. I've lost count of how many of them have children. I just know that Christmases cost a small fortune."

Her mouth falls open. "All those siblings and yet you were an only child?"

I laugh. "When you've produced perfection the first time around, why try again?" But then I sober pretty quickly. "In truth, my parents struggled for years with infertility. They'd just about given up on the idea of a pregnancy when, miraculously, at age forty-two, my mum got pregnant with me."

Skye reaches for my hand and links our fingers. "I'm sure they were beside themselves with joy when they had you."

I nod. "They were the best parents any kid could ask for. They showered me with love. They made sure I had the best education money could buy. I really couldn't have asked for a better upbringing."

"Where are all your cousins, aunts, and uncles now?"

"A lot of my mum's family live in Glasgow."

She perks up, eager. "You're Scottish?"

"Half." I flip through more pages of the photo album, pointing at my aunts. "My mum's sisters own a chain of fashion boutiques. Her brothers own a chain of restaurants all over Scotland. My cousins on my mum's side are dotted all around Scotland."

"And your father's side?" she asks with growing interest.

"They're based in the Midlands. My uncles run a highly successful soliciting firm, whilst my aunt Nancy heads up a charity organization in London." I pause, wondering if this is the right time to ask her to the wedding. "My cousin Esme is getting married in a couple of weeks, at my parents' estate in Surrey. Would you like to be my plus one? I'd love for my family to meet you."

"Are you sure?"

Tilting her face up to mine, I plant a kiss on her soft lips. "Yes, I'm sure. I'd like nothing more."

She looks away.

My heart starts pounding as I turn to face her. "What's wrong?"

"Will, I—" She pauses a moment as if collecting her thoughts.

My heart slams against my ribcage, and I quickly backpedal. I'll say anything to put her at ease. "It's just a wedding, Skye, not a lifelong commitment. You wouldn't want me to show up at my cousin's wedding alone and be the odd man out, would you? I'd never hear the end of it. You'd be doing me a favor. We'll bring Kennedy if you like. And Connor. We'll make a group outing of it. It'll be fun."

She looks far from convinced.

"Will you at least think about it? Please?"

She nods. "I'll think about it."

Shit.

For the first time in my adult life, I'm the one facing the prospect of getting my heart broken. Usually it's the other way around.

I set the photo album back on its shelf and hold out my hand to Skye. "Come outside with me. Let me show you why I love this place so much."

26

Skye

We make a pitstop in the kitchen on our way outside. Will grabs a wooden cutting board and a sharp knife and starts slicing up some apples.

"These are from our own orchard," he says. "The ponies love them."

He tosses the pieces of apple into a small container, which he hands to me. Then he takes my hand and leads me out the back door.

"This farm has been in my nan's family since the late seventeen hundreds. She inherited it from her father when he passed, and she gave it to me a few years ago when she went to go live with my parents in Surrey."

Will's in a good mood as he leads me by the hand to a pasture fence. He whistles, and three little dappled ponies trot up to the fence, their heads bobbing eagerly.

"D'you know how to feed a horse?" he asks me.

"No."

He demonstrates by placing a piece of apple on his flattened palm and offering it to one of the ponies. "Keep your hand flat so you don't accidently get nipped."

The little brown pony gingerly lifts the treat off Will's palm with its nimble lips.

"Now you try," he says, handing me a piece.

A little brown and white pony gingerly takes the piece from my hand, her soft, fuzzy lips tickling my palm. "They seem quite friendly."

"They are. Alice babies them."

We feed the rest of the apples to the ponies, and then we head for the barn.

I can't stop thinking about Will's invitation to attend a family wedding. I'm torn, because I really would love to go with him, but weddings can be a slippery slope. And meeting his family... expectations are bound to come from that. Plus, my plans haven't changed. I'm going home after my internship is done. My life is in Ohio. I *can't* let myself get seriously involved with someone here.

Will opens the barn door, and we step inside. It's dark in

here, the air cool and redolent with the sweet scent of grain and freshly-cut hay. There are six horse stalls, all empty at the moment while their occupants are out roaming the pasture.

"How much land do you own?" I ask him.

"One hundred and six acres. It's mostly fallow now, and a lot of it has been reclaimed by nature. It hasn't been a proper working farm in decades, but that's okay. We have pastures, and we grow our own hay. There's a sizeable vegetable garden and a small orchard."

Behind the barn is a large chicken coop. The door is open at the moment, and scores of chickens scour the ground for bugs.

Will grabs a bucket of corn and grain and tosses the contents onto the ground. The chickens flock madly to partake in the meal.

We peek into the nesting boxes, which are currently empty.

"Alice collects the eggs every morning," he says. "She keeps some and trades the rest with our neighbors for fruit and honey."

Then Will returns the empty bucket to a workbench in the barn.

"I can easily see you living here, Will."

The corners of his eyes crinkle as he laughs.

"I'm serious," I say, following him out of the barn. "Why don't you do it? You said you feel cooped up in the city. Why not live here?"

His expression sobers. "Because I have responsibilities—to my family, to the company."

"Don't you have a responsibility to yourself, first? To be happy?"

His jaw clenches. "It's called Carmichael & *Son* for a reason. I'm to take over one day. I'm an only child—there's no one else. The responsibility falls to me."

He walks ahead, down a gently sloping hill toward a small lake.

"You could easily work from here, you know," I say as I catch up to him. "There's Internet out here. You could work remotely. People do it all the time."

He shakes his head dismissively, frowning. "I wish it were that easy."

"It can be," I argue. "It's your family's company. You can make the rules, Will. Just give it some thought, please."

He steps out onto a rickety old wooden dock that extends several yards over the water.

I join him, and we stand at the end of the dock and watch a group of ducks paddle around.

I peer down into the surprisingly clear water and see tiny silver fish darting in and out of the shadows cast by the wood beneath our feet. When a frog hops into the pond, making quite a splash, I jump. Will grabs my arm to steady me.

"Care to go out paddling?" He nods toward a little wooden rowboat resting on the bank.

"I'd love to."

He opens a small shed nearby and pulls out a life vest, which he hands to me. "Buckle up, Miss America."

"You're not wearing one?"

"No. I swim like a fish."

"Then I don't see why I should have to wear one. I can swim perfectly fine."

He leans down and kisses the tip of my nose. "Because I said so, Miss Williams. I'm not going to risk your pretty neck."

After I'm suitably buckled into my life vest, Will hands me into the rowboat, and I take the front bench.

He pushes the boat into the water and steps in at the last moment, taking the back bench and grabbing the oars.

"Try not to tip us," he says with a laugh.

"Ha! Funny."

For an hour, we paddle around in companionable silence, both of us enjoying the quiet serenity. The ducks don't take very kindly to our intrusion, and they let us know by quacking their heads off at us as they depart for the opposite end of the lake.

I find myself glancing back at Will, watching his strong arms pull the oars through the water. "How big is this lake?" I ask him.

"About three acres."

"Are there a lot of fish in here? I saw some small ones swimming underneath the dock."

"Oh, sure. There's all kinds of wildlife here. Roy used to bring me out here fishing all the time. We'd catch trout and catfish. When I was a kid, I'd chase tadpoles and frogs. It was the perfect setting for a boy to roam and explore."

As the sun begins to set behind the trees, Will rows us back to shore, where we climb out. He stows the boat on land and then returns my life vest to the shed.

"Hungry?" he asks, as we head back to the house.

"Starving."

"Let's go see what Alice has made us for supper."

* * *

After a delicious meal of roast beef, mashed potatoes, and salad, Will lights a fire in the living room hearth and we sit on the sofa and relax.

I answer a call from my mom and chat with her for a while, telling her about my weekend getaway to the countryside. She catches me up on what's happening at home and how her semester is going at the university where she teaches.

After I say goodbye to my mom, Will pours us both a glass of wine. He grins. "No comments. Can I help it if I like good quality wine?"

I shake my head. "You're impossible."

"No, *you're* impossible," he says, tapping the end of my nose.

As we sit on the sofa and drink our wine, Will plays with my hair, brushing it back from my face and tucking some strands behind my ear.

"Would you be terribly offended, Miss Williams, if I kissed you?"

I swear the wine has already gone to my head. "No."

"Good." He sets our glasses on the table and leans close to press his lips to mine. My hands skim up his broad chest to his shoulders, and when I begin to knead his muscles, he groans.

When a muffled moan escapes me, he nudges my lips apart and deepens the kiss, his lips warm and hungry on mine. "Skye?"

"Hm?"

He pulls back and brushes his thumb across my cheek. His beautiful green eyes, full of seriousness and intent, meet my gaze. "Come to bed with me."

It's not quite a question. My belly quivers as liquid heat pools low. Swallowing hard, I nod.

Up the stairs we go, and he pulls me into his room. He reaches for the hem of my top and pulls it up and over my head.

His heated gaze lands on my breasts, cradled in a pale pink bra. He traces the curved edge of one bra cup, making my skin tingle. "As pretty as this is, it's got to go." And then he reaches behind me and deftly unfastens my bra, catching it as it falls and tossing it onto a chair.

He proceeds to unbutton my denim shorts, and tug them, along with my panties, down my legs and off.

I'm not sure how this is fair. Before long, I'm standing completely naked before him, and he's still fully dressed. There's something incredibly arousing about being naked in front of him. I shiver.

"Are you cold?" he says.

"No."

He grins. "Nervous?"

"Maybe. Or maybe I'm just wondering why you're still dressed when I'm not."

He laughs. "Because your body is a thing of beauty, and I can't get enough of it."

"It hardly seems fair."

"All right," he says, unbuttoning his shirt. Once that's discarded, he starts to unfasten his jeans.

I still his fingers. "Wait." My body flushes with heat, and ignoring the pounding of my heart, I brush his hands aside and do it myself, carefully lowering his zipper past a rapidly growing erection.

I pull his jeans down, along with his boxer-briefs, and sink to my knees on the thick rug below.

His hands catch mine. "Skye."

I shake my head. This is something I want to do—something I *need* to do—and if I don't just push through with it, I'll lose my nerve. He's done it for me, and it's only fair that I return the favor.

I take his thick length into my hands, mesmerized by the velvety-soft skin over hot steel. Moisture glistens at the tip.

"Christ," he says, his warm hands dropping to cradle my face. He tilts my head up so I meet his gaze.

His green eyes are gentle as they skim over me, almost reverent. "You don't have to, Skye," he says gently. "No one's keeping score."

"I want to."

His hands soften as he brushes my hair back from my face.

"I'll be honest. There's nothing I'd like more than to feel your mouth on me, but I don't expect it."

That's all the encouragement I need. I lean forward and hesitantly lick the tip of his cock, tasting salt and heat and *man*. My belly clenches tightly with arousal.

Groaning, he shudders, and his hands tighten reflexively on my head, just for a moment, before he relaxes his hold.

Burying my trepidation, I take him in my mouth. I've been reading romance novels since I was a teenager, and I've watched porn before, so I'm not entirely clueless as to how this goes. Still, until you actually do it yourself, it's all a bit theoretical.

I figure I'm probably doing this badly, but Will doesn't seem to mind. His hands are on my head, stroking me, as he murmurs incoherent words that I think are supposed to encourage me.

He groans as I lick his length, stiffening when I take him into my mouth, as far as I can. His thigh muscles clench as he cries out, "Jesus, Skye! Fuck!"

I can't help smiling—I've never heard him sound less like a gentleman. I keep at it, stroking and licking him, sucking him into my mouth as far back as I can manage. I swirl my tongue around the head, tasting more and more of his saltiness.

Suddenly, he takes me by the arms and hauls me to my feet. "No more," he says, his voice practically like gravel. "I want to come inside you."

He steers me onto the bed, and then he opens the top drawer of his nightstand and grabs a condom, tossing it onto the mattress. Quickly, he kicks off his jeans and boxers, dropping them unceremoniously to the floor before climbing onto the bed with me.

I fall back on the mattress, shivering with anticipation. He's staring at me, his gaze taking in every inch of my body, and it's unsettling.

He kneels between my legs, looming over me with a dark expression his cheeks taut and his nostrils flaring. His gaze sweeps my body, and then he leans down and takes my left nipple into his mouth. His hand molds my flesh, plumping it and shaping it as he suckles the tip.

I feel the pulling sensation all the way down my body, between my legs, where suddenly I'm hot and flushed and aching. I cry out. "Will!"

As he shifts to my other breast, one of his hands slides down my torso to the aching spot between my legs. He dips his finger inside me, gathering wetness, and then he begins rubbing tiny circles on my clitoris. Immediately, my thighs stiffen, and my belly clenches hotly. A heavy breath escapes me, and my restless hands fist the bedding.

My hips start rocking on their own accord. Sounds escape my lips, shameful, high-pitched keening cries. When his finger slides down and slips into my opening one more, deeper this time, I gasp. He rubs me there, deep inside, and pleasure coils inside me. He works my body, persistent and measured. Then his mouth is there, hungrily devouring me, his tongue tormenting my clit as his finger strokes me deep inside.

Pleasure coils tightly inside, and I'm panting for air.

When he sucks gently on my clit, my body bows off the bed. My core detonates, and exquisite sensations radiate outward and make my body sing. I swear I see stars.

After quickly rolling on the condom, he hooks his arms under my legs and spreads me wide. Leaning forward, he positions his cock right against my opening.

His expression is taut, his jaws clenched, lips tight. His eyes are locked on mine, unwavering. "You okay?"

I nod, incapable of coherent speech.

And then he presses forward, the head of his erection pushing inside me. My body is soft and wet, but still the pressure of him sinking inside me steals my breath.

I'm still a bit sore from the first time, and it burns a little as he stretches my body. He sinks inside slowly, an inch at a time, watching my expression and gauging my reaction.

Seeing his concern floods me with emotion, and my eyes tear up. His eyes are locked on mine, as if he's studying every single nuance. I reach up, my thumbs brushing his short beard.

My heart swells with emotion, and I'm on the verge of embarrassing myself by saying something stupid when he kisses me again. His breath is hot and heavy, matching mine, and we strain together—both our mouths and our bodies—as he rocks into me.

My hands slide around to his back, my nails digging into his muscular shoulders, and he groans.

When I clamp my muscles on his erection, squeezing him

tightly, he bucks in my arms. The tendons in his neck pull taut and he grimaces with pleasure. As his climax hits him, he throws his head back and cries out, rough and guttural.

Thank God we're alone in the house.

His erection throbs deep inside me, and he thrusts slowly until his orgasm wanes. Then he withdrawals and collapses beside me, with one hand on his heaving chest as he tries to catch his breath.

His face turns toward mine and he kisses me. Then, he leaves the bed to dispose of the condom in the bathroom. I hear the water running just before he returns to climb back in bed with me.

Pulling the sheets over us, he takes me in his arms and kisses my forehead. "I didn't hurt you, did I?"

"No." Truthfully, I am a bit sore, but I guess that's to be expected.

He switches off the bedside lamp and settles down again beside me, holding me close. Rolling to face me, he traces the shape of my nose and the edge of my cheek. Then his thumb gently brushes my bottom lip.

He opens his mouth as if to say something, but nothing comes out.

I wonder if there are things he wants to say, but—like me—feels it's too soon.

❧ 27

Skye

When I wake Sunday morning, I find myself draped over a firm and beautifully sculpted chest. Will's body is lean, his muscles well-defined. He says he likes looking at my body, but I could stare at him forever. I'm tempted to skim my fingers up and down his pecs, or better yet kiss him awake. He looks so blissful in his sleep, though, I can't bring myself to disturb him.

I slip quietly out of bed, and instead of reaching for my discarded clothes, I pick up his gray t-shirt. Giving into temptation, I hold it up to my nose and breathing in deeply. It smells like *him*, like his cologne and his natural scent. The combination is incredibly arousing, and I'm so tempted to crawl back into bed with him.

But there's something I really want to do, and that requires me to slip something on and head downstairs to the kitchen. I want to surprise him with a proper British breakfast.

After pulling on his t-shirt, which just barely covers my butt, I head down the stairs to the kitchen.

Alice is just coming in the back door, juggling a basket of fresh produce on one arm and a sack of groceries in the other. She takes one look at my state of dishabille and grins. "Oh, sorry, love. I should have knocked first."

I can feel my face heating as I tug the t-shirt lower. "It's okay. Here, let me help you," I say, taking the basket from her.

Alice gives me a knowing smile. "I hope you slept well last night."

"I did, yes."

"You know, I've never seen Will so happy and relaxed. I'm glad you're here with him."

My blush deepens as I set the produce basket on the kitchen counter. Inside are tomatoes, apples, and cucumbers. "Are these from your garden?"

"They are. And you won't taste better tomatoes anywhere. I guarantee it."

Alice sets down the sack of groceries and begins putting the items away.

"I thought I'd surprise Will this morning by making him

breakfast," I say, hoping she doesn't think I'm interfering. "I'd like to try my hand at making a Full English."

Alice's eyes widen. "Oh, he'd like that. Can I help you?"

"Thanks, but I'd like to do this on my own. I think I can manage."

"All right, then. Give me a ring if you need anything. My number's there on the counter." She points to a pad of paper. And then Alice graciously heads back to her cottage, giving me full rein of the kitchen.

I have to admit I'm relieved. Having someone watching over my shoulder will only make me more nervous than I already am.

I locate all the ingredients I'll need—bacon, sausages, eggs, baked beans, bread, black pudding, tomatoes, and mushrooms—and place them out on the counter. Before I dive in, I remove my charm bracelet and lay it on the kitchen windowsill so it doesn't get dirty. I wash my hands and put the sausages in the pan. Just as I start slicing the tomatoes and mushrooms, the kitchen door opens.

"Did you forget something?" I say, assuming it's Alice again. But when I turn to look, my heart jumps into my throat. It's not Alice standing in the doorway, but a gorgeous redhead. She looks as startled as I feel. My heart hammers in my chest. "I'm sorry. I thought you were Alice."

The young woman's smooth brow wrinkles into a scowl. "Who the fucking hell are *you*? And what are you doing in this house dressed like a whore?"

Oh, my God.

I feel practically naked standing there in Will's shirt and nothing more. Yes, it covers my ass, but barely. I feel incredibly exposed.

My stomach turns, and my head starts spinning. "I'm Skye. Who are you?"

The volume of her voice increases with each word. "I'm Rachel—Will's fucking girlfriend—that's who!"

My face goes ice cold as her words sink in. That's not possible. "He said you two broke up."

She rolls her eyes. "Is that what he told you? Figures. Yes, I'm his girlfriend. Who the hell did you think I was?"

"But...but—he told me—"

"Did he tell you we're practically *engaged*?" She flashes her ring finger, which is adorned with a huge diamond ring. "That cheating fucker! I go on holiday for a few weeks, and *this* is what happens. I came home a few days early and thought I'd surprise him. Well, it looks like I'm the one who got the surprise. It's not the first time, though, to be honest."

My heart is slamming against my ribcage like that of a trapped animal, and I can't catch my breath. "I—"

There's a roaring sound in my head.

He lied to me.

"I have to go," I say, choking on the words.

I race up the stairs to the blue room, where most of my things are. I rip off Will's shirt and dress quickly in my own clothes. I stuff my bag with the rest of my things.

Where are my boots?

Oh, crap.

They're in Will's room.

I head across the hall and peer into his room. The bed's empty, and I hear water running in the bathroom. He's in the shower, thank God. I sneak in to grab my boots and socks. Not even bothering to put them on, I run back to my room and grab my bag and my purse and run back downstairs.

Rachel's standing right where I left her. "D'you want to borrow my hire car?" She nods behind her. "It's right out back. You're welcome to use it to drive to the train station."

I'm desperate to be gone, and I have no transportation. I suppose I could ask Roy or Alice to give me a ride to the station, but I can't bear to face anyone right now. "You wouldn't mind?"

"Of course not. I don't blame *you*. You seem like a perfectly nice girl who's been lied to by a right cheating arsehole. Take my hire car—the keys are in the ignition. Just leave it at the train station, and I'll have Will collect it later."

I hastily pull on my socks and boots. "He's in the shower," I say, and then wish I could beat myself over the head.

Who cares where he is right now?

And why the hell am I explaining anything to her?

She gives me a sad smile. "Shall I give him a message when he comes down?"

I shake my head as scalding tears burn my cheeks. "No. I have nothing to say to him." And then I walk out the back door.

There's a light blue Mini Cooper parked in front of the garage. I throw my stuff onto the passenger seat and slide in behind the wheel. Just as Rachel promised, the keys are in the ignition. I start the engine, and with my heart in my throat, I drive to the end of the lane.

It feels wrong sitting on the right-hand side of the car. Everything is backwards. I tell my phone, "Give me directions to the nearest train station," and Siri tells me to turn left.

Dear God, I hope I can do this without running off the road. Holding my breath, I pull out onto the main road. Driving on the left-hand side of the road just feels so *wrong*. "Left side, left side," I keep reminding myself as fresh tears blur my vision. "Stay on the left side."

I just hope I can make it to the station in one piece.

* * *

The train jolts as it starts moving, rocking me forward in my seat. We're leaving the station and heading to London.

I lucked out and got a seat to myself.

I sit completely alone, clutching my bag and my purse in my lap, as if they're my lifelines. I'm numb inside, completely frozen. My brain plays the events of the last hour on a loop in my head. I'm not sure which one of us was more surprised, me or Rachel. All things considered, she was pretty decent to me. It must have been as big of a shock to her as it was to me.

He lied to me.

Will lied.

I think back to all the times someone warned me about him—my father, Connor, Kennedy, even Mr. Sinclair. Each time, I shrugged off their concerns, thinking they were overblown or simply mistaken.

Will seemed so genuine, so caring.

But no. I was a fool for wanting to think the best about the guy I'd fallen head over heels for.

I'm such an idiot!

My chest is tight, and it hurts to breathe. My heart aches. And no matter how much I rub at the spot, the pain's not going away.

How could I have been so stupid?

I pick up my phone and send Kennedy a text.

Me: On my way home. Taking a train. You were right about Will. I'm such an idiot.

A moment later, Kennedy texts me back.

Kennedy: WTF? What happened?!?

Me: He has a girlfriend.

Kennedy: You mean Rachel? I thought she left him.

Me: Apparently not.

Kennedy: That motherfucker!

The rest of the train ride passes in a blur. I'm nauseated and praying I won't get sick. I'm mortified enough as it is without having to puke in public.

My heart is shredded, and I'm bleeding on the inside. The past few days keep replaying in my mind, over and over on automatic rewind, and I can't stop.

I trusted him!

I had sex with him!

I remember all the things we did, everything we shared, and it sickens me.

I lean my head back on the seat cushion and close my eyes. I think I've finally run out of tears. My eyes hurt from crying.

Everything hurts—most especially my shattered heart.

28

Will

After waking from a deep, restful sleep, probably one of the best night's sleep I've had in ages, I found myself alone in my bed, the sheets beside me cold. But I heard sounds coming from the kitchen... Alice and Skye talking. That puts a smile on my face. They seem to be taking to each other really well.

I decide to head straight for shower before I join my darling girl downstairs.

After getting dressed, I step out of my bedroom and I'm struck by the delicious aroma of frying sausages. Still barefoot,

I jog down the stairs and step through the kitchen doorway to see Rachel Whittingham standing at the stove—in *my* fucking kitchen. She's holding a spatula in her hands, poking at the frying food.

Skye is nowhere to be seen.

My heart stops cold. "What in the bloody hell are you doing here, and where the fuck is Skye?"

Rachel turns to face me, her eyes wide as she puts on a brave smile. "Will, good morning. Breakfast is—"

"You didn't answer my fucking questions, Rachel. Where's Skye?"

Her smile turns vicious. "You mean the slapper I saw wearing nothing but your God-damn shirt? She's gone, and good riddance."

"What do you mean she's gone?"

Rachel waves the spatula toward the back door. "I mean, she's gone. She left. Bolted for the train station."

Blood is pounding in my head, and there's a rushing sound in my ears. My chest tightens and my lungs can't keep up with demand.

She's gone?

Skye's gone?

"Why would she go?"

Rachel scowls at me. "Maybe because I told her to get the fuck out of my boyfriend's house?"

I rush to the window and look outside. Nothing.

"I let her take my hire car to the train station," she adds.

My stomach sinks at the idea of Skye behind the wheel of a car. She hasn't driven in the UK. She's had no practice driving on the left side.

She could get hurt!

"You fucking bitch!" I yell, absolutely seething.

Rachel has the audacity to look affronted. "*Me?* I walk into this house and find a half-naked floozy in your kitchen, and *I'm* the bitch? Oh, that's rich, Will."

I'm so livid I could scream. "Rachel, what are you doing here?"

"I changed my mind. I've come back to you."

My mouth drops open and I'm shouting loud enough to bring the rafters down on our heads. "I don't give a flying fuck that you've changed your mind! We're done! We were done when you left me for David Markham."

I glance out the kitchen window again, this time to see Roy and Alice heading this way as if their hair is on fire. But as soon as they are close enough to see in the windows, and they get a good look at Rachel, they reverse course.

Smart folk.

"Will, don't be impulsive," Rachel says, trying to placate me. "You know we're perfect together. Even your parents think so. I'm willing to take you back."

I drag my fingers through my still damp hair, tugging hard on the strands as my mind races.

I've got to find Skye.

Jesus, where is she?

I jab a finger in Rachel's direction, so angry I can barely manage a coherent sentence. "Get the fuck out of my house, Rachel! I don't ever want to see your face. And I swear to God, if you ever talk to Skye again, I'll make you wish you'd never been born. Is that clear?"

She goes white as a sheet, her mouth falling open. "How dare you speak to me like that! I'll have you know—"

I take a menacing step forward. "Get out of my house—now!" I've never in my life raised my hand against a woman, but I'm tempted to do so now.

"I can't. Skye took my hire car."

"Oh, bloody hell." I need to be gone—I need to go after Skye—but I can't leave Rachel here for Roy and Alice to deal with. "Fine. Get your arse in my car and I'll drive you to the station so you can collect your car." I point toward the stove. "Shut everything off. We're leaving as soon as I pack."

"But what about breakfast?"

"Fuck breakfast!"

I rush back upstairs to gather my things. When I'm back downstairs, Rachel's standing by the back door, a mutinous pout on her face, her arms crossed over her chest.

"Did you turn off the stove?" I say.

"Yes."

I notice something shiny glinting in the sunlight coming through the window above the sink. When I step closer, I see Skye's charm bracelet laid out on the sill. She must have taken it off when she was cooking.

I tuck the bracelet into my pocket and point toward the door as I glare at my ex. "Get your arse in my car."

* * *

After dropping Rachel off at the train station—I'm more than happy to leave her to her own devices—I head back to London. I'm assuming Skye left the keys in the hire car, but if she didn't, then tough luck for Rachel. She deserves whatever comes her way.

If I spend one more second in her company, I'm likely to strangle her.

I call Skye, but she doesn't answer.

I wait a few minutes and try again. And again. And again. Each time my call goes to her voice mail. I try texting her. I even text Kennedy. But I get no replies from either of them. Knowing how close the two girls are, I'm sure Kennedy already knows about this morning's debacle.

Fuck!

I leave Skye voice messages, pleading with her to contact me and let me explain. I try to reassure her that whatever Rachel told her was a lie.

But Skye doesn't answer my calls.

And she doesn't return any of my messages.

It's like she's fallen off the face of the Earth, and that scares the bloody shit out of me. My poor, sweet girl. She's running. She's hurting. And the knowledge rips me to pieces.

I make a quick call to Roy and update him on what's happened.

His gruff voice fills the line. "Alice and I pretty much figured that out for ourselves."

"There's a mess in the kitchen," I tell him. "Sorry about that."

"Alice is cleaning it up now. She said Skye wanted to surprise you with a fry-up this morning. She wanted to make it herself."

"Shit. I'm sorry, Roy. Please tell Alice."

"I will, son. Just go find your girl. Don't worry about anything else."

I race back to London, ignoring speed limits. All I can think about is getting to Skye. I can't bear the thought that she thinks I deceived her.

I drive straight to Skye's flat, double parking in front of her building.

When I buzz their flat, no one answers. But I know the girls are home because I pull a stalker move and peer inside their front window. I see Skye's handbag on the coffee table in the lounge, and her overnight bag on the floor. I even catch a glimpse of Kennedy walking down the hall toward the kitchen.

They're ignoring me.

I knock again.

No answer.

I pound on the outer door, hoping someone in the building will let me in.

Still no answer.

Shit.

I'm desperate enough to try peeking in Skye's bedroom window, but she's closed the blinds.

I try calling again, and then texting, but there's no response. She's completely shut me out.

29

Skye

S kye?" Kennedy sits at the foot of my bed, facing me, concern stamped across her fine features.

I'm seated on the overstuffed chair in my bedroom, my knees drawn up to my chest, my body closing in on itself, in the upright version of a fetal position. Kennedy had covered me earlier with the quilt off my bed. My arms are wrapped around my pillow, which I'm hugging for comfort.

When I catch myself rocking, I stop, attempting to shake myself out of it. I'm completely numb.

Will finally left.

He stood outside our building for over an hour, pounding on the door, shouting loudly enough to bring curious neighbors outside to see what all the fuss was about. I'm still surprised no one called the police.

At least he's quit calling and texting. He called me at least two dozen times and texted repeatedly all day.

Will: Call me please!

Will: Rachel lied to you

Will: Please, sweetheart. Let me explain.

Will: I never lied to you. Rachel and I were over before I met you. I swear.

Will: Skye, for God's sake, don't shut me out

He also texted Kennedy, over and over.

Neither of us replied.

My mind keeps going through the morning's events, from Rachel's sudden appearance at Will's house, to my impromptu train ride back to London.

Kennedy was waiting for me at the train station. When she took me into her arms, I sobbed on her shoulder.

Now Kennedy reaches out to put her hand on my knee. "Is there anything I can do?"

I shake my head and rub at my face. My cheeks itch from all the crying. Somehow, I have to figure out how to get past this.

I have to go to work tomorrow.

"So many people warned me," I mutter to myself, my voice

raw from crying.

Kennedy sighs. "I wish we'd all been wrong about Will. I really do."

I swallow past a painful knot in my throat. "I should have known better. He was too good to be true."

His face keeps flashing in my brain. Memories bombard me—memories of us together, naked, our heated bodies surging together, rocking gently, Will thrusting into me, pleasure stealing my breath and making me see stars. I remember the sounds I made, the ones that'd come from him. It was incredible, and at the time I thought it meant something.

Obviously, I was wrong.

My face screws up and I'm struck once more by the sheer ferocity of the pain tearing through me.

I gave him a blow job!

It was my first, and now I'll regret it for the rest of my life. I feel like such an idiot.

Everything we did over the weekend—every moment, every word—is now a tainted memory.

I cover my face with my hands as fresh tears fall.

Kennedy growls, like a mama bear protecting her cub. "I could kill that rat bastard!"

I peer up at her through tear-filled eyes. "How am I going to face him again? We had *sex*, Kennedy!" I'm so frustrated I could scream.

"Maybe Rachel was the one who lied. Have you considered that?"

I shake my head. "Why would she do something like that?"

Kennedy gives me sad smile. "Honey, people lie all the time. Not everyone is as honest as you are. Anyway, you don't have to face him again. Carmichael's is a big company. Technically, your job and his don't cross paths. We'll just have to make sure you don't run into him at work. I'm sure Connor will help."

The thought of working in the same building as Will makes me feel sick. If I run into him, I'll be mortified.

"Can I get you anything?" Kennedy says. "Some dinner? Or tea? Ice cream?"

"No thanks." I lay my head on the pillow I'm cradling in my arms. "I'm just going to wallow in my pain until I pass out."

Smiling regretfully, Kennedy stands. "Call me if you change your mind. I'll leave you alone, unless you want me to stay?"

I shake my head. "I need to be alone for a while, if you don't mind."

She sighs "Okay. Holler if you need me."

Kennedy leaves my room, closing the door on her way out.

It's dark outside now, and the streetlights are on, but I think sleep is going to elude me tonight.

I head for the bathroom to get ready for bed. Then I crawl under my covers with my phone in my hand and try to read, but that fails epically. Not even my favorite books can hold my interest right now. So instead, I watch some YouTube and try to get my mind off Will.

I had put my phone on silent earlier to block out any calls or texts, but notifications are popping up on my screen in rapid fire. He still hasn't let up.

I put my phone on *Do Not Disturb*, lay it on my nightstand, and turn away.

I don't ever want to hear from Will Carmichael again.

* * *

Monday morning, my heart is in my throat when our bus pulls up to the stop, just two streets from Carmichael & Son. My pulse is pounding.

I'm not ready for this.

I'm terrified that I'll run into Will, and I just can't face him.

Not yet.

Maybe not ever.

As we walk briskly to the building, I stare down at the sidewalk in complete avoidance mode. Kennedy's right beside me, step for step, geared for battle.

When we reach the steps to our building, I glance up to see Connor standing at the front entrance, alert and on guard. Kennedy had called him early this morning to give him explicit instructions.

"He's not arrived yet," Connor says, waving for us to come up the steps before he opens the door for us. "The coast is clear."

Kennedy and I enter the building and head straight for the elevators. We're inside a crowded car and riding up to our floor a moment later.

Kennedy walks me to my desk. "I'll come check on you later," she says. "Text me, or call, if you-know-who makes an appearance. If he does, I'll make good on my threat."

I nod. "Thanks."

Kennedy told me that she texted Will early this morning and told him to stay away from me, or she'd report him for sexual harassment.

After giving me a quick hug, Kennedy leaves to make her way to her own department. I watch until she rounds a corner and is out of sight. Then I take my seat and boot up my PC. The best thing for me now is to get to work, focus on my tasks at hand and dive right in to a new portfolio. I'll bury myself in work.

No more fraternizing. No more dating. I'll concentrate on work, my dad and his family, and Kennedy.

Thank God for Kennedy.

The morning passes quietly. There's no drama. My gaze keeps wandering to the entrance of my department, and I'm half expecting to see Will standing there. But he doesn't show up.

And that's a good thing, I keep reminding myself.

Kennedy checks in late-morning with a text.

Kennedy: Want to grab lunch in the cafeteria?

That seems like a safe option, as Will never eats in the cafeteria if he can help it.

Me: Yes

Kennedy: I'll stop by at noon

I get back to my reading, and then do a little bit of market research on this new potential client I'm assessing.

Half an hour later, Kennedy arrives at my desk. "Ready for lunch?"

"Sure."

No, not really.

My appetite is shot, but I need to eat something.

We take the stairs down to the ground floor and enter the employee cafeteria. Both of us head for the salad bar.

Halfway through our lunch break, Kennedy catches my attention. "Don't look now, but Will's here, and he's staring right at you."

I'd been doing a great job of keeping my eyes on my plate, afraid Will would somehow materialize in the cafeteria. Covertly, I lift my eyes and take a quick look. He's leaning in the open doorway, his shoulder propped against the door jamb. His arms are crossed over his chest, and he looks miserable.

Just like I feel.

I look back at my plate.

"Uh-oh. Here he comes," Kennedy mutters. "What do you want me to do?"

I grab her sleeve. "Don't leave me."

"I won't."

Kennedy and I are seated at a table for four, both of us on one side.

Will pulls out the seat directly in front of me. "May I sit?" he asks, his voice low and a bit rough.

I nod, not wanting to make a scene here in the cafeteria.

He sits and lays his arms on the table, facing me. At first, he doesn't say anything. My attention is focused on my plate, as I poke at my salad though my appetite has vanished.

"Does *she* have to be here right now?" he says, and I know he's referring to Kennedy.

"Yes."

He sighs. "Very well." His tone changes when he says, "No offense, Kennedy, I'd just rather speak to Skye alone."

"None taken," she says in a tight voice. "But you lost your right to speak to her alone, so now you get me, too. Deal with it."

He makes an exasperated noise, but he doesn't rise to the bait. Instead, he addresses me. "Skye." He pauses a moment, like he's gathering his thoughts. Like he's planning a strategy. "I was just as shocked as you to see Rachel show up at my estate. She broke up with me just before you arrived in London. She actually ran off to marry someone else. I honestly thought she had, until yesterday morning."

My throat tightens painfully as my heart pounds. Still, I don't look at him. I'm in over my head right now. I have no experience with guys, no dating experience to speak of before Will. I don't know how to handle myself in the best of circumstances, let alone in the worst.

He extends his arm across the table, his palm facing up, as if offering me his hand.

I ignore it.

"There are shadows under your eyes," he observes. "I'm

sorry."

"You should be sorry," Kennedy mutters.

"D'you mind?" Will says tersely.

I can just picture him glaring at Kennedy. Biting my lip, I suppress a grin. He sounds so put out.

"Skye." He lets out a heavy breath. "Look at me, please."

I look up, and I'm shocked by the stark pain I see in his expression. He looks like he didn't sleep any better than I did last night.

He leans closer. "I swear to you, Skye, on everything I hold dear, that Rachel lied to you. She broke up with me and ran off to marry David Markham before you and I met. Apparently, David got cold feet at the last minute and left her standing at the altar. She was just trying to cut her losses by coming back to me, thinking we would pick up where we left off. Problem is, she didn't count on me not wanting her back. I only want *you*."

All the air in my lungs escapes in a rush. I open my mouth to speak, but nothing comes out.

"Everything that happened over the weekend was *real*, Skye," he says. "Every second of it. Nothing's changed. You and I are still the same people we were up until the moment she arrived and attempted to ruin everything." He holds his hand out, silently asking me for mine.

When I place my hand in his, his fingers close over mine.

"We need to talk, sweetheart," he says. "Can we go somewhere—alone?" He glances at Kennedy. "Somewhere without a bloody audience?"

Hearing the strain in his voice makes my heart ache. He seems sincere. And logic tells me, if he really wanted Rachel, he wouldn't be here with me right now, tolerating Kennedy's glaring disapproval as he pleads his case.

He's telling the truth.

Rachel lied.

Will squeezes my hand. "Come to my office, please, so we can talk in private."

I glance at Kennedy, who's rolling her eyes even as she continues to glare at Will. Clearly, she's not ready to let this go. But as he rubs the back of my hand with his thumb, his touch gentle, the frayed edges of my heart start to slowly knit back together.

"All right," I say.

Relief sweeps his features. "Are you finished eating?"

"Yes."

He stands, still holding my hand, and pulls me gently to my feet. "Let's go."

Once we're out in the hallway, he asks me, "Stairs or lift?"

I smile, touched that he's asking my preference. But the truth is, the thought of walking up four flights of stairs is a bit too much right now. "Lift."

We take the elevator up to his floor. Since we're not alone in the car, we refrain from speaking. But he's right beside me, standing so close that our bodies touch. His hand is on my back.

We're the first ones to exit the elevator, and we walk down the hall toward his office. My gaze lands on the nameplate outside his department.

Fitzwilliam Carmichael, II
Senior Account Manager

The moment we walk in, his administrative assistant waves her hand. "There you are, Will. Your father would like to—"

"Not now, Lois. Hold my calls, please. I'm not to be disturbed."

Once we're in his office, he closes the door and wastes no time in getting to the point. "When I came downstairs yesterday morning and saw Rachel in the kitchen, I knew you'd gone. My heart went into overdrive. I actually had a full-blown panic attack." He laughs harshly. "I haven't had one of those since I was a schoolboy."

"What happened?"

"We argued very loudly, so loudly that Roy and Alice came to investigate. Then I packed my things and drove Rachel to the train station so she could collect her hire car. How nice of her to help you escape, by the way. At that point, I left her to her own devices."

He cups my face in his hands. "All I could think about was getting back to London. Getting back to *you*."

And then he kisses me, stealing my breath and making me weak in the knees. When I stumble, he sweeps me up into his arms and carries me to the sofa by the window.

❧ 30

Will

I'm not letting go of her—*ever again.* The past twenty-four hours were a nightmare, and I don't want a repeat. I hug her close. "Please don't ever do that to me again. I swear, you took ten years off my life."

Groaning, Skye covers her face. "I'm so sorry. It was a completely emotional reaction."

I hug her close. "You have nothing to be sorry about, love."

When she presses her face against my chest and slips her arm around my waist, a knot forms in my throat. "You believe me then, don't you? About Rachel?"

"Yes. If I'd just waited and talked to you first, gotten the whole story, our weekend trip wouldn't have been ruined. I panicked, and all I could think about was getting away."

I kiss the top of her head. "Rachel showing up like that must have been quite a shock." I tip her face toward mine and kiss her, our lips melding gently. "I'm sorry, Skye. I wish I'd been with you when it happened. I would have put her in her place."

She traces the tendon running along the back of my hand, and her touch makes me shiver.

"Before I forget…" I reach into my shirt pocket to retrieve her charm bracelet and dangle it in front of her. "You left this on the kitchen windowsill. Give me your wrist."

She holds out her arm, and I clip the bracelet on her.

"That's better," I say. And then I press a kiss to her temple. "Come home with me tonight. Spend the night with me, please."

She hesitates, and I suspect she's not quite over yesterday's events. Finally, she says, "Or… you could come stay with me tonight at my flat. That is, if you don't mind roughing it."

She gives me a devilish grin, and I think she's just issued a challenge.

"I'd love to," I say without pause, surprising her.

"Really?" She tugs gently on my tie. "With no one to wait on you?"

I'm right. It is a challenge.

"Yes, really. I just want to be with *you*. Nothing else matters. After work, I'll head home and pack a bag and come to your place. You sure Kennedy won't mind?"

She shakes her head. "She won't."

I relax into the settee and pull her closer, my mouth finding hers. We kiss, gently, sharing a quiet moment together. She rests her hand on my chest, and the slight pressure makes my body stir.

When there's a knock on the door, Skye slides off my lap and sits beside me.

"Come in," I say, regretting the interruption. If it's Connor, I'll have his head.

The door opens and Kennedy walks in, her gaze going right to Skye. She looks her friend over. "Are you all right? I came to check on you."

Skye smiles. "I'm fine."

Kennedy looks relieved. Then she nods toward the clock on my office wall. "Good. Now back to work before your boss notices you're late getting back."

Skye shoots to her feet, smoothing her trousers. "Yes, ma'am."

I rise too and snag Skye's hand before she gets away. I pull her to me and kiss her lightly on the lips. "I'll see you this evening. I'll be round about seven."

"Sounds perfect."

Kennedy raises a brow, but she doesn't say anything. At least not in earshot. I'm sure Skye will get an earful on her way back to her office.

A moment after the girls depart, Lois pops her head in my doorway. "Will, your father has called *again*. He said it's important—something about a wedding."

Oh, right.

My cousin Esme's wedding is this weekend, to be held at my parents' estate. I can't miss it. Of all my cousins, it's Esme I'm closest to. "Thank you, Lois. I'll go see him."

I head to my father's office and knock once before opening the door.

"Will. Have a seat, son," he says, motioning me forward.

I do as he asks. "Lois told me you wanted to see me."

"Yes, indeed." He steeples his fingers as he observes me from across the desk. "Rachel Whittingham is coming to the wedding, you know. As one of Esme's closest friends, she'll be a bridesmaid. I just heard through the grapevine that Rachel's very ill-considered wedding to David Markham fell through, which is a good thing for you. It means the girl is still available. Why don't you ask her to attend Esme's wedding as your guest?"

I'm tempted to explain to my father just how much of a conniving bitch Rachel is, but I don't want to drag Skye into it. So I decide to take the high road. "Actually, I'm already bringing someone to the wedding."

My father leans back in his chair, brows rising. "And who might that be?"

"Skye Williams."

He frowns. "Frank's daughter?"

"One and the same."

"Frank's *American* daughter?" he clarifies, as if there's another.

"Exactly."

"Will, you know your mother and I think Rachel would make a good wife, and—"

"Dad, if you don't mind, I'll choose my own wife. I don't need your input."

He bristles. "You listen here—"

And that's my cue to leave. I stand. "No, Dad, you listen. I don't need you and mum to choose a wife for me. I'm perfectly capable of doing it myself. And it sure as hell isn't going to be Rachel Whittingham."

* * *

"Are you quite sure, sir?" Hamish asks for what seems like the hundredth time whilst driving to the girls' flat.

"Quite."

"If you need me—"

I raise my hand, cutting him off, and we share a look through the rear-view mirror.

Hamish frowns. "If you're sure you'll be okay."

Seriously?

He's not my bloody nursemaid. "I'm spending the evening with a beautiful girl, one I'm rather fond of. Why in the world wouldn't I be okay?"

The corners of his eyes crease as he smiles. "Yes, sir."

When the car stops outside the girls' building, I lean forward and tap Hamish on the shoulder. "Here you go." I tuck a fifty-pound note in his jacket pocket.

He looks at me for a beat.

"If you so much as think about giving that back to me, I'll fall out with you," I warn him. "Take the night off. The car is yours for the evening."

"Yes, sir. Thank you, sir."

His eyes crinkle again as he breaks into a full-faced grin. In a very uncharacteristic move, he loosens his tie and unfastens the top button of his shirt.

I exit the car, carrying the case of beer I've brought with me. I'm walking on cloud nine as I make my way to the building's front step. I decided to go for a casual look this evening—jeans and a black t-shirt—because I need to show Skye I'm not just an Armani suit.

I'm buzzed in before I even have a chance to press the intercom. Skye's already at the door, dressed in a knee-length gray tunic dress. She throws herself into my arms. This moment definitely feels like something right out of a chick-flick, but in this instance I'm more than happy to play the leading man.

We kiss, rather passionately I'm happy to say. I'm optimistic all that mess is behind us now. I lace my fingers with hers, and we walk hand-in-hand into the building.

Kennedy is waiting for us at the door to their flat. "Don't think you get any special treatment, Mr. Fancy Pants." She tosses me a curious look as she eyes the crate of beer. "Well done, mate." She holds out her hand. "Give me your bag and I'll take it to Skye's room. You put the beer in the fridge."

Skye steps aside as I enter. On impulse, I pick her up and

toss her over my shoulder and carry her through the flat to the kitchen.

"Put me down!" she shrieks, laughing as she grasps the back of my shirt to steady herself, simultaneously trying to prevent her dress from falling down around her ears.

I don't take her words too seriously as she hasn't stopped laughing. Upon reaching the kitchen, I plonk her down on the worktop and laugh as she squeals whilst I stow the beer in the fridge.

We're alone in the kitchen, and I can't resist stepping between her legs, running my hands up her bare thighs and beneath her dress. I clamp my hands on her hips and lean in for a kiss.

She smiles as our lips meet.

I deepen the kiss, opening her mouth and seeking her tongue with mine. She makes a breathy sound, followed by a quiet moan. And when I slide my hand around to her backside and slip my fingers into the back of her knickers to grip her butt cheek, she shivers.

"Will." Her voice is shaky and a bit hesitant.

I imagine it's the fear of being caught making her nervous. Kennedy could walk into the kitchen at any second. Since I don't want to make her feel uncomfortable, I withdraw my hands. After all, I have all night to touch her, caress her, have her.

Very slowly I push her hair behind her ear, nibble gently on her lobe and whisper, "You've no idea what I want to do to you right now."

The way she shivers makes me harder.

I groan. "Fuck, you're torturing me."

"Get a room," Kennedy says as she strolls into the kitchen.

Skye jumps at the sound of Kennedy's voice. I don't immediately turn to face our audience because I'm sporting a very noticeable erection, and my jeans do very little to hide it. If anything, the fabric is hugging my cock, drawing attention to the damn thing.

I look at my watch. It's seven-thirty, too early to take her to bed.

Damn it.

I'll have to suffer through the next few hours until I can get Skye alone in her bedroom.

I turn my head to see Kennedy prop her hands on her hips and stare right at me. "So, what's for dinner, Carmichael?"

"We could order something in," I suggest, feeling hopeful they'll take the hint.

Kennedy shakes her head. "I have a better idea. Let's test your culinary skills." She nods toward the fridge. "It's pretty well stocked. Impress us. Make dinner."

"Me?" I say, incredulous. Skye's friend is a bit of a ballbuster. My erection wanes almost instantly. "I don't cook."

"Yes, you," Kennedy says. "If you want to date my girl Skye, you need to know how to feed her."

Skye laughs. "I can feed myself just fine, Kennedy."

"You hush," Kennedy says, keeping her eyes on me.

Kennedy loves to challenge me, to test my worthiness. "Fine. I'll cook dinner," I say, feigning complete confidence.

How hard can it be?

Jesus, famous last words. After staring for ten minutes at the contents of their fridge, I end up phoning my housekeeper. Maggie finds the situation highly amusing, of course.

Once she stops laughing, her final words are, "You're a big boy, Will. Figure it out."

"Maggie, please," I say, as I stare into the fridge. "At least give me something to go on. A starting point."

"Well, what have you got to work with? Are there eggs?"

"Yes."

"Cheese?" she asks.

"Yes."

"Mushrooms? Peppers?"

"Um, yes."

"Then make an omelet." And then she runs through the basic steps. "It's easy, Will. You can do this."

"Right. Thanks."

You can do this, Will.

And now I'm talking to myself.

Taking the leap, I pull all the necessary ingredients out of the fridge. There are loads of eggs.

Eggs are easy, right?

Grabbing my phone, I search YouTube for videos on how to make an omelet.

* * *

Nearly an hour later, after having cut up the veggies and cracked a half-dozen eggs, I emerge from the kitchen victorious. With a plate in each hand, I make my way to the lounge where the girls are sitting on the settee watching a sit-com on Netflix. I hand each girl a plate and stand back to await the verdict.

Kennedy eyes her food, and then she glances at Skye's plate. "This looks... interesting, Will."

The YouTube food vlogger whose advice I followed stressed the importance of *presentation*. What I've concocted looks like something you'd find dead on the side of the road, but I smile. "*Bon appetit.*"

Skye frowns. "Where's your plate, Will? Aren't you eating?"

"I ate mine already, while I was cooking. I was absolutely famished, and it looked so good."

Total lie.

What I should have said was I didn't think there were enough eggs to go around, so I nibbled on cheese and crackers whilst I was cooking.

Kennedy pokes her fork at the scrambled mess on her plate. Then she takes a tentative bite, chewing slowly, with caution as if she expects to bite down on a bit of eggshell. It is entirely possible, although I'm pretty sure I successfully fished out the bits that fell in.

Skye takes a good bite and chews thoughtfully.

I've got to hand it to them, they're at least attempting to eat something I made. I don't miss the conspiratorial looks they pass to each other.

Holding my hands up I laugh. "I won't be offended if you don't finish it." The truth is, the eggs are a bit dry, more like overcooked and burned in places. "I might have added too much salt."

It's comical how quickly both forks hit their plates.

Kennedy jumps to her feet and confiscates Skye's plate. "I give you marks for trying, pal," she says to me as she carries their plates to the kitchen. She calls back over her shoulder, "There's leftover curry in the fridge. We won't starve."

I drop down beside Skye on the sofa. "You girls could have mentioned the curry about an hour ago, you know—saved us a lot of bother."

Laughing, Skye lays her head on my shoulder. "I'm proud of you for trying. Even Kennedy's impressed, I can tell."

Skye reaches for my hand, linking our fingers and placing our joined hands in her lap.

"What's this?" I ask her, meaning the show playing on the telly.

"*New Girl.* It's one of my favorites."

So, I sit back, relax, and watch American TV with my American girlfriend, while Kennedy heats up curry for the three of us.

Life doesn't get much better than this.

31

Skye

Slowly, as the early morning light seeps through my curtains, my brain comes back online.

Will's in my bed.

I know this because there's a strong arm tucked around me, and my backside is pressed up against a warm body. His muscular legs, long and toned, are entangled with mine.

I smile as I remember how funny he was last night, how sweet he was as we tried to make love quietly, shushing each other and trying to muffle our groans.

I'm not sure how successful we were, but at least Kennedy

didn't pound on my door and tell us to keep it down.

Will's phone starts beeping. He groans and tightens his hold around my waist. Then he kisses the back of my head before releasing me to reach back and grab his phone from the nightstand.

The beeping stops.

"Did you hit the snooze button?" I ask him.

He grunts, clearly not quite ready to wake up. He turns back to me and wraps his arm once more around my waist, drawing me closer to the heat of his body. When I feel his erection pressing against my backside, my belly quivers.

I could definitely get used to having him in my bed.

Warm lips press against my bare shoulder.

"I'll need a shower this morning," he says, his voice gruff from sleep.

"You'd better hurry, then. Kennedy gets up first to use the bathroom. Then it's my turn to get ready."

"Right. Only one bathroom—one bathroom and two girls. How in the world do you manage?" He chuckles as he slips his hand between my thighs. "I can think of something a lot more satisfying than a shower. Maybe we could skip work altogether and stay in bed all day."

I press my thighs together, trapping his hand between them, and the pressure feels so good. I'm dangerously tempted to take him up on his offer, but I can't. I sigh with regret. "I have a meeting with Mr. Sinclair this morning."

Scoffing, Will says, "Forget bloody Spencer Sinclair."

He starts tickling me, and laughing, I say, "I can't. He's my boss."

Will turns me onto my back and rolls onto me, sliding one thigh between mine. He presses against the heated spot between my legs, making me groan.

"My God, you're so perfectly wet."

He rubs his thigh against my wetness, and it feels so good, I moan helplessly into his mouth.

Without another word, he reaches for a condom packet on the nightstand and tears it open. A moment later, he's sheathed. And then he's pressing into me, slowly, steadily filling me until I'm gasping.

"Will!" He feels so good, sliding inside me, making every inch of me tingle.

"I can't get enough of you," he whispers. His breaths grow rough as he starts thrusting.

When he sucks one of my nipples into his mouth, pleasure shoots down to my core and my thighs start trembling.

He rocks gently into me. "Come home with me tonight," he murmurs as he shifts to my other breast. "I want you in my bed." He kisses me, then rubs his nose against mine. "Say yes."

"All right, yes."

He smiles down at me. "That's a good girl."

Then his thrusting picks up tempo, and soon he's driving into me—long, steady strokes that propel my arousal higher. He reaches between us and teases my clitoris, sending me even higher. Relentlessly, he torments my clit until I'm gasping. Pleasure explodes deep within me, and my body stiffens as I cry out.

He captures my cries with his mouth and comes in a heated rush, our mouths sealed together as we muffle our climaxes.

Finally, after catching his breath, Will hauls himself up and off the bed and disposes of the condom, wrapping it in a tissue. He stands there stark naked, his body ridiculously perfect, from his sculpted chest and arms to his ridged abdomen.

I can't help watching him as he picks up his phone. "Checking messages?" I say.

"I'm summoning Hamish, telling him to be here at seven-thirty to collect the lot of us. He'll drive us to work."

I bite back a grin, knowing how he feels about public transportation. "You mean we're not taking the bus?"

"No, we most definitely are not." He grabs his toiletry kit and pulls on his boxers. "I'm off to the shower. I just hope I beat Kennedy." And then, with a wink and a grin, he shuts my bedroom door on his way out.

I hug the pillow he slept on, breathing in his lingering scent. A moment later, I hear the toilet flush, and then the shower comes on.

His suggestion to take the day off and stay in bed is tempting. But duty calls.

When Will returns to my room, he's damp from his shower, with a towel wrapped around his waist. As I watch him put on his suit and tie, I marvel at how effortlessly he transforms into this debonair man.

I'm just here to work, I remind myself. But I think it's too late.

He kneels on the bed and looms over me, dropping kisses on my forehead, on my nose and my lips. "Kennedy is in the bathroom now. I told her to be quick and not to use all the hot water so there'll be some left for you."

"Thank you."

He grins. "You're very welcome. In the meantime…" He shifts lower, pushing the bedding down to my waist, and draws a soft nipple into his mouth. Immediately, the tip puckers into a tight bud, and I feel a fresh surge of pleasure at my core. I moan, helpless not to.

Will's nostrils flare, and his green eyes darken. "God, I love it when you make those sounds." He cups my breast in his hand, caressing the mound gently, his thumb brushing over the tip.

A moment later, there's a knock on my bedroom door. We both jump and then laugh.

"Bathroom's all yours, Skye," Kennedy calls through the door. "You better get a move on. We have to leave soon."

* * *

After a quick breakfast of coffee and toast, the three of us head outside, where Hamish is waiting with the car. He has the Bentley idling at the curb. When he sees us, he jumps out of his seat and opens the rear passenger door. Kennedy slides in on the bench seat first, and then me.

Will hands our overnight bags to Hamish. "Skye's coming home with me tonight. Will you see that these get delivered to the master suite?"

"Certainly, sir."

While Hamish stows my bag in the trunk, Will slides in beside me.

Hamish returns to the driver's seat and pulls into traffic as we three buckle our seat belts.

Hamish observes Will through the rearview mirror. "I trust you had a good morning, sir?"

"Yes, quite," Will says, as he lifts my hand to his mouth to kiss.

"I'm glad to hear it, sir."

Kennedy nudges me with her sharp elbow. "I should say he did," she mutters.

It takes far less time to drive to work than it does to take the bus. In record time, Hamish pulls up to the front of the building and lets us off at the main entrance.

The three of us get out and walk up the stone steps to the glass doors. Will stands back to let us go in first.

"Hey, wait up!" Connor calls, running in behind us. "Good morning, Kennedy. You're looking lovely, as usual."

"Oh, please," Kennedy says, and she heads for the elevators.

Connor races after her, following her into the car.

Will and I follow at a more sedate pace, neither of us in a hurry because we know we'll have to part soon as we head to our respective offices.

Just as we reach the elevator, which Kennedy's holding for us, Will leans close and whispers, "Let's take the stairs."

"Sure," I say. I'm all for getting in a few extra steps. "We're taking the stairs," I tell Kennedy, waving goodbye.

As we head for the stairwell, we're both dragging our feet, not wanting to go our separate ways. When we reach the landing at my floor, Will pulls me aside. He leans against the wall and pulls me to him.

He fingers the hem of my sweater. "Have lunch with me. I can't go all day without seeing you."

His sincerity tugs at my heartstrings. And the truth is, I'm loathe to part from him too. "That sounds wonderful. How about the cafeteria? After all that pizza last night, I need a salad."

"I'll pop by your office at noon to collect you."

And then he draws me into his arms and kisses me. One hand goes behind my head, cradling it, and the other slips around my waist.

I slide my hands beneath his suit jacket, splaying them against his back.

Finally, we break the kiss.

"Noon then," he says. "Have a good day, Miss Williams."

"You too, Mr. Carmichael."

* * *

When I arrive at my desk, my boss once again waiting for me, seated in my guest chair and looking none too happy. I surreptitiously check the time to make sure I'm not late. I'm not, thank goodness. I have five minutes to spare. "Good morning,

Mr. Sinclair."

He gazes up at me, looking a bit harried and distracted. "Good morning, Skye."

I walk around to the back of my desk and open the drawer where I keep my purse. Out of habit, I immediately power on my computer.

He leans back and crosses his arms. "I was just wondering if you had a chance to reconsider your assessment of Hoffman Enterprises like we discussed last week."

I pull my chair out from my desk and take a seat. "I did review my notes when you asked me about it."

"And?"

"I'm afraid my assessment hasn't changed. Based on their flagging market share, and all the missteps they've had when it comes to new product development, I can't recommend them. I'm sorry."

His expression darkens as his eyes narrow on me. "I thought I made it quite clear to you that I wanted you to re-assess."

"I did review the portfolio and reconsider, but my original conclusion still stands." My pulse starts racing. I don't like how he's putting me on the spot like this. Others in the department are openly staring.

He grits his teeth. "Do I have to spell it out? I want you to revise your conclusion and recommend them for funding. I'm pretty sure I'm a better judge of which companies should be approved than you are. You're an *intern*, Skye. You're here to learn, so learn—starting with how to follow directions from your superiors."

"Mr. Sinclair—"

He stands, hands braced on his hips. "I'll give you until the end of the day to reconsider your position. If you haven't thought better by then, there will be consequences. Is that clear?"

And then he turns and stalks across the room to his private office. My face is hot, and as I look around, my coworkers quickly redirect their attention to their work.

I'm pretty sure Spencer Sinclair just threatened me. And the problem is, I have no intention of backing down. My call on that client application was a no-brainer. It was a textbook example of *bad* risk.

For the rest of the morning, I go back through my notes and reevaluate Hoffman Enterprises one more time, to be sure I didn't miss anything. But no matter how I look at it, I see nothing but red flags. I compare what they present in their application to their public company financial records. I study the performance of their company stock. I examine what customers say about them on social media. And every single thing I see only reinforces my conclusion.

And they're certainly not worth betting the ten-point-five million pounds they're requesting from Carmichael & Son.

* * *

At noon, Will shows up at my desk, a smile on his face.

"Ready for lunch?"

I stand. "Yes. I'm starving." I grab my purse, and we head for the cafeteria.

"Want to take the stairs?" he asks.

I smile.

He listens to me.

He remembers.

"Yes."

When we reach the cafeteria, I head for the salad bar, and Will waits in line for a hot entrée. I have my food first, and I find us a table near a window overlooking the rear courtyard. He joins me shortly, sitting down with a plate of fettuccine Alfredo with grilled chicken, steamed asparagus, garlic bread, and a cup of tea.

"That looks good," I say.

He takes a bite of the pasta. "Not too bad. It's not as good as Maggie's, but it will do. How's your salad?"

I glance down at my plate of lettuce, two halves of a hard-boiled egg, diced tomatoes, thin slices of cucumbers, shredded cheese, and croutons. "Not nearly as exciting as your lunch, but it'll do."

Will twirls a length of pasta on his fork and offers me a bite. Grinning, I take it. "Mmm. That's good."

He shakes his head at my plate. "You eat like a rabbit."

"I eat like this at lunch so I can have fattening things for dinner."

He nods. "I'll tell Maggie to make us an extra fattening dinner this evening, then."

As we eat our lunches, we chat about how the day is going. When I tell him about the incident with Spencer Sinclair, he frowns.

"You're quite confident in your assessment of Hoffman?" he asks in all seriousness.

I nod. "Absolutely."

Will shrugs. "Well then, case closed. Stick to your guns. I have full confidence in your judgement, Skye. Don't worry about it. There's no telling what's motivating Sinclair."

"He said there would be consequences, though. Can he fire me if I refuse to change my assessment?"

"No, he can't." He reaches out to lay his hand on mine, and the warm weight is comforting. "I'll tell you what. E-mail me all the pertinent files you have on this applicant, and I'll have a look."

"You wouldn't mind?"

"Not at all," he says, and then he starts fiddling with the charms on my bracelet. He fingers the double-decker bus. "D'you remember when we found this?"

"Of course. At that little vintage shop in Bibury."

He brushes his fingers along my forearm, making my nerves sing. "D'you remember what we did the night before?"

My face heats. "Yes." It was the first time we made love.

He turns my arm over and strokes the tender skin of my inner wrist, sending my pulse rocketing. Then he raises my wrist and kisses my pulse point. "Tonight, when I've got you in my bed, I'm going to kiss every inch of your delectable body, from the crown of your head to the tips of your toes."

He turns my hand over and traces the sensitive skin of my palm, sending a shiver through me. Then he smiles at my reaction.

"My cousin's wedding is this weekend," he reminds me.

I nod as I absently pick at my salad. My belly is quivering madly, and my appetite is shot. "Can I wear the dress we bought at the boutique, the night we ate at *La Traviata*? It's not fancy, but it's pretty."

His brow furrows a bit as he considers my question. "Of course you can. Though I'd be happy to take you dress shopping again, if you'd like—my treat this time."

"Oh, no!" Laughing, I shake my head. "I've had enough dress shopping for a while, thank you. Unless we find something suitable at a second-hand shop."

Will makes a face. Then, smiling, he shakes his head at me. "My mum won't know what to make of you, Miss Williams, and I have a sneaking suspicion my nan will adore you." And then he kisses the back of my hand. "Just like I do."

❧ 32

Will

The afternoon drags, and I have to force myself not to go see Skye. I miss her already, and I'm looking forward to having her stay with me this evening. Also, I'm a bit concerned about the undue pressure Spencer is putting on her. I don't know what he's up to, but I'm sure it's no good.

I took a few minutes to review the materials she'd collected on the Hoffman application, and I agreed wholeheartedly with her assessment.

Finally, five o'clock rolls around. Anxious to collect Skye and go home, I close up my office and head down to her department.

Connor catches sight of me along the way and joins me step for step. "Where are you off to in such a hurry?"

"Just getting Skye and heading out. She's coming home with me this evening."

His brows rise. "Things are getting serious with you two, aren't they?"

I give the kid a smile, but I refrain from commenting. I'd say yes, things are getting serious, but I don't want to be presumptuous and put words in Skye's mouth.

With Connor in tow, I take the lift down to her floor. We intercept Kennedy in the hallway as she's heading to the same destination we are. Skye's a popular girl.

"Hello, Kennedy," Connor says, abandoning me to fall in step beside her.

Kennedy gives him a nod. "Connor."

I may be imagining this, but it seems that Kennedy's hard outer shell has softened somewhat towards our young friend. She's still short with him occasionally, and her words often drip with sarcasm, but lately she's been looking at him differently. Her dark eyes would sweep him in an assessing fashion, and I could swear I'd see a bit of a flush in her cheeks. I'm not sure if she's aware she's even doing it, but it shows he's certainly making headway where she's concerned.

"My cousin's getting married this weekend," I tell them. "Skye's coming with me as my plus one. Would you two like to tag along?" I'm thinking Skye will be more comfortable if she has some familiar faces keeping her company.

Connor lights up as he looks to Kennedy. "What do you say, Ken? Sounds like a good time to me. Lots of free food and alcohol. And you should see me on the dance floor!"

Despite Kennedy's shrug, she seems keen enough on the idea. "Sure, why not? I don't have anything better to do this weekend."

Connor pumps a fist. "Excellent!"

"But only for Skye's sake," Kennedy clarifies. "Not to hang out with the likes of *you*." She rolls her eyes. "Get over yourself, slick."

I walk on ahead, leaving the two bickering youngsters behind me. As we near the risk assessment department, a deep voice cuts through the air, ricocheting off the walls like a boomerang. My pulse immediately kicks up a notch because I recognize that voice, and it doesn't bode well. And then I hear an answering voice, soft-spoken, yet resolute.

For fuck's sake!

That wanker is yelling at Skye!

I quicken my pace. Spencer may be the head of the department but that doesn't give him the right to speak to *anyone* in such a derogatory manner—let alone Skye.

I push open the door to their department and do a bit of quick assessing of my own. I do a double-take when I spot Spencer Sinclair standing red-faced, yelling at Skye. He's looming over her, trying to intimidate her, but she's holding her own.

Who the fuck does he think he is?

Anger like barbed wire wraps around my gut, cutting into

my flesh as it tightens. I look around the room at all the staff, who are staring in shock like a bunch of sheep. Everyone's glued to their spots. But Skye stands her ground, her face flushed as she goes nose-to-nose with Sinclair.

He is absolutely irate as he practically screams at Skye, jabbing his fat finger in her face. "When I tell you to jump, you ask how fucking high! Is that clear? Apparently, I have to spell it out for you. I specifically told you to re-assess that applicant and give me a different answer!"

Skye's beautiful blue eyes are wide and a bit frantic, but not a single tear falls. She doesn't budge an inch, and I'm so damn proud of her.

Kennedy stops short beside me. "Holy shit. That idiot has lost his mind."

"Damn right, he has," I mutter. Then louder, I snap, "Spencer!"

All heads shoot in my direction, including Sinclair's. His mouth drops open. Kennedy runs to Skye and throws an arm around her friend—girl power solidarity and all that.

"Get out of here, Will," Spencer says, sneering at me. "This is none of your damn business."

"Actually, this *is* my business. Carmichael & Son? In case it's slipped your mind, I'm the fucking *son*, and you are gone. Get the fuck out of my building! You're fired."

Spencer's face reddens even more. "You can't do this. I have rights, you know. The union—"

I glance at Connor. "Call security."

Spencer sputters in anger. "You have no idea what this insubordinate little bitch has done!"

"Actually, I do know. I reviewed the data she collected on the applicant, and I agree completely with her assessment. I only have one question. What's in it for you, Spencer? Is this a favor you owe a friend? Or worse yet, is someone blackmailing you?"

When Spencer pales to a sickly shade of white, I think I have my answer.

He scowls at me, and then at Skye. "I see what's going on here. You've coming running to defend your new bit of office fluff, have you? How long is this one going to last, Will? Tell me—is she a good fuck? Better than your last one—the redhead? Rachel, wasn't it?"

I lunge forward, but Connor pulls me back.

"Come on, Will, he's not worth it," the kid says, standing between me and the object of my ire.

Connor's right, but all I want to do right now is rearrange Spencer's fucking face.

How dare he behave this way with an employee?

Spencer comes at me, pointing at his cheek. "Right here, Carmichael," he taunts. "Go ahead and hit me, but make sure it's hard enough to leave a mark so I can bring you up on charges."

I'm itching to take him up on his offer, but Skye materializes at my side and tugs on my sleeve. In an instant, I unclench my fists and reach for her hand.

"Let's just go, please," she says quietly.

I suppose if she can keep her cool, so can I.

When two uniformed security guards arrive, I tell them, "Escort Mr. Sinclair out of the building." Then to Spencer, I say, "I'll have HR send your personal belongings to you. Our lawyers will be in touch to discuss the terms of your separation."

Spencer smiles sardonically. "You can't do this. I have rights. The union will be all over you like a rash."

"With all the written warnings you've received in the past six months, your job was already hanging on by a thread."

Skye shakes her head. "He's not worth it, Will. Don't give him the satisfaction." Then she turns to Spencer. "All I'd like is an apology, and we can all forget this ever happened."

Spencer grunts. "I'd rather clean toilets than apologize to the likes of you."

"That can be arranged," I say.

Skye looks hurt. She gave him an olive branch, and he pissed all over it.

"Take the remainder of the week off, Sinclair," I say. "I'll have HR review your contract. Our lawyers will be in touch."

I nod at the security guards, who escort him out of the building.

* * *

After the security guards lead Spencer out of the department, several staff members come forward, sheepishly admitting they've also been pressured by Spencer in the past to change their opinions on certain assessments. Apparently, this isn't the first time. It's all more ammunition to use against him.

Skye collects her handbag, and then we head downstairs.

Hamish is waiting for us out front, so I don't waste any time ushering Skye out of the building and into the car. Then I ring up my dad and inform him of what's taken place, along with the allegations other employees were now making.

"I'll handle it," my father says. "Sinclair is through."

Ending the call, I relax back in my seat and pull Skye against me. She's shaking in the aftermath, her body undoubtedly bombarded with adrenaline.

"I'm sorry, Skye," I tell her.

She shrugs. "It's all right."

"No, it's not." Turning to face her, I trace the edge of her cheek. Then I lean forward and kiss her lightly. "You were in the right, and besides, no one should be treated like that."

Once we're in my penthouse, I wrap Skye in my arms and close the door on the world. We lounge on a settee out on the balcony with a view of the River Thames at our feet. The sun is just starting to lower in the distance.

The glass door slides open, and Maggie clears her throat. "Dinner is ready."

I'm about to stand when Skye says, "Do you mind if we eat out here?"

"Of course not," Maggie says. "I'll bring your dinners right out."

When Maggie's gone, I squeeze Skye a little tighter. Pushing her hair aside, I whisper in her ear. "D'you know what I love about you?"

"What?" she says, turning her face toward mine, our noses practically brushing. Her cheeks are turning a pretty pale shade of pink.

"Everything."

I can see Maggie in my periphery. She's watching us through the glass wall as though she has a front row seat at the cinema. Her smile is so big I swear her face is going to crack. When I raise my brow at her, she snaps out of it, scurrying off in the direction of the kitchen.

She returns soon after, pushing a trolley holding two covered plates, two wine glasses, and a bottle of wine in an ice bucket. "Here you are," she says. "I made some dessert too—chocolate mousse."

I stand and uncover the dishes, handing one to Skye. She peers down at a steaming salmon filet on a bed of fresh greens, a creamy sauce drizzled on top, steamed asparagus and sautéed mushrooms. The presentation is spot on.

Skye smiles gratefully at Maggie. "This looks amazing! Thank you." Then she reaches for a fork and dives into her meal.

I think my girl's hungry.

She takes a bite of the salmon and groans with pleasure, her eyes drifting shut. "So good."

Maybe I'll ask Maggie to give me some cooking lessons. I'd love to be able to surprise Skye with a home-cooked meal—one she'd actually like.

As we're eating, I decide to broach the subject of Esme's

wedding again. It's kind of been the elephant in the room. She's agreed to come, but she doesn't seem quite happy about it. I've told her Rachel will be there, as one of Esme's bridesmaids— there's no helping that. But perhaps she'll feel better about the whole thing when I tell her I've invited Connor and Kennedy to join us.

"About the wedding this weekend," I begin.

She frowns. "I said I'd go with you, even though she-who-shall-not-be-named is going to be there."

I smother a laugh. Woman are jealous creatures by nature and those who say otherwise are lying.

"Do you think they'll like me?" she asks as she stabs her fork into the salmon.

"Who?"

"Your family."

I ponder her question for a little longer than I was meaning to. When I don't reply, she looks up with a hesitant glance.

"No, they won't *like* you. They'll love you." I look her up and down. "I mean, what's not to love?"

Smiling, Skye bites off a piece of asparagus and chews.

Following the meal, Maggie brings us dessert, which is decadently delicious. Skye's practically having an orgasm over it.

"Ohmygod," she moans, savoring a bite of the fluffy chocolate.

After finishing, we remain seated—hand in hand—and watch as London slowly descends into darkness. The moon is full tonight and high in the sky, demanding admiration as she casts her silvery spell on the River Thames. Streetlights far below us begin to flicker on, one by one, as they light up the city. People look like ants from up here, barely visible as they scurry along the pavement.

I'm about to lean in for a kiss when she beats me to it. Her arms wrap around my neck and she pulls me to her. It's not a soft, dainty kiss either. It's full of heat and desire.

"I know it's a little early, but let's go to bed," she says against my lips.

My heart thunders at her unexpected invitation. And it's all the encouragement I need. I stand and scoop her into my arms and carry her into the apartment, ignoring Maggie's amused grin as she watches us pass through the lounge on the way to the master suite.

I head straight for the bed and toss her gently down onto the mattress. I'm too turned on to mess around with pleasantries. I want her, and I'm having her—now.

I climb onto the bed, looking over her, as I unbutton her blouse, revealing smooth, supple skin. I smother her quivering body with soft kisses, from her throat to the valley between her soft breasts. I peel the lacy material of her bra aside to expose a soft pink nipple, which I draw into my mouth to suckle.

My free hand finds its way beneath the waistband of her trousers and into her knickers. I slide a finger between the lips of her sex and revel in her slippery wetness. She's already so aroused, wildly aroused, as evidenced by her hands, which are frantically clutching my shoulders.

"Spread your legs," I instruct, my mouth on hers.

Obediently, she complies, and I push my finger inside her opening. Her wet, swollen flesh makes way for me, and soon I'm rubbing the sweet spot inside her.

Soon her fingers are working my belt free, then unfastening my trousers and lowering my zip.

I reward her with a swipe of my tongue across her nipple. When I suckle once more on her nipple, she groans and arches her back beneath me.

And then everything turns into a race as we frantically undress each other.

In a way, this feels like my first time all over again. We're both all fingers and thumbs, rushed and clumsy, like two overly excited teenagers.

This is a side of Skye I'm more than happy to experience. She's usually so meticulous, her words and actions so measured, but right now, she's throwing caution to the wind.

Our clothes end up in a pile on the rug. When we come back together, it's skin on skin. Flesh on flesh. Two warm bodies gravitating toward each other, seeking and searching.

I want my mouth on every inch of her at once, which is regrettably impossible. I'm desperate to go down on her, but before I can get into position, she takes my cock in her hands. Immediately, my brain short circuits, and she has my undivided attention.

I'm already hard as can be and my balls are drawing up tight. *Shit!*

I wanted to make this last all night long, but my greedy girl has other plans apparently, as she begins working my shaft with insistent, clever fingers.

Groaning, I pull a condom packets from the top nightstand drawer and rip it open.

"Let me do it," she says, holding out her hand as she eyes the condom. "I've seen it done in videos."

Oh, fuck.

She's been watching porn?

Just the thought makes me hard. "Sure." I lie back on the mattress and give myself to her like an offering.

Biting her lip in concentration, she positions the condom just right and carefully rolls it down my shaft.

Dear God, please don't let me blow my load right this moment.

Once I'm sheathed, I roll her onto her back, nudge her legs wide open and kneel between her silky-soft thighs.

Just as I push the head of my cock into her lush opening, she clutches my shoulders and digs her nails into my flesh. "Will!"

Succumbing to temptation, I sink slowly inside her. She moans softly as I fill her completely.

"Oh, my," she breathes, panting. "That's... you're... a lot."

I grin as I cover her trembling lips with my own. "And you are exquisite."

I withdraw and roll us so that Skye's on top of me. Her eyes are huge, but she doesn't waste any time positioning herself astride me.

I help her guide the head of my cock to her opening. And

then she slowly sinks down onto me, staring down to observe the process. She bites her bottom lip, and it takes everything in me not to thrust up into her to quicken the process.

"Will," she breathes once she's fully seated on my shaft.

"Yes?" My voice is as quiet and reverent as hers.

With a little encouragement from my hands on her hips, she starts moving.

She closes her eyes as she rocks on me, slowly, languidly, her long hair falling forward and brushing my chest as she leans closer. She breathes out a sweet sigh. "Oh, my God, Will. This feels... so... *good.*"

I smile as my heart expands in my chest. I am a slave to this girl.

* * *

I lie on my back with Skye cuddled up against me, her arm across my waist. One of her legs is draped over mine. It feels perfect.

She's perfect.

Together, *we're* perfect.

At the moment, I've got sex and weddings on my mind. "How do you feel about kids?" I ask her.

She laughs softly. "They're usually cute and adorable. Sometimes they're loud and messy."

I turn to her and kiss her forehead. "D'you fancy having some of your own one day?"

She stills, clearly recognizing the seriousness of my question. It's not a random question. I want kids. I want a family. My future partner has to want that too.

"Yes, Will, I want children. Someday. Just not today."

I laugh. "Of course not. You're still so young. But someday?"

She leans her head on my chest. "Yes. Someday."

33

Skye

The ceremony was lovely. Will's cousin Esme looked like a princess in her flowing white wedding dress, with sprigs of baby's breath tucked into her upswept chestnut hair. The groom was equally dashing in his black tuxedo, white dress shirt, and gray cummerbund, with a deep burgundy silk tie for a splash of color.

I wasn't too nervous at the wedding ceremony, but now, as we're approaching the very exclusive country club where the reception is being held, I'm a nervous wreck.

Out of my peripheral vision, I see Will studying me. He hired a limo for this trip, so there'd be ample room for Kennedy and Connor to ride with us. They're seated together on a bench seat opposite ours.

Will reaches for my hand and strokes the back of it with a gentle index finger. "You okay, love?" His voice is low, soothing. As always, his accent makes me a bit weak in the knees.

I nod. "I'm fine." *I'm not.*

I'm not looking forward to attending a fancy social event with Will's extended family and their friends. Worst of all, Rachel will be there. I know Will has no interest in her, but I'm not good with confrontation. If she ignores me, I'll be fine. But if she doesn't...

Who am I kidding? I caught her staring longingly at Will more than once during the ceremony. She's not ready to give up on him. That much is obvious

Will looks incredibly handsome in a black Armani suit, with a white dress shirt and a striking, cobalt blue silk tie. He said he'd chosen the tie because it matches the color of my eyes.

In an attempt to mask my nerves, I busy myself with smoothing the fabric of my dress. I decided to wear the same blue dress I wore the evening we ate at *La Traviata*. I just couldn't justify buying another dress, especially one I'd probably never have an opportunity to wear again.

I look perfectly presentable, even if I don't look like I just stepped off the cover of a fashion magazine. Kennedy spent an hour this morning putting my hair up in a glamorous upswept style, with a couple of ringlets dangling at the sides. I sent a selfie to my mom so she could see.

I didn't realize Will was visible in the photo, barely in the frame. My mom asked me who the handsome guy behind me was. I told her he was a friend from work, and then I felt guilty for not being upfront with her.

I haven't told my mom about my relationship with Will, nor my dad. I'm afraid my mom will just worry about me, and my dad has already made it perfectly clear he wouldn't approve of us being together. But, as things get more and more serious between us, I know I'll have to come clean with both of them at some point.

Kennedy looks stunning in a form-fitting, black A-line dress, with her dark eyes enhanced with a kohl, cat eyeliner and her sleek black hair cut at chin-length bob.

Connor—well he always looks handsome. Today, he's in a black suit, white shirt, and emerald green tie. He cut his hair short, and the new style somehow makes him seem older, more mature. I've caught Kennedy, on more than one occasion, watching him when he wasn't looking.

"I'm starving," Connor says as he loosens his tie. He looks to Will. "There'd better be good food at the reception, and lots of it."

Will laughs. "Oh, there will be. I promise you, Esme's parents will spare no expense."

Kennedy catches my gaze. "You look gorgeous, Skye."

"Oh, stop." She's just being nice.

"No, seriously. You look hot. If I was a lesbian, I'd be all over you."

Connor shoots Kennedy a sharp look as he clutches his chest. "You're not a lesbian, Ken. Right?"

"I only meant, if I *was*," she says.

"Don't do that to me," Connor mutters.

Will brings my hand up to his lips and kisses the back of it. "Sorry, Kennedy. She's taken."

The vehicle comes to a stop.

"We're here, sir," Hamish says from the front seat.

We all look out the window at the front of the reception venue's main entrance.

"That's a fucking castle," Connor says, fixing his tie.

Kennedy leans down for a better view out the window. She whistles. "It must be nice having money."

A footman dressed in a crisp uniform opens the rear passenger door. "Welcome, sir," he says to Will.

Will steps out of the vehicle and offers me his hand. Kennedy and Connor follow after us.

A uniformed hostess holds open an ornate arched door and ushers us inside. "Straight ahead, ladies and gentlemen. You'll find name placards at the tables to indicate your seating assignments."

"Ooh, assigned seating," Kennedy mutters. "*Fancy.*"

We stroll down the main corridor, Will to my left and Kennedy to my right. Connor follows closely behind Kennedy, towering over her petite form like he's her personal bodyguard.

A woman dressed in a cream-colored suit stands at the reception hall door, a clipboard in the crook of her arm and a gold pen in her fingers. She smiles brightly at Will. "Mr. Carmichael, how lovely to see you, sir." And then she skims the rest of us, her smile not quite so bright.

"Party of four," Will says.

The woman consults her clipboard. "I have you and Miss Williams seated at table five, up front." She glances curiously at Kennedy and Connor. "Your names, please?"

"Kennedy Takahashi and Connor Murphy," Will says. "They're with me."

The hostess frowns as she checks over her roster. "I'm terribly afraid I don't have their names on the guest list. But not to worry. I have a spare table—table twenty-seven—set up for unexpected arrivals."

Will gives the woman a smile that doesn't quite reach his eyes. "Would you be so kind as to move them to my table? Thank you."

"I'm sorry, sir. I can't. There are other people assigned—"

"I'm sure you can work it out. We'll go find our seats now, thank you." Will links his arm with mine and leads me into the room.

Kennedy and Connor follow close on our heels.

"That was fucking dope, dude," Connor says, shaking his head as he slaps Will on the back. "I'm impressed as hell."

"Money talks," Kennedy says.

Connor tries to link his arm with Kennedy's, but she skillfully slips out of his reach.

"Nice try, kid," she says.

We find table five pretty quickly. It's near the front, and the tables are in numerical order. We'll be sitting near the wedding party, who will be seated at a long row of tables facing the guests.

Great.

That means I'll have a front-row view of Rachel, and she can stare at Will all she wants.

Will pulls out my chair for me, and I take my seat. He points to the chair to my left. "Kennedy, sit there, beside Skye. And Connor, you're next to Kennedy." Will pulls out the seat to my right and takes a seat.

The wedding party hasn't arrived yet. They're probably still back at the church taking photographs.

Delicious aromas waft our way from the direction in which I assume the kitchen is located. There's an orchestra setting up in the front of the room, to the left of the bridal party's row of tables. The back of the room is reserved as a dance floor, and a full-service bar is located in the back corner.

Guests continue filing into the reception hall. And it's not long after that the bridal party arrives, laughing and smiling. They take their places at the front of the room, and after a few toasts to the bride and groom, dinner is announced.

It's a sit-down dinner, and we're waited upon by a uniformed catering staff. For starters, they wheel out carts laden with covered dishes. We're served salads first, and then bowls of Italian Wedding Soup, warm crusty bread, and fresh butter.

Our servers offer us a choice of three different entrees. Will and Connor choose the filet mignon with a baked potato. Kennedy and I both opt for a pasta dish with pesto, grilled chicken, and steamed veggies.

The food is exquisitely prepared, absolutely perfect, and paired with a delicious assortment of wines, tea, and coffees. By meal's end, I'm a bit stuffed.

After dinner, the guests start mingling.

Will stands and holds his hand out to me. "Come meet my parents and my nan."

My stomach plummets, and I feel a bit queasy.

"It's okay, Skye," Kennedy says. "They won't bite your head off. Not in such polite society."

Will beckons me to take his hand. "Come on, love. Kennedy's right. They won't bite."

I place my hand in his, and Will pulls me to my feet. Then, he leads me across the room to a table where some older couples are seated, along with an elderly woman in a wheelchair.

Everyone at the table watches us approach.

I swallow hard.

Will tightens his grip on my hand. "Mum, Dad, Nan, I'd like for you to meet Skye Williams."

His parents eye me with perfectly neutral expressions, the pair of them, as if they're studying me. I can't tell if they're happy or not.

His grandmother, on the other hand, beams up at me, lifting a wrinkled, shaky hand in greeting. Will takes her hand and leans in close to kiss her cheek. "You look lovely this evening, sweetheart."

His grandmother grins up at Will. "So do you, my boy." Then, to me, she says, "Hello, dear. I'm so happy to meet you. I've heard so much about you."

I'm not sure how that's possible, as I don't think Will has said much of anything about me to his family, but I smile nonetheless. "It's a pleasure to meet you."

"What did you think of the ceremony?" his mother asks me.

I smile. "It was lovely."

When she nods, I relax a fraction. I guess that was an acceptable answer.

"Did you enjoy your dinner, Skye?" Fitzwilliam Sr. asks.

"Yes. It was delicious."

More nods from his parents.

"Come here, child," his grandmother says, holding out her hands to me.

I join her, standing beside her wheelchair, and she takes my hands in hers, squeezing mine. I know Will's parents are in their mid-seventies, and that must make his grandmother in her mid-nineties at least.

"I'd dance, you know," she says, winking at me, "but no one can keep up with me in my chair."

Will's standing behind us, his arms crossed, a pleased expression on his face as he watches the exchange between me and his grandmother. I know he's very close to his her.

His parents remain polite, yet cool, as if they're not sure

what to make of me. Or perhaps they're trying to ascertain the exact nature of our relationship. I wish I knew the answer to that, too.

The orchestra begins tuning their instruments, and there's a buzz of excitement in the room. There has to be nearly two dozen musicians. No DJ or dance music for this reception. My suspicions are proven right when they strike up a lovely waltz by Johann Strauss, if I'm not mistaken.

Will wraps his arms around me and leans down to whisper in my ear, "Dance with me."

I smile, wishing I could. "I don't know how."

"You don't need to know. I'll lead you."

Will's grandmother grins up at me from her chair. "Go have fun, Skye." She waves us on. "Go dance with my handsome grandson."

Will leads me to the area of the reception hall reserved for dancing. There are already tons of couples already on the dance floor, waltzing skillfully to the music.

I guess everyone here has had dance lessons, except for me.

Will draws me to his side. "It's easy. Just follow my lead." Then he kisses my forehead and says, "You look ravishing, by the way."

My face heats at his compliment. "Thank you."

He sweeps me out onto the dance floor, one hand firmly at my back, and the other grasping mine. With subtle pressure, his hand directs my movements, indicating which direction to move, and I'm surprised at how easy he makes this. After a few missteps, I get the hang of it, and we're waltzing through the crowd.

The first waltz leads into a second, and I'm quickly relaxing in his arms, trusting him to keep me from falling on my backside.

As the second dance comes to an end, Kennedy sidles up beside me. "Time out for a potty break," she says.

I don't really need to go, but I could use some girl time for sure. "Excuse me," I say to Will. "I won't be long."

Will nods. "Right. No problem. I'll be waiting patiently for your return."

Kennedy grabs my hand and pulls me toward the women's restroom. "He's pathetic."

I laugh. "No, he's not."

"He is. Mr. Perfect. Mr. Polished. It's pathetic."

I'm still laughing as we push through the door into the women's room. The bathroom is easily half the size of our flat, with fancy sofas, mahogany coffee tables, and gilded mirrors hanging on walls covered in dark blue velvety wallpaper.

I stop abruptly when Rachel walks out of one of the bathroom stalls. When she sees me, she freezes, and we stare at each other for a moment.

Then she finally heads for the sinks.

I disappear into a stall, and Kennedy takes the one next to mine. I procrastinate as long as I can, hoping to give Rachel plenty of time to finish up and leave the restroom before I show myself again.

A few moments later, when I exit the stall, Rachel's still there, obviously waiting for me, her arms crossed over her chest. I'm relieved when I hear Kennedy flush, because that means she'll be out here any second to lend moral support.

Ignoring Rachel, I cross the room to wash my hands.

"You're wasting your time," Rachel says.

I can feel her gaze drilling into the back of my head.

Hurry up, Kennedy!

As I'm drying my hands, Rachel adds, "His father will never accept you. You're a nobody. You're beneath him."

Kennedy's stall door slams open, and she comes charging out. "So, you're the bimbo I keep hearing about."

Rachel's lips flatten, and her freckled cheeks flush hotly. "Excuse me?"

"You heard me," Kennedy says as she violently scrubs her hands. To me, she says, "Come on, Skye. Your Prince Charming eagerly awaits."

I fight a grin, knowing Kennedy said that last little bit just to irritate Rachel.

Tired of her backbiting, I turn and face Rachel. "Enough, Rachel. I know everything about you and Will. I know you left him for someone else, and that it backfired on you. I'm sorry about that, but it doesn't mean you get to reclaim Will just because you want to. He's moved on."

Kennedy motions toward the door, and I take a step.

Rachel steps in front of me, her hands on her hips. "You don't get it, do you? He'll never marry you. You're an *outsider*—

an American. His family will never accept you, and trust me, he won't marry without their approval."

Kennedy steps between us. "I guess you missed the part when his grandmother practically fawned over Skye."

Rachel frowns dismissively at Kennedy. "I'm not talking to *you*."

"Look, bitch," Kennedy says, going up on her toes to get in Rachel's face. "Give it up."

I grab Kennedy's arm and pull her toward the door. "Don't bother. She's not worth it."

When we exit the ladies' room, Will and Connor are standing not ten feet away, deep in conversation. The pair of them look dashing standing shoulder-to-shoulder, one auburn haired and the other blond, both tall, strikingly handsome, and debonair.

The moment Will sees me, he breaks into a huge smile.

"Told you," Kennedy mutters, elbowing me. "He's pathetic."

Will holds his hand out to me. "Ready, love?"

I take a deep breath. "Yes." If I can face Rachel in the ladies' room, I can face a dance floor of waltzing strangers.

And without further ado, he takes me in his arms and sweeps us back onto the dance floor, effortlessly guiding me through the steps.

"Everything all right?" he asks, eyeing me curiously.

"Fine," I say, forcing a smile. I'm not going to let Rachel get to me. "Peachy keen."

He frowns. "Why don't I believe you?"

34

Will

"Tell me what's upset you, love," I say. Clearly something happened in the loo.

She glances up at me, her eyes glittering suspiciously. "I ran into Rachel in the ladies' room."

Immediately, my blood pressure skyrockets. That bitch is determined to fuck with my relationship with Skye. "What did she say to you?"

Skye shakes her head. "It's not worth repeating. Let's just forget it."

I tip her chin up so that she's meeting my gaze. "Tell me,

Skye."

She sighs. "She said I'm wasting my time with you, and that your family will never accept me."

"That's absolute rubbish! I'm tempted to hunt Rachel down right this minute and wring her bloody neck."

Skye smiles at my outburst and squeezes my hand. "It's okay. Really. I know she's just resentful that we're together." Her hand leaves my shoulder to straighten my tie. "She really regrets leaving you, Will."

"Well, that's too damn bad. She actually did me a favor. I should thank her."

Skye tugs on my tie, bringing my attention on her. "I'd rather you didn't talk to her at all. It will only encourage her."

I lean down and drop a light kiss on her lips. "Fine. Your wish is my command."

* * *

Maybe it's the atmosphere or the ambience, or maybe it's just being with Skye. The young woman I'm holding in my arms has managed to completely captivate me. In a room full of people, I only have eyes for her. I know it sounds overly dramatic and very romantic, but I think I've found my true love.

The waltz playing in the background reaches its crescendo. I spin Skye around as we dance. The room becomes our beautiful carousel where faces lose their definition and colors merge and bleed into one another.

I lead her through the steps, and we take a turn around the room. Thank God my mum insisted that I take dance lessons when I was a teen. Otherwise, I'd have nothing but two left feet, and I'd be crushing Skye's delicate toes beneath my size-twelve shoes.

I'm careful not to run us into another couple. But keeping a watch proves difficult because Skye is gazing up at me with a beautiful smile on her face, and I am loathe to look away from her even for a second.

One dance turns into two, and then three. She's really getting the swing of it now, and she smiles as we take another turn around the room. Connor cuts in, stealing Skye from me, and I take the opportunity to dance with the bride. Esme is beaming, and I'm beyond happy for my cousin.

"You look radiant, Esme," I tell her. "Are you quite content with your choice of groom?"

She grins at me. "Absolutely. He's all I could ask for."

Esme and I chat through the duration of our dance, and all the while, I'm keeping a discreet eye on Skye and waiting for the chance to reunite with her.

When the music comes to an end, we all stop and applaud the orchestra. My Aunt Mildred, the mother of the bride, informs us that it's time for the happy couple to cut the cake. The bride and groom shove pieces into each other's mouths, as wedding couples often do. Frankly, it's messy.

Note to self: Don't do that to Skye when it's our turn.

After eating cake, the girls suggest we go outside for a bit.

The gardens out back are truly splendid, so everyone's on board with the idea.

The girls walk ahead of us along a paved path, Connor and I taking up the rear. Connor flags down a waiter carrying a tray of champagne flutes. He takes one and guzzles it down. Then he sets the empty glass on the tray and reaches for another one.

I grab his wrist as he attempts to take the second glass. "I'm afraid not, mate." And then to the waiter, I say, "Inform the staff that Connor's had his last alcoholic drink for the evening."

"Yes, sir," the waiter says.

Connor narrows his eyes at me. "You wanker."

I place my hand on his shoulder and give him some fatherly advice. "You don't need to get drunk to get up the courage to kiss Kennedy."

"Am I that obvious?"

I give him a sideward gaze. "Utterly transparent. Pathetic love-sick puppy is what comes to mind."

Connor sighs, his shoulders dropping as he saunters ahead. The evening is dark, but not pitch black. The full moon hangs low in the sky, lending her light on this beautiful summer evening. We continue walking in the direction the girls went, passing small clusters of people chatting or having a cigarette. My Uncle Harold is handing cigars out to all the gentlemen. I shake my head when he angles one my way.

Connor stops in his tracks and turns to me, looking more than a little discourage. "I've got no chance with her, have I?"

I glance down the path at the girls, who've stopped to wait

for us. Kennedy's tapping her foot impatiently, as though she's wondering what's keeping us.

"We'll catch up," I call, waving them on.

I motion Connor over to a stone bench at the edge of the path. "Sit."

He slumps forward, his head in his hands.

This is new territory for me. Connor's usually jovial and self-confident. I'm not used to seeing him so discouraged.

"D'you need a hug?" I joke, raising my arm as if I'm about to follow through. When he says nothing, I allow my hand to drop to my lap.

Staring forward, Connor rakes his hand through his hair. "I really like her, man. In fact, I think I'm in love her. But she doesn't take me seriously. She treats me like I'm a kid."

"Well, you are just eighteen, and she's twenty-three. Girls mature faster than boys, you know. She probably sees you as a kid."

I pat his leg. I don't know why I feel so protective of this kid, so fatherly all of a sudden. I want to comfort him, but I don't know how. "You're awfully young to be in love," I tell him. "Don't be in such a hurry. Bide your time."

"Look at her!" he says, nodding toward the girls who are now walking away. "She's amazing. But I'll always be younger than her. I feel like I'll always be playing catch-up."

"Give it time. Eventually, the age difference won't mean so much."

He scoffs. "She's not going to wait for me. Some bloke will

come along and sweep her off her feet. I haven't got a chance."

"Why don't you tell her how you feel? Maybe she'll surprise you. You'll never know unless you ask."

"What if she turns me down, and I fuck everything up between us? At least now we're friends. I don't want to lose that." His hands are fidgeting in his lap.

"She won't," I say with complete confidence.

"But how do you know?" Exasperation edges his voice.

For a guy who usually exudes confidence in every area, Connor is suddenly anything but. I wonder if he's ever had a girlfriend.

Maybe it's time to change my approach. "Haven't you noticed how she acts around you?"

Connor shakes his head. "What d'you mean?"

I've not got the time to go into the science of body language, so I settle on a condensed explanation. "She watches you when you're not looking. I've caught her staring at you on numerous occasions. Bottom line, she likes you. Find somewhere pretty to take her—girls like romantic gestures—and go for it. Tell her how you feel."

He gives me a lop-sided grin. "You really think she could be interested in the likes of me?"

I clap him on the back. "There's only one way to find out, mate."

Connor shoots to his feet just as Rachel appears out of nowhere. Even though daylight has ebbed, I can see her face clearly enough to know that her eyes are puffy and mascara is running down her cheeks. Her gaze is locked on me like she's a heat-seeking missile, and I'm a bonfire.

I can't let this charade carry on any longer. It's enough we have to breathe the same air, but her going all *psycho-ex* on me isn't going to work. Not if I want to have an enjoyable evening with Skye.

"Connor, you go," I tell him. "I'll be right behind you."

Connor frowns at the sight of Rachel, but he doesn't argue. Giving her the evil eye, he walks off, heading toward a fountain where the girls are peering into the water.

After he's out of earshot, I turn to Rachel with a sigh. Her face is red and blotchy, and I can't tell if she's sad or angry. Maybe it's a bit of both. Any affection I might have felt for her is long gone, and now I feel nothing but pity.

I point at the spot beside me that Connor just vacated. "Rachel, sit."

She nearly stumbles on her heels as she sits, and I wonder how much she's had to drink tonight. This close, I can see that her eyes are a bit glassy. "How much have you had to drink?"

"Will, I'm sorry! I made a terrible mistake. I never should have gone off with David Markham. It was an utterly stupid thing to do. I still love you, and I want you back. We can still have what we had before. I know it."

"No, Rachel, we can't."

She attempts to throw herself into my arms, but I hold her off.

Her eyes fill with fresh tears. "Will—"

"No, Rachel. It's over. *We're* over. Nothing you say is going to change that. You need to move on."

"It's because of that *American*, isn't it?" She sneers. "She's turned you against me. She's just a money-grubbing slut."

I choke back a laugh because Skye is the furthest thing from a money-grubber than anyone I've ever met. "Rachel, how can I be any clearer? We're done. You made your choice, and now I've made mine. And I'm a hell of a lot happier for it."

"But, Will—"

"I love her, Rachel. Can you get that through your head? *I love her.*"

Love isn't a word I throw about. In fact, I've never said it to a woman before. I wasn't even sure I knew what love was before I met Skye.

If love is feeling like you can't breathe when you're not with someone, or if love is the inability to stop thinking about someone every waking minute—if love is knowing you'd do anything, give anything, for the happiness and welfare of someone—then I'm in love.

I used to think that loving someone was a weakness, and I never wanted to give any woman that kind of power over me. But now I'd gladly lay that power at Skye's feet.

Rachel sits beside me, practically shaking. Her cheeks are streaked with tears, and her mascara's running. I don't think she's faking this, and it makes me sad for her.

"You don't love her," she whines under her breath. "She's just a novelty for you. And I'll bet she's a boring fuck."

My eyes widen at her vulgarity. "You will not talk about my girlfriend in such a disrespectful way."

Her eyes practically bulge. "Girlfriend! What the fuck, Will? We were together for four months, and I didn't even get that title. Exactly how long have you been seeing her? Were you fucking her behind my back? Tell me!"

"That's pretty rich coming from you." Then I lower my voice because I notice we're garnering some unwanted attention from curious bystanders. "Throw your stones at another glass house, Rachel."

I'm done with trying to tiptoe around her feelings. She needs to get it through her head that we're done.

Without warning, Rachel slaps me across the face. "You cheating bastard!" she cries. "I go on a short holiday, and you fuck the office whore. For your information, Spencer Sinclair's the one who told me she's a lousy lay."

I stand. "That's enough. This is Esme's wedding, and you're making a scene. You need to leave."

"Who's going to make me?" she screams, sobbing now.

"I am," a deep voice cuts in.

We both turn to see my father, standing there with his arms crossed over his chest. Rachel's shocked parents are at his side.

My father looks at Rachel with disgust. "My son has brought a lady with him to this event, and I'd hate to think you were eating into their evening."

Rachel falls silent, her mouth agape as she stares at my dad and her parents. Then she stands abruptly and straightens her dress. "She'll leave you, Will. She'll go back to America and carry on living her life. When she does, call me. I'll be here to pick up the pieces."

I'd be lying if I said Rachel's parting words didn't hit a nerve. As spiteful as she's being, she might also be right. Skye's made it clear that she's leaving London after her internship is over and returning home.

I swallow against the lump in my throat.

And then I catch Skye's gaze. She's standing at the back of the small crowd that has gathered around us, staring at me. She looks utterly shell-shocked.

Fuck!

Rachel's father grabs his daughter's arm and marches her out of sight. It's cliché as hell, but the people standing around start clapping.

As I make my way to Skye, my father gives me a curt nod before he heads back into the reception hall. In that one small gesture, he's given me his approval. It's not something I require, but it's certainly nice to have.

As I pass through the small crowd, the onlookers drift away and return to whatever it was they were doing. I stop in front of Skye, facing her directly, looking down into her face. She looks up at me.

"I'm sorry you heard that," I say.

"I'm not. You said you love me."

Ahh, she heard that part.

She sounds surprised.

"Of course I did," I say. And then I take her in my arms and kiss her. I'm generally not big on public displays of affection, but it feels right. It's a soft kiss, almost reverent. This moment will be forever encapsulated and stored in the recesses of my mind.

Pulling away, I tuck a wayward strand of hair behind her ear. There's a tear in her eye, threatening to fall. "What is it?"

Her voice breaks. "That was my wish."

"What was?" I say.

She nods down the path. "Kennedy and I found a wishing well, and I threw in a coin. That was my wish—that you loved me."

I stand speechless, the back of my eyes pricking as tears threaten to form. "Of course I do. Skye..."

My chest tightens with emotion and my pulse starts racing.

This isn't the time or place that I had planned to declare myself to her, but it looks like Rachel has forced my hand.

"Come with me," I tell her, taking her hand and leading her off onto a little side path that leads through some trees. Fairy lights are strung overhead, making it a pretty little spot for romantic interludes. The only sound is the soft and gentle chirp of insects.

Stones crunch under our feet as we carry on down a shingled path. We stop as we catch sight of Kennedy and Connor's silhouettes in the distance. They're standing in front of the wishing well, and in sync they both throw a coin into the water. I squeeze Skye's hand when Connor turns to Kennedy and strokes her face. Connor leans forward and kisses her.

I'm so fucking proud of him. "Look, Skye, the kids are all grown up."

Laughing, she pulls me in another direction. I can tell by her quickening steps that something is up.

"Where's the fire?" I say.

She stops and turns to me, melting into my arms. "I love you, too, Will."

Hearing her say the words sends my pulse into overdrive. I sense a *but* in the tone of her voice, though—which steals some of the joy from the moment.

Rachel's words come back to haunt me.

"*But*? You're going to leave me, aren't you?"

When she doesn't immediately answer—when she doesn't deny it—I cup her face between my hands and make her look up at me. "Please stay."

Stay is the word I selfishly shackle her with. Shackling her is exactly what I'd be doing, bounding her to the UK and to me.

How could I ask her to stay when her home—and her mother—are back in the States?

And yet, the idea of letting her go is unthinkable.

"This was only supposed to be a job," she says. "A gap year. And now, everything has gotten so complicated."

I fidget with the bracelet around her wrist. I refuse to be nothing more than just another bloody charm, like a souvenir collected on her travels.

"You said you love me," I remind her. "Did you mean it?"

Shit, she actually said it.

It registers in my mind loud and clear. She loves me. Not my money, not my status—because that doesn't mean anything to her. She loves *me*.

She nods. "With all my heart."

I place my hand over her heart. "Wherever your heart leads you, wherever you go, that's where I'll be. If I have to uproot myself from everything I know and love to be with you, then so be it. I'll buy us both first class tickets to anywhere you want to go. If you want to live on the moon, I'll be there, right by your side."

She grins. "You know, economy class is a better value."

I sweep her up into my arms and kiss her like there's no tomorrow.

That's my sensible girl.

"Fine, we'll fly economy. Just promise you won't go without me."

She beams up at me with a teary-eyed smile. "I promise."

Epilogue

Skye
Two months later...

O n an early Saturday evening, Will and I sit on the sofa in the living room of his Bibury house watching the fall foliage through the front windows. It's late October, and the days are getting shorter, the temperatures colder. I'm looking forward to lots of snuggling with Will this winter.

We've come here for the weekend, like we often do, to escape the hustle and bustle of London. As much as I love the city, and all the cultural and culinary amenities it has to offer, I admit to loving this house—and the countryside—even more.

It's almost dinner time, and we're killing time cuddling beneath a blanket on the sofa as we wait for Alice to call us to eat. That woman spoils us rotten.

I hear the sound of a leaf blower outside as Roy clears the drive. We're expecting my dad and his family tomorrow morning for a visit.

My stomach growls loudly enough that people from the next farm over probably heard me.

Will kisses my cheek. "Someone's hungry."

"I'm starving." It's not surprising after the busy day we had.

We took a drive into the village earlier this afternoon and had lunch at our favorite pub. I visited the little vintage shop where we found the double-decker bus charm and I bought another one on this trip—a thatched-roof cottage. We took a leisurely walk through Bibury and stopped in at the village shop so I could send another postcard to my mom.

I still haven't told her about how serious things have gotten between me and Will, and that's making me feel very guilty. I dread telling her. I'm afraid she'll think I'm abandoning her, but I could never do that.

"What's wrong?" Will says as he coils a strand of my hair around his index finger.

"Nothing."

He reaches for my hand and gives it a squeeze before bringing it to his lips for a kiss. "That wasn't a *nothing* I just saw. It looked more like a flash of panic to me."

I sigh. "I was just thinking about my mom."

"You miss her."

"Yes."

"And you still haven't told her about us, have you?"

I shake my head again.

He kisses the back of my hand. "You're going to have to sooner or later. You don't want me showing up on her doorstep unannounced, do you?"

I smile. "No."

We've been back from our excursion into the village just long enough to warm up in front of a log fire in the hearth and sip hot tea.

Alice pops her head through the doorway. "Dinner's ready, you two. I've got roast beef sandwiches for you, with home-made chips, and there's an apple crumble for dessert."

After thanking Alice profusely, we carry our plates into the dining room. Will chooses a bottle of wine from the cellar and brings it and two glasses to the table.

He pours us each a glass and offers a toast. "To us," he says. "To all the excitement and adventure our future holds."

I *am* excited about the future. Now that Spencer Sinclair is gone from the company—fired because he'd been pressuring staff members to falsify assessments of potential clients—I'm really enjoying my job. The new manager of the risk assessment department, Eleanor, is a joy to work with, and she's taught me so much in the short time she's been with the company. She's already offered me a permanent, full-time job if I'm interested in staying. She said Carmichael & Son would be only too happy to sponsor me for a work VISA.

I still have a number of months to go on my internship. Next summer seems like a long time away, but I know it will be here sooner than I imagine.

And then I'll be faced with a choice.

After we finish eating, Will reaches for my hand. "You're looking far too serious for what's supposed to be a relaxing Saturday evening. Tell me what's on your mind."

"I'm wondering what will happen at the end of my internship."

"I see." He pops his last French fry into his mouth and chews as he studies me. "You look so melancholy."

"I feel melancholy."

"Please don't worry. If you want to return home, I'll go with you."

"Will, be honest. You don't want to leave England any more than I want to leave my country. Your family is here. Your heart is *here.*" I wave my hand around, indicating this house he loves so much.

"And your heart is back home with your mum. Don't try to tell me it's not."

I squeeze his hand. "Part of it is. The other part is right here with you." I frown, knowing my heart is going to be torn in two.

"I've been thinking about this," he says. "And I have a proposition to make."

"What's that?"

"Like you've said, I can do my job from anywhere in the world, as long as I have a phone and Internet. You can do your job anywhere as well."

My pulse starts racing as I anticipate his next words. "Yes?"

"How about we split our time between London and Cincinnati? We can both work remotely from anywhere, so why don't we? We'll split our time between the two countries."

"Can we do that? Do you think the company would let us?"

He gives me an exasperated look. "Skye, it's my family's firm. I can do what I damn well please."

"But would your father go for it?"

"If the alternative is me emigrating to the States, then yes. He'll go for it and jump for joy in the process. Darling, we can make this work."

Tears blur my vision, and my throat tightens. "It sounds too good to be true."

He scoots his chair back and stands. Then he offers me his hand. I take it, and he pulls me to my feet.

Without saying a word, he leads me up the stairs.

Once we reach the landing, he sweeps me up into his arms and carries me into our bedroom, closing the door behind us.

The room is dark, and the drapes are open. Moonlight falls over the countryside, with the twinkling lights of the village in the distance.

Will walks me over to the window and stands behind me, his body flush with mine. I lean back against his hard chest, soaking in his warmth.

He wraps his arms about me and leans down to rest his chin on my shoulder. "D'you see that? It's magical, isn't it?"

"Yes." From our vantage point up here, I can see the River Coln as it winds its way through Bibury, the bright moonlight reflected on the water's surface. It *is* magical. It's no wonder Will loves this house so much. "It's your own little slice of heaven."

"It is. And I want it to be your slice of heaven, too."

He brushes my hair aside and drops a kiss on my neck, making me shiver. "It doesn't matter where we are," he whispers against my skin, "as long as we're together. If you fancy living in an igloo at the North Pole, we'll make it work, assuming they've got Internet up there."

I laugh. "You're serious."

"I am. Now, say yes."

"To what? What's the question?"

After turning me to face him and getting down on one knee, he reaches into his pocket and pulls out a ring—a dainty gold band with a lovely amethyst setting. He holds it up to me. "It was my nan's, and she wants you to have it. Skye Williams, would you do me the honor of marrying me?"

My heart skips a beat before it lodges in my throat. "Will, you can't be serious."

"Why not?"

"We haven't known each other that long."

He shrugs. "I know all I need to know. I want to spend the rest of my life with you, and I'm hoping you feel the same."

Tears spring from my eyes. There's only one answer that feels right, deep in my soul. "Yes."

His eyes widen, almost in surprise, and he surges to his feet and pulls me into his arms. He kisses me before pulling back and slipping the ring on my shaking finger.

It fits perfectly.

He scoops me up into his arms and carries me to the bed, laying me down. He pulls off my shoes and kicks off his own. Then he joins me on the bed, pulling me into his arms and sealing our future with a heated kiss.

* * *

Sunday morning, my dad, Julia, and the kids arrive. We go out to meet them as they pull up to the house.

Julia gets out of the car and unbuckles Rebecca from her car seat.

Rebecca jumps down to the ground and runs to me, jumping into my waiting arms. "Skye! Is this your house?" she asks me as she looks wide-eyed at the pasture fence, where the ponies are peeking through the rails.

"It's not mine," I say. "It's Will's."

Will comes up behind me, placing his hand on my shoulder as he gently ruffles Rebecca's hair. "Why yes, it's hers," he says.

Charlie runs to the fence and bends over to stare at the ponies. "Can I ride one?" he says, looking back at us.

"Sure," Will says. "I'll get one saddled up and take you for a ride. If it okay with your parents?"

As my dad and Will take Charlie off to the barn, so he can ride a pony, Julia, Rebecca, and I head inside the house.

"I've got to go wee," Rebecca whispers loudly.

I smile. "I'll take you to the bathroom."

"No, I need the *toilet*," she says.

Julia laughs as she ruffles her daughter's hair. "The bathroom is the toilet, dear."

After Julia helps her daughter take care of business, the three of us sit in the living room to visit.

Julie eyes the engagement ring on my finger. "That's new," she says, grinning.

"Yes. He popped the question last night."

"Have you told your mum?"

"Not yet. She knows we're dating, but she doesn't know how serious it is."

"You need to tell her," Julia says. "It's not going to get any easier."

"I know." My stomach sinks like a stone. "I'll call her tonight."

Julia and I take Rebecca outside so she can ride a pony, too. Will has saddled Snowflake, a dainty white pony with a slow, steady gate and a wonderful temperament. Julia and I watch on as Rebecca takes her turn around the paddock.

After the pony rides are over, we let Charlie and Rebecca feed the chickens, which results in fantastic squeals of delight. Then we walk down to the lake and spot fish darting in and out of the shadows beneath the dock.

Alice rings the bell when lunch is ready, and we all head inside for a roasted chicken and mashed potatoes.

After lunch, Julia and I play board games with the kids at the dining room table, while Will and my dad shut themselves up in the study.

"They're having a man-to-man talk," Julia says to me, winking as she rolls the dice.

"My turn!" Charlie says, and he picks up the dice and shakes them.

"About what?" I say.

"You know," she says, shrugging. "The usual things a father asks of his daughter's beau. What his intentions are. How he intends to support you. The usual questions."

We both laugh at the obvious absurdity of that.

"Maybe I'll support Will," I say. "My boss, Eleanor, has offered me a permanent job at Carmichael & Son, when my internship is up."

It's a full hour later when Will and my dad finally rejoin us. We all decide to go into the village and have a look around. After I mail my weekly postcard to my mom, we stop in at the ice cream shop for sundaes.

Later, we walk along the River Coln and watch the ducks.

My dad pulls me aside as the others walk on. "How's everything going? With Will, I mean."

"Fine." Suddenly, I'm feeling a bit leery as I don't know where this conversation is headed.

"I had a talk with him this afternoon, as you know. I have to say, I was wrong about him. He's very much in love with you, and he's given this a lot of thought. We talked about your mum, too, and Will said he's perfectly willing to live wherever you want to live."

"We're going to split our time between the US and England."

He nods. "That's what he said. I admire him for his willing-

ness to compromise. You shouldn't be the only one making sac-
rifices." He puts his arm around my shoulders. "You need to tell
your mum, sweetheart. Very soon."

I swallow hard. "I know. I'll call her tonight. I'm just worried
about how she'll react."

"She just wants you to be happy, Skye—same as I do. That's
all we've ever wanted for our daughter."

* * *

That evening, after my dad and his family depart for home,
I tell Will, "It's time."

He nods. "Let's do this."

When I send a Facetime request to my mom, she answers
with a beaming smile on her face.

"Hello, sweetheart," she says. "How are you?"

"I'm good. How are you?"

"I'm doing just fine. I'm getting ready to prepare final exams
for my students. How's Will?"

Will leans into the camera frame so that she can see us both.
"Hi, Brenda. It's good to see you."

I know I need to get this over with before my nerves get the
best of me. "Mom?"

"Yes, honey?"

"I have some news," I say, stalling as my pulse starts racing. I
lift my hand, showcasing the ring on my finger. "Will asked me
to marry him, and I said yes."

Her eyes widen in surprise, just for a moment, before she smiles. "Skye, sweetheart, that's wonderful. I'm so happy for you." Her eyes tear up.

My heart is pounding. "You are?"

"Of course I am. I've suspected for a while now that you're in love with him, and I couldn't be happier for you both."

I'm stunned. "My boss has offered me a permanent position with the company after my internship is over. I'm going to accept it, but... I want you to know that Will and I are moving to Cincinnati at the end of my internship. We'll both work remotely from there."

My mom looks shocked.

Will slips his arm around my waist. "We're going to split our time between England and Cincinnati," he says.

My mom bursts into tears, averting the camera for a moment. We hear muffled sobs over the phone, and when she comes back on a few moments later, there's a teary smile on her face as she dabs her eyes with a tissue. "I just assumed you'd stay in England," she says to me.

I shake my head. "We're going to have the best of both worlds, Mom."

* * *

That night, snuggling together under a thick, warm comforter, we lie with our limbs entwined, our naked bodies hot and flushed from sex.

Outside, the wind has whipped up ferociously, and rain lashes the windowpanes. Inside, it's warm and toasty, and I couldn't be happier. My dad gave his official blessing to Will this afternoon, in their little man-to-man talk, and tonight we told my mom.

"It's beautiful," I say, admiring my engagement ring in the glow of the fire in the hearth.

"No, you are," he says, rolling on top of me.

He's hard again already, and since I started taking birth control pills, and we no longer use condoms, he slides inside me and begins gently rocking. His slow, steady thrusts stoke my pleasure and steal my breath.

His mouth captures mine, stealing my breath, as his finger begins teasing my clitoris. He makes it a point that I come before he does.

When his mouth drops to my breasts, and he tugs on my nipples with gentle lips before suckling them, I feel the response between my legs, where my body is hot and aching. Before long, I'm gasping, and then keening, as the sensations swell inside me, swamping me.

Pleasure detonates deep inside and radiates up my spine. As I cry out, Will kisses me, drinking in the sounds. His thrusts pick up tempo and force as he chases his own climax.

Afterward, we lie in each other's arms, neither one of us wanting to move. Will languidly strokes my back, sending shivers skittering down my spine. I close my eyes and relax into his hold, feeling utterly at peace.

"I suppose we should get cleaned up before you fall asleep," he says.

"Mm," I murmur, burrowing closer. "In a little bit. I don't want to move quite yet. I could stay like this forever."

He chuckles and then kisses me. "As always, your wish is my command, Miss America."

* * *

Thank you for reading *Charmed*, the first book in our British Billionaire Romance series! We hope you loved Will and Skye's story. If you'd be so kind, please leave a review for us on Amazon. We'd be very grateful if you did. Stay tuned for Connor and Kennedy's story, which is coming next in the series.

* * *

For news on future releases, sign up for our mailing lists.

Join April's mailing list: www.aprilwilsonauthor.com

Join Laura's mailing list: http://eepurl.com/cztorz

Books by April Wilson

McIntyre Security, Inc. Bodyguard Series:

Vulnerable

Fearless

Shane (a novella)

Broken

Shattered

Imperfect

Ruined

Hostage

Redeemed

Marry Me (a novella)

Snowbound (a novella)

Regret

With This Ring (a novella)

A Tyler Jamison Novel:

Somebody to Love

A British Billionaire Romance:

Charmed (co-written with Laura Riley)

Dedications

April's dedication:

Laura, your friendship has enriched my life greatly.
I'm thankful for you every single day.

Laura's dedication:

To April, my bestie, for always being there for me,
always believing in me, and giving me a voice.
I treasure our friendship.

Printed in Great Britain
by Amazon

40557542R00225